FAIRIES AT THE BOTTOM OF THE GARDEN

Cheryl Headford

Chapter One

KEIRON HURRIED HOME at the end of a very long day, anticipating some peace and quiet. He liked a quiet life, so what had possessed him to take on a boyfriend like Bren Donovan was anyone's guess. Whatever else it might be, life with Bren was certainly not quiet, and it was slowly wearing Keiron out.

It was almost a relief Bren wouldn't be staying at the flat that night. Although they were practically living together, Bren had his own place and sometimes felt the need to stay there. This was usually because a member of his family—or particularly flighty friend—was coming to stay. It wasn't as if his family wasn't aware of their relationship, but Bren was shy about "rubbing it in their faces". Keiron didn't understand because Bren's mother seemed to like him a great deal and considered him to be a stabilising influence on her son.

Keiron was a conservative person and so different to Bren, they might as well live in different worlds. As for Bren's friends, they were usually very like him—loud, messy, and irresponsible. Keiron couldn't stand them. He was lucky if nothing got broken, and they always left the flat in a complete mess. If Bren wanted to live in a pigsty, so be it. He could do it in his own home.

This weekend, with the bank holiday, Bren was getting both. His friends were congregating on Saturday. Then his parents and sister were coming on Sunday, and staying through until Tuesday morning. Keiron had a Bren-free weekend and was looking forward to it.

If it hadn't been for their differences on this point, they'd have moved in together a long time ago. Bren chafed for it, but Keiron couldn't handle his flat descending into chaos, and it wasn't even as if Bren helped tidy up afterwards. Keiron cringed at the thought of having that chaos and therefore stress every day.

Not only that, but Bren was the most jealous person Keiron had ever come across. Keiron was constantly accused of looking at other men, and

God forbid he spoke to one. Bren was a firebrand, completely living up to his fiery red-headed Irish-descended promise. Sometimes it was exciting, even invigorating, yet at other times Keiron longed for the peace and stability he used to have before Bren burst in on him. Maybe at twenty-two, he was just getting old.

Keiron ordered takeaway and, while he waited for it to arrive, wandered down to the bottom of the garden, a beer in his hand, his hair damp from the bath. The sun was still high and warm enough for him to be wearing a thin T-shirt and shorts. The smell of a barbecue drifted over from a neighbouring garden and his mouth watered.

Savouring his drink, he sank onto the stone bench under the rose arbour. It afforded a good view of the whole garden. It was a big one. A long lawn stretched ahead of him to the decking immediately outside the house, where a large wooden table, a number of items of garden furniture, and a shiny silver gas barbecue sat.

Sometimes, he had Bren's friends around for a barbecue. They weren't so bad out here in the garden, although they made such a mess of the barbecue itself that it took him days to get it properly clean. He smiled to himself. Sometimes, living with Bren was like having a teenage son. Fortunately, Bren was very good at things he'd hate to think any son of his could do.

The lawn was bordered on either side by flower beds and bushes, which hid the wooden fences separating his garden from the ones on either side. To his left, screened from the arbour by a yew hedge, was a garden pool with a rock fountain and fat koi swimming under lily pads. There used to be more fish—before Bren's friends found the pond. He pursed his lips at the thought.

To the right was a shrubbery. A large variety of plants made up a wild area of about thirty square feet. Bren loved it, of course. He'd burrowed into it and, within a week, had made a green cave right in the middle. He'd floored it with an old piece of carpet he'd found on a skip. It had taken a long time and a lot of carpet-cleaner to persuade Keiron to enter it, but he had to admit, making love outside under the bushes in the darkness was something he'd come to enjoy very much.

Bren had been surprised he had such a wild place in his neat garden, in his neat life. Perhaps it was the thing that sealed the deal with Bren, who'd been reluctant to get involved with someone so unlike himself, and likely to "cramp his style".

"But why?" he'd asked. "It doesn't seem like you to have a wild place like this. It's so out of place—with the garden and with you. Why haven't you 'tamed' it? Everything else in your life is tame. You're the most vanilla person I know—except for this."

They were in the "cave" at the time. It was dark but warm, and they were holding each other in the afterglow of amazing sex. Keiron had smiled lazily and sighed.

"My mother used to live out in the country somewhere when she was a child. My grandmother never took to city life. She told me once there was no room in a city for life, real life. Nowhere for roots to reach the earth. No place for the fairies."

"Fairies?"

"Oh yes, she was very superstitious about fairies. Never had anything made of iron in the garden. Put out saucers of warm milk if there was a deep frost or snow. And always had a wild place in the garden—for the fairies."

Bren had smiled at him. "I never thought you had any of that in you, Keiron. I guess there's hope for you yet."

Keiron had grinned and held Bren tightly in his arms.

Keiron smiled at the memory and took a drink of his beer. Something caught his eye, and he turned towards the shrubbery. He was sure he'd seen something move, shooting across his vision, behind the trees. He stared hard, but there was nothing there. It must have been a squirrel. He saw them now and again, scrabbling for nuts under the hazel tree or acorns from the enormous oak that overhung the garden from next door.

With a sigh, he settled back and took another drink. His stomach rumbled, and he glanced at his watch, wondering when his pizza would get there. The deliveryman was a regular, and if there was no answer at the door, he'd text to say he'd arrived. So Keiron could relax and not worry about—

There was definitely something there. It moved again. He'd seen it— a flash of white. A cat? Most of the neighbours had cats, and they liked to hang about in the shrubbery, waiting to pounce on unsuspecting birds. It had taken a lot of work to get rid of the smell of cat pee from the carpet.

Ah well. Although...something nagged at the back of his mind. It wasn't a cat. It couldn't have been a cat because it hadn't looked like a cat. It had looked like a person. A small person with a pale pointed face.

But it had only been a fraction of a second, a flash, an impression. It was nonsense, of course.

Maybe it was one of the fairies. He smiled.

There was no further movement in the bushes, so when the text came to herald the arrival of his pizza, he wandered back into the house.

He decided to eat his stuffed-crust vegetable supreme at the kitchen table. It was a beautiful night. Other than distant strains of music drifting over from the barbecue, there was the type of silence that magnified the slightest sound. Like the silence that came with snow. It was magical.

Keiron laughed at himself. Magical? That's what you get for thinking of fairies.

Something flashed at the window and he glanced up sharply. There was nothing there, but there had been. In that fraction of a second between his head beginning to move and his eyes orienting on the window, there had been something or someone peeping in. Someone with a small pointy face. Shit.

Take it easy. If something was there, he didn't want to frighten it away before he found out what it was.

He took up the uneaten pizza, making a show of putting it onto a plate and into the fridge. The back door was open to let in the summer warmth, and the bin was next to it, out of sight of the window. He folded the pizza box, and headed for the bin—only he wasn't going to the bin at all. He lifted the lid, so the sound carried out into the garden, but before he let the lid drop, he dived for the back door.

There was nothing there, but there had been. There had been someone crouching under the window, peeping in. It was someone with long white hair, a pointed face, and unnaturally blue eyes. It was all seen in the blink of an eye, and after he'd blinked, there was nothing there and no sign there ever had been.

"I know you're there. I've seen you three times now," he called into the silence. "I know what you are." Why had he even said that? It couldn't have been anything but a figment of his imagination. Human beings couldn't move that fast, and it was certainly no animal. Then what? A fairy? Hah.

Smiling at his own foolishness, he went back into the house and closed the door.

He was halfway through the remaining pizza, drinking his third bottle of beer and feeling pretty mellow, when there was a soft tapping at the back door. This surprised him very much. No one ever knocked on the back door. Why would they? How could they? They'd have to be in the garden, and there were only two ways into it, the door at which they now tapped or a tiny gate right at the bottom, which would have necessitated them traipsing right through the garden. Who would do that?

With a frown, gripping the bottle in his hand like a weapon, he walked through the kitchen to the door. He could see a vague form through the frosted glass. There was definitely someone there. He wondered if they'd disappear by the time he opened the door.

When the door opened, Keiron froze. He'd never seen anything—or anyone—remotely like the creature who stood on his back doorstep.

Neither spoke.

Keiron blinked, half expecting the creature to vanish before he opened his eyes. He didn't. He seemed human enough. A boy of seventeen or eighteen years old, with long silvery-white hair and a pretty elfin face. Long white lashes swept over the downturned eyes and skin so pale it appeared translucent, seeming almost to glow in the gathering dusk. He was slender, willowy, and completely naked.

"Who the hell are you?" Keiron eventually asked. The boy looked up and Keiron recoiled. Nothing with eyes like that could be human. They were blue, but it wasn't any blue he'd ever seen before. It was a brilliant electric blue with a metallic sheen that marked him as something very different to anyone Keiron had ever encountered.

"Draven," the boy said automatically in a light singsong voice.

"What do you want?"

"Whatever you want."

"I...want...I want to know who you are and why you're standing naked on my back doorstep."

"I'm...Draven," he said with an anxious little smile. "I'm yours."

"Mine?" Keiron shivered when he spoke the word. It seemed to ring in his head, and he rubbed his temple absently. "What the hell are you talking about? What do you mean, mine?"

"I'm your slave," Draven said matter-of-factly, although there was something in his eyes that seemed to flinch as he spoke.

Keiron took a deep breath and released it slowly. "I don't know who you are or what the hell you want from me, but I'm not into that stuff—whips and handcuffs and—" He trailed off. Draven seemed stricken.

"You…you're going to…whip me? Why? What have I done?"

Keiron's mouth dropped open at the real fear on Draven's face and in his voice. "I…. Of course I'm not going to whip you. Isn't that what I said?"

Draven frowned deeply, then smiled. "I could probably get a whip for you, if you wanted. As long as you're not going to use it on me." He frowned again. "I suppose I shouldn't make that a condition. You have the right to whip me if you want to. Of course, I'd much prefer if you didn't. I could make one out of plaited grass if you'd like. You don't have the right kind of grass in your garden, but I bet I could find some close by. I wouldn't run away. I promise."

Keiron was stunned. Draven spoke so fast, he could barely follow what he was saying. "Wait. Stop. I…I've already told you—I don't want a whip."

"Oh. But you said…. Oh. What do you want?"

"Nothing. I don't want anything. I want you to go away and leave me alone."

Draven blinked at him. "I can't," he said sadly. "I can't leave you. I'm your slave now."

Keiron raised his hands and took another step back. Draven advanced over the threshold and gazed around curiously.

"Look, I've no idea what's going on, who you are, or what you want, but you are not my slave and you are not coming into my house."

Draven frowned at him, his head tilted to the side. "But I am your slave, and I am inside your house."

"I…. Well…. Leave, then."

"Leave?" Draven gaped in apparent astonishment. "But I can't leave."

"Why not?"

"Because," Draven said slowly, as if explaining something obvious to a child, or an idiot, "I'm your slave."

"Please, I have no idea what game you're playing, but whatever else you might be, you are not my slave."

Draven sighed. He gazed at Keiron through his insanely long lashes, flashing his violently blue eyes. From the expression on his face, he seemed to be deep in thought, chewing on his lip and frowning.

Eventually he shrugged, his face clearing to an apologetic smile. "I can't go away. I have to stay."

"Why do you have to stay?"

"Because I'm your—"

"Slave. Yeah, yeah. Whatever. Come in. I can't stand here all night. I'll get you something to wear, and you can tell me what the hell's going on. I'm obviously not going to get rid of you any other way."

Of course, he could have called the police, but the idea repelled him. He was sure the boy wasn't going to hurt him. Besides, he was intrigued now. He wanted to know who the strange boy was, and more importantly—what he was.

Ten minutes later, Draven was settled on the sofa with his feet tucked under him, wearing Bren's bathrobe. It was pretty much brand new. Bren hadn't appreciated it when Keiron bought them matching robes. He'd suggested that he buy Keiron a pipe and slippers to go with them.

Draven was even smaller than Bren, making the robe far too big, but it was the best Keiron could think of. There was no way any of his clothes would fit the boy.

Keiron sat in the chair as Draven explored. It seemed as if he'd never been inside a house before and everything was a wonder to him. The emotions flickered across his face too fast for Keiron to catch. With a little shake of his head, Draven focussed on what was in front of him. He gently stroking the leather of the couch with his fingertips, then rubbed his cheek against the soft towelling of the robe and gave a huge sigh.

Keiron smiled. There was something about Draven that made him feel curiously protective. Draven was soft and sweet and childlike, but there was a hardness underneath that made Keiron a little wary of the hyperactive creature.

"Draven?"

Draven glanced up as if surprised there was anyone else in the room. Then he sat up straighter, trying to look contrite and failing. "Oh. I'm sorry. I'm supposed to be your slave. What do you want me to do?"

"I want you to tell me why you're here—without mentioning the word *slave*."

Draven frowned, then shrugged.

"You saw me," he said.

"In the bushes?"

"Yes, and at the window—twice."

"And—?"

Draven shook his head. "You're very slow, aren't you?"

"What are you talking about?"

"I let you see me three times. That's a very bad thing. It's not allowed. You broke the magic. My punishment is that I have to be your slave. Not forever. Just for three months."

"Just. Three. Months?" Keiron was dumbstruck. His mind couldn't process what he was hearing. He stared at Draven who seemed uncomfortable at first, then lost interest, seduced by the wonders of the house.

"What's that?" he asked, pointing to the television. It was a sixty-inch flat-screen, mounted on the wall.

"What?" Keiron blinked, snapping back into action.

"That big black thing."

"What big black— Oh, that's the television."

"What is it? What does it do?"

"It.... Haven't you ever seen a television?"

Draven shook his head, his eyes still on the screen. "I've never been inside a house. I've looked through the window, but I've never seen one of those." He got up and drifted across the room, pausing to crouch down and bury his fingers in the soft carpet. When he got to the television, he ran his fingers over it, peering at his reflection in the surface. He was only barely tall enough to do so.

Still in shock, Keiron picked up the remote and switched on the television. Draven screamed and flipped backwards over the sofa. When he didn't come back out, Keiron went to investigate, worried he might have hurt himself. Draven crouched with his back against the leather. His eyes were darting everywhere.

"What's wrong? Did you hurt yourself?"

Draven's strange eyes focussed on him, and the expression made Keiron shiver. He was clearly frightened, but that hardness was more prominent now—a hint of steel.

"Where are your weapons," he asked in a shaky voice. "I-I don't think I can fight them all, definitely not if we have no weapons." He gazed up at Keiron, vulnerability replacing the harder expression. "Can you? Can you fight them? Can you protect me?"

"What are you talking about?"

"The...people. They were.... They had weapons."

"That was the television, Draven. Remember? You were asking about it. That's what it does. It shows pictures."

"P-pictures?"

"Yes. Come and see. Let me show you. Do you trust me?"

Draven stared at him. His strange eyes gave Keiron chills. "Okay," Draven whispered and held out his hand. Keiron took it and helped him to his feet. When he saw the television, Draven whirled and threw his arms around Keiron, burying his head in his body. Keiron's first impression was how small and insubstantial Draven felt. His arms barely reached all the way round and the top of his head was level with Keiron's chest.

"I can't—"

"Draven...Draven, look. It's big and bright, but it's only pictures. I promise it won't hurt you."

Draven raised his eyes. Keiron found he was getting used to them, and they didn't seem so strange anymore.

Keiron smiled. "Trust me."

Draven searched his eyes for a moment, then nodded, and holding tight to his hand, turned and stared up at the screen.

Keiron watched Draven watch the television. At first it was with fear, but that gradually changed to curiosity. As if forgetting to be afraid, he let go of Keiron's hand and drifted across the floor. Keiron stood back and let him do what he wanted, wondering what the hell he'd got himself into. There was no getting around the fact that, alien and strange as he might be, Draven was very beautiful and the thought of him naked under the bathrobe made Keiron's heart flutter a little. That was one of the many reasons he had to get rid of him as soon as possible.

Draven stared at the screen for a while, then reached out a trembling hand to touch it. He spun, his face split in a grin. "It's pictures on a wall...moving ones," he said excitedly.

"Yes, that's what a television is."

"They talk," he said, turning back to the television. "They're real people, moving and talking and—what are they doing?" He tilted his head to the side, and Keiron concentrated on what was happening on the screen. It was a vampire film. The rampaging mob had gone, and the vampire had gained the bedroom of the vapid heroine. She of the heaving breasts was in full flow, her cotton nightdress straining, while the vampire, mesmerising her with his hypnotic gaze, was about to sink his teeth into her neck.

"He's a vampire. He's about to bite her."

"Why would he do that?"

"Because he's a vampire. That's what they do."

Draven turned to him and frowned. "No, it isn't," he stated baldly.

"Know many vampires, do you?" Keiron asked.

"Not many. But I know they don't do it like that."

"Do what?"

Draven huffed and rounded on him, his hands on his hips. "That," he said, pointing back at the screen, "is not a vampire. Why is he pretending to be something he isn't? That is a human."

Keiron's eyes widened a little at the word *human*, but he said nothing. He knew—of course he did. He knew, but he didn't believe, not yet.

"That's what television's all about. It's about people pretending to be other people or other things."

"Why?"

"For entertainment. Like...like a moving picture book."

"Ooh yes, books." Draven grinned. "I've seen them. I've seen books. They have pictures in them. They have symbols...words. I can read some of them," he said proudly. "Fenn taught me. Fenn knows lots of things. I don't know how she learned to read, though. I mean, we're not supposed to have those things, human things. And we're not allowed to talk to humans—not even allowed to show ourselves to them." He gave a sad little smile and hung his head.

"And you did. You showed yourself to me."

Draven bit his lip and lowered his eyes, the picture of unrepentant guilt. "I...I let you see me."

"You let me see you. But you weren't supposed to, were you?"

Draven shook his head. "No, it's not allowed."

"And now you're being punished?"

He nodded. "Yes. I have to stay here, with you, for three months to pay for what I did."

"I don't understand. If you're not supposed to show yourself to me...us at all, why would you have to stay here, in full view, for three months?"

"Because I've been warned before, lots of times. You've almost seen me before, lots and lots of times. They said the only way to break the habit was to force me to face it."

"They?"

"The Council. They're in charge—at least here." He waved his hand vaguely. "There are lots of them, I think. The king and queen live a long way away. I've never seen them."

"Oh. Draven. You know you can't stay here."

"I can't?"

"This isn't your home. This isn't your world and I…I have my life, my boyfriend. He'd freak if he found you here. This just isn't your place."

"I know," he said sadly, "but there's nothing I can do about it. I have to stay."

"And if I won't let you stay here?"

He shrugged. "There's a place in the bushes. It's warm and comfortable. I've slept there before and—"

"I'm not letting you sleep outside under a bush."

"Why not? That's where I usually sleep."

Keiron shook his head. "What am I going to do with you?"

Chapter Two

DRAVEN COMPLETELY SWEPT Keiron away that evening. He was excited about everything. Naturally curious, he thoroughly searched the living room, picking things up, exclaiming over them, demanding an explanation, then moving on to the next thing. Keiron indulged him, relaxing more and more, as he was infected by Draven's childlike enthusiasm.

When fingers of exhaustion began to tug at him, Keiron realised it was past midnight.

"Draven, it's getting late. It's time to think about getting to bed."

"Oh. Shall I leave this inside the house? It will get wet and dirty outside." Slipping off the robe, he let it fall to the ground and headed, naked, for the back door."

"Wait? What are you doing? Where are you going?"

Draven stopped and turned to him, his head tilted in surprise. "You said you didn't want me to stay in the house. I'm going to—"

"Oh no, you're not. Put your robe back on. You can sleep in the spare room. We'll think this through in the morning."

"Okay."

After making sure Draven was safely tucked back into his robe, Keiron led him up the stairs. Draven trotted obediently behind. When Keiron opened the bedroom door and switched on the light, Draven cried out in delight.

"Can I sleep here? Can I really?"

"Of course you can."

Draven spun on light feet and gazed at Keiron. "Is that the thing you call a bed?"

"Isn't that what you call a bed?"

Draven shook his head. "We sleep in flowers or in the branches or roots of the trees. All kinds of places. Sometimes we weave nests. If we're inside, we sleep on big piles of cushions or woven cots, but I've never seen anything like this. I've heard people talk about them and wondered what they were like. They don't understand. They can't see why I should be so interested in humans. Most of us stay well away because we're scared or scornful or just not interested. But I'm interested. I'm interested in everything." He beamed at Keiron. "Most of all, I'm interested in you."

"In me?"

"Yes. That's why I let you see me. I wanted to talk to you."

"You did? Why?"

"I've watched you in the garden. Both of you. You look sad when you should be happy. I've never understood that. Either you're happy or you're sad, and if you're doing something happy, you shouldn't be sad. But you do happy things, lots of happy things, but you are still sad." Draven paused, frowning. Keiron took the opportunity to catch up after the breathless tumble of words. Draven brightened. "And, of course, you're very beautiful. My friends say all humans are big and clumsy and ugly, but I think you're beautiful."

"You...er...do?"

"Oh yes. I like your eyes. They're blue, but not like mine. Like the sky after rain. Clean and fresh. You smell fresh too, like lemons. But they aren't real lemons, because lemons taste different."

"Taste different to what?"

"To how you smell?"

"You can...er...taste smells?"

"Can't you?" he asked, his eyes wide.

"Er...no, no I can't."

"Oh."

"I think you should go to bed now. I know I want to. Do you want to shower first?"

"Shower? What's that?" Draven yawned widely, showing neat little pearly-white teeth. Keiron had the irrational desire to run his tongue over them. He shook his head.

"Never mind. Get into bed."

"Into?" Draven regarded it, his eyes glittering with curiosity. "Does it open?"

"It's a...a saying. You don't open the bed, just pull back the covers and get inside...um...lie underneath them."

Draven pulled at the duvet curiously. He tugged and pulled, seeming to be trying to tear it open.

"You don't get inside the quilt, Draven," Keiron said, amusement colouring his words. He was beginning to get used to the way Draven thought. "Here, let me help you. Get up on the bed."

Draven obeyed, fluffing the pillows delightedly. Then, he realised the bed was bouncy and started to bounce on it. The robe fell open and slipped off his shoulders. He just kept on bouncing, like a child on a trampoline. Keiron closed his eyes and gritted his teeth.

"Beds aren't for bouncing on, Draven."

"They're not?"

"No, they're for sleeping in."

"But they're bouncy."

"Yes, they are, but right now, you're supposed to be sleeping, not bouncing."

"Why do you have your eyes closed?"

"Because I don't want to see your...you...bouncing."

"Why not?"

"Just get into bed."

"But I can't," Draven said sulkily. "I don't know how."

With a sigh, Keiron opened his eyes, trying not to look at Draven's body. "Give me the robe." Draven wriggled out of it and handed it over. "Right, lie down."

Obediently, Draven curled up in the centre of the bed.

"You should try putting your head on the pillows. That's what they're there for."

Draven blinked at him. He suddenly appeared very tired. "Okay," he said and scooted up. His head sank into the pillow and he sighed, an expression of bliss on his face.

Keiron pulled the duvet up and tucked it around him. "Goodnight, Draven," he said. "Sleep well."

Draven yawned a sleepy little yawn and, to Keiron's amazement, was instantly fast asleep.

"Draven?" he called softly, but the little creature was oblivious, wandering somewhere in dreams, a smile on his face. Keiron stared in amazement.

What the hell?

Leaving the door slightly ajar, Keiron turned off the light and went to his own bed. He lay awake for a long time, pondering the fairy creature in the next room. There was no doubt in his mind Draven was a fairy, as crazy as it sounded even to himself. After all, what else could he be? *So, what the hell am I going to do about it? I can't have someone like that living here for three months. Christ, Bren would have a fit.*

Keiron fell asleep, imaging the look on Bren's face if he'd seen Draven standing naked on the doorstep. The next morning, he woke thinking of Draven standing naked on the doorstep. For a moment, until reality crashed in on him, he smiled and hugged himself, then a light flashed "danger, danger" in his head and he sat up.

The sound of someone moving about downstairs startled him. His first thought was, *Oh my God, Bren's here.* His second was, *Oh my God, Draven's downstairs on his own.* He didn't know which of the two possibilities scared him most.

Throwing himself out of bed, Keiron pulled on a pair of jeans and a T-shirt. He turned and tripped over his shoes, almost falling on his face. "Dammit." With a growl, he savagely kicked the shoes aside and ran for the door.

He found Draven in the kitchen. Draven's face and hands were covered with jam, and he was completely naked. He hummed to himself as he tried to smear jam on a piece of bread with his fingers. It was such a funny sight that Keiron paused in the doorway, watching.

Draven scanned the kitchen, not seeing Keiron. He thrust his fingers into his mouth, spreading jam over even more of his face, then stamped his foot angrily and put his hands on his hips, getting even stickier.

"Where is the water?"

"Try the tap."

Draven jumped and spun around. Keiron laughed out loud. There was jam all over Draven's face, jam in his hair, jam on his hands, and now it was smeared down his hips too, not to mention all over the kitchen table. Even the handle of the fridge seemed decidedly jammy.

"It's not my fault," Draven said indignantly. "I could smell strawberries, but I didn't know it was going to be like this, and I couldn't find where you keep the water."

"It's in the tap."

"Where's the tap? I thought it would be somewhere in the cooking room. I didn't want to make a mess in your pretty room, and anyone in their right minds should keep water in a cooking room."

"I do. I told you, it's in the tap."

Draven stamped his foot and glared. "But I don't know where the tap is."

"It's in the sink."

"Where's the door?"

"What door?" Keiron was still amused but now also bemused. Draven confused him more with every word. Draven heaved a huge exaggerated sigh.

"The door to the sink, of course. Is it in the floor?" He started peering at the tiles, and said thoughtfully. "I didn't think of looking in the floor, but if it's sunken, I guess it's under there."

"There's nothing under the floor, Draven." Keiron crossed the kitchen and turned on the tap. "This is the sink and this is the tap."

Draven gasped and stared at the water gushing out of the tap. "You have a mountain stream? In your cooking room? Inside your house?"

"It's a tap, Draven. It's attached by a very, very long pipe to a reservoir somewhere. All houses have taps. I have another in the bathroom."

"What's a bathroom?" Draven asked distractedly as he turned the tap on and off, twisting to peer into it as if expecting to see something inside—a mountain stream, perhaps.

"It's the place where you shower and bathe."

"Oh." Draven glanced up with a puzzled expression on his face. "So you do have a pool in your house. Why do you need a...tap, then? Can't you just get water from the pool?"

"I don't have a pool in my bathroom, Draven."

"But you said that's where you bathe."

"It is." Keiron sighed. "Let me show you. You can take a shower while I clean up this mess."

"What's a shower?" Draven asked, as he trotted along beside Keiron. Thankfully, he seemed to be taking care not to touch anything. He was very close and smelled strongly of strawberries. Keiron was able to sneak glances at him, watching the emotions fly like shadows across his face. Draven didn't notice. He was completely absorbed in everything around him. Keiron realised the whole house was filled with strange new things—things Draven had never seen or heard of before. The realisation was quite a shock.

When they reached the bathroom, Draven stopped in the doorway, as Keiron turned on the shower.

"Where's the pool? Isn't it supposed to be—" Draven was pointing towards the bath, but cut off suddenly when the shower started. His eyes and mouth went round, and he froze.

"What's the matter?" Keiron asked, startled by the shock on Draven's face.

"How did you make it rain? Not even weather witches can do that. Not so fast and all in one place."

"It's not rain, Draven, it's a tap; a different kind of tap." Turning the shower on and off a few times, he had Draven's undivided attention. Draven was utterly enchanted and bounced, clapping his hands every time the water started.

"Do it again. Do it again," he pleaded when Keiron stopped, leaving the shower running.

"I'm getting wet. You can do it, but not until you've cleaned off every bit of that jam, understand? I don't want to have to clean the bathroom as well as the kitchen."

Draven gasped and suddenly looked utterly wretched. He bowed his head, kicking at the back of one foot with the other, his hands clasped behind his back, like a naughty boy, being told off.

"What's the matter?"

"I'm supposed to be your slave," he muttered. Then his head came up and he grinned. "I'm not a very good one, am I?"

"Um...no, not really, but—"

"The High Lord—he's the leader of the Council—said that being a slave would help me learn how to follow rules. He said he hoped you could get me to listen to authority because he's damned if he can. He didn't actually say that, of course, those words, in human. The High Lord doesn't associate with humans at all, not free ones. He doesn't like to speak human language. There aren't many who can; at least not as well as I can." He puffed his chest proudly.

"You speak it very well," Keiron said weakly.

"I know. I listen a lot."

"Listen? To humans? You eavesdrop?"

"I don't know what that means. I...." Draven had the grace to look embarrassed. "I like to watch people and listen to what they say. I follow them—sometimes too far. I've almost got caught, lots of times. And I like to peep through windows. Not just yours," he added hastily, as if that made a major difference.

"If you spend so much time peeping through windows, how come you don't know more about what goes on inside houses. Why haven't you seen a tap or television working?"

Draven shook his head. "I can only look in when I know people aren't looking out. I can hardly watch someone when they are standing in the cooking room, in front of the window, can I? And I think the...taps are mostly in front of the window. I've seen them, but I had no idea what they did. As for the...television...." He shrugged. "They mostly have their back to me. I guess I must have seen the pictures on them some time, but I don't remember. I must have been concentrating on something else. I get like that. When I'm concentrating on something, I don't see other things." He frowned. "Sometimes, quite important things. The High Lord says that one of these days I am going to get into serious trouble because of it. Oh." He glanced up and grinned. "I think I did, didn't I?"

"I think you did," Keiron agreed with a smile, slightly dazed at Draven's breathless speech. Draven had a tendency to take a breath and not stop until it had gone, at least that's how it seemed. Keiron found it endearing, but it was sometimes difficult to follow. The High Lord, whoever he was, had Draven's measure right enough. Sending him to Keiron had been a stroke of genius on the High Lord's part, Keiron just wished he'd sent him somewhere else. He groaned inwardly. Maybe he could talk to the High Lord and get him to change his mind. It felt as if this was a punishment for him, too. He glanced at Draven, who was staring hungrily at the shower, rubbing jam into his eye. More of a punishment for him...much more.

"Take a shower and dry off with the towels on the rack over there. Make sure you dry your hair thoroughly. I'll get some clothes and put them on the bed in your room."

"Why?" Draven asked, dragging his attention away from the shower.

"So you can get dressed."

"You want me to wear clothes?" Draven asked, wide-eyed.

"Of course I do. You can't walk around naked."

"Why not?"

"Because someone might see you."

"It hardly matters now, does it? I'm already being punished once and sending me here doesn't suggest that the High Lord wants me to continue to hide. I mean, if I'm your slave, I have to go wherever you tell me to—even outside." His eyes glittered as he said that, as if he would like nothing more than to be told to go outside, and he wasn't thinking of the garden.

Keiron sighed. "It's not because you're a fairy, Draven. It's because people don't just walk around naked."

"They don't?" His face fell. "I wondered why I never saw any of them naked. Do I have to wear clothes all the time?"

"All the time—except when you're in the bathroom."

Draven brightened and Keiron groaned inwardly. He had a feeling that Draven was going to spend a lot of time in the bathroom.

"I'll leave you to it, then."

"Yes." Draven was gazing at the shower again. Keiron shook his head. If he'd thought living with Bren was like having a teenager around, this was like having a child. Draven might not look it, but he had the innocence, curiosity, and playfulness of a child. This was going to be interesting, but he was damn sure it wasn't going to be for three months.

Keiron sorted through Bren's things to find something that might fit Draven. As he set aside item after item, he was shocked to realise just how small Draven actually was. It wasn't just his height, which was only an inch or so less than Bren's. He was evenly proportioned and well-muscled but very, very slender. Keiron could easily have put his hands around his waist, and Draven's hands would have been only half his size if it weren't for the length of his fingers.

Ah well. He found a pair of skinny jeans, which were extremely figure-hugging on Bren but would still be big on Draven, and a crop top that would probably slip off his shoulder. He did his best with underwear, but there was no chance it was going to fit, and he didn't even bother with shoes.

Keiron paused, staring at the clothes laid out on the bed, and simply couldn't visualise Draven wearing them. In fact, he couldn't visualise Draven wearing anything, but the alternative was...uncomfortable. Tossing a pair of sneakers onto the floor beside the bed, he turned and headed for the kitchen, welcoming the distraction of cleaning up the jam.

After twenty minutes, he changed his mind. A whole pot of jam, at least the part that hadn't been coating Draven, had been spread all over the kitchen, from the table, to the door handle, to the fridge. There were sticky finger marks over cupboards and even on the floor. It took three bowls of soapy water before he was able to declare the room unstuck.

It was still early, and Keiron set about making breakfast. Pausing with his hand on the bacon, he changed his mind. He had no idea if Draven ate meat. He knew he liked fruit, though, so he set out a selection of cereals, fruit, and fruit juice, with milk and sugar.

When he was done, he realised over half an hour had passed, and there was no sign of Draven. With a sigh, he climbed the stairs and knocked on the bathroom door. There was no response. From within, he could hear water and singing. The singing seemed to blend with the water, so it was hard to tell where one ended and the other began.

He cracked open the door and called, "Draven?" The singing stopped. Moments later, the door was yanked out of Keiron's hand, and Draven stood in front of him, dripping and still very naked. Draven grinned.

"It's wonderful, Keiron. Come and have a go." He grabbed Keiron's hand and dragged him into the bathroom, which was steamy from the open shower door. Keiron tugged his hand free.

"Not now, Draven. I'll shower later, after breakfast. I've got it all set out. Hurry up. Dry and get dressed."

Draven grinned. "Yes, of course. I like your shower. It's like rain, only warmer." His eyes turned dreamy. "I could stay in there all day."

"No, you couldn't. For one thing, my electricity bill would be through the roof, and for another, you'd wrinkle up like a prune."

As he spoke, Draven stared at him in intense concentration. "I have no idea what you just said. How can the shower go through the roof, and will the water really turn me into a prune? What's a prune?"

Keiron smiled. "Go get dressed."

"Yes." Draven shook his head like a dog, sending his long hair whipping out and droplets of water flying everywhere.

"Hey...watch it. I'm soaked."

Draven seemed surprised. "You sound like that's a bad thing."

"It is when I'm dressed."

"You see? I told you being dressed is a bad thing." With a self-satisfied toss of his head, Draven slipped past Keiron and disappeared into the bedroom.

Keiron stared after him for a long moment, then smiled in bemusement and hurried to switch off the shower and clean the water off the bathroom floor.

He was pouring coffee when he heard the soft footsteps that told him Draven was on his way. He glanced up and smiled, then frowned. There was something different about him. Draven looked good in clothes, almost as good as he did without them, and strangely they seemed to fit him just fine.

"I thought those clothes would be way too big for you."

"Oh, they were," Draven said, sniffing at the coffee, "but I made them fit."

"You made them fit? You made them smaller?"

"No, I made me bigger."

Keiron stared and realised it was true. Draven was taller and wider and generally bigger. In fact, he was pretty much the same size as Bren, and filled out his clothes just as well. He swallowed hard at the sight of Draven's tight midriff, clear between the cut-off and the waist of his jeans. Ah hell.

"You can change your size?"

"Of course. Can't you?"

"No. Is there anything else you can change?"

"Of course," Draven said again, leaning closer to the coffee jug and sniffing.

"What? What can you change?"

Draven straightened. "Anything," he said, "I mean, I can make myself bigger and smaller, change colour and—"

"Change colour?" Keiron gasped, startled. "What do you mean, change colour?"

Draven frowned. "Well...make my...colour...different." He seemed to be struggling to think of another way to say the words.

"But...."

"Like this," Draven volunteered before his skin turned sea green and his hair deep blue. If it hadn't been so shocking, it would have been extremely attractive. The hair was almost the same shade as his eyes, and had a slight metallic shimmer, too. Draven seemed anxious, nervous of Keiron's reaction.

"It...Um...It's...It...."

Abruptly, Draven reverted to his original colour, his face falling into a pout. "You don't like it."

"No, no, it...it isn't that I don't like it. It's just— I've never seen anything like it before. It was a bit of a shock."

"Can't you do that?"

"No. Nothing like it."

"I wondered. Why humans don't change, I mean. I kind of figured it's because they can't." Now his voice was full of pity. Then he sniffed again at the coffee. "What's that?"

"It's coffee. A hot drink. Would you like some?"

Draven grinned at him. "Ooh yes, yes please."

"Would you like sugar and milk?"

"Ooh, you have milk? I love milk. What did you milk? A cat? A stoat?"

"Draven, you can't milk a cat."

"You can't?" He turned thoughtful. "Maybe I should tell them."

"Tell who what?"

"The cats. Tell them they can't be milked. They won't like it. Neither will the High Lord. He likes cat milk and—"

"You milk cats?"

"Well...yes. I didn't know you weren't supposed to."

"It's not that you're not supposed to; it's just—" Keiron broke off. He could imagine the conversation. There just wasn't any point. "It's cow's milk."

"Cows?" Draven's eyes went wide. "You milk cows?"

"Not me personally, but yes."

"But they're so...big." His eyes were round, and his mouth hung open. Then he shook his head. "Of course. You're big too. Ah. I suppose cats would be too small, huh? They don't give very much, and only when they want to."

"Will you stop talking about milking cats? Do you want milk in your coffee or not?"

"I've never tasted cow's milk. I'd like to try."

Keiron poured a cup of coffee while Draven watched, fascinated. He carefully poured in milk and handed it over. Draven closed his hand around it, then yelped and dropped it. "Ow, ow, ow," he sang, dancing on the spot and clutching his hand. "It hurt me. It hurt me."

"It's hot, Draven. It's made with boiling water. Of course it's going to hurt if you hold on to it like that."

"Boiling water? What do you mean? How do you make it hot?"

"It's boiled in a kettle. Let me see that hand."

Obediently, Draven held out his hand. It was red but there was no sign it was going to blister. Keiron led him to the tap and ran the cold water over his hand. Draven smiled and gazed up into Keiron's eyes. His face was streaked with tears, which had already dried. He looked...

Keiron dropped his hand and turned away. "You've made another mess."

"Oh. I'm sorry. Let me clean it up." Draven pushed past Keiron and started moving things out of the puddle of coffee. All he succeeded in doing was allowing the puddle to get bigger. The box of cereal was soaked and, as Draven lifted it, the bottom gave way, spilling cereal all over the table. Yanking back his hand, he knocked over the jug of orange juice and sent fruit rolling onto the floor.

"Oh. Oh, I'm sorry. I'm so sorry. I'll fix it. I'll—" In his haste to try to catch the rolling fruit and stand up the jug and gather the cereal, his foot turned on a rolling apple and he fell backwards, landing on his bottom on the floor with the cereal in his lap and a puddle of spilled milk spreading from between his legs.

With a trembling lip and tear-bright eyes, Draven sat on the floor and stared up at Keiron, sniffing. He was dejected and so comical, Keiron just couldn't stop himself from laughing. After a shocked look, Draven grinned and started to giggle too. Keiron held out his hand and Draven took it, hauling himself to his feet while trying ineffectually to brush himself down.

"I think it might be a good idea if you changed out of those wet clothes and leave the clearing up to me. Again."

The giggling stopped and Draven looked crestfallen. "I'm sorry."

Keiron grinned. "Don't worry about it. Go get changed."

As Draven skipped towards the stairs, dripping milk on the carpet, Keiron turned back to the mess that was his kitchen. He groaned. If he'd thought Bren's friends were bad, this was so much worse. It was crazy. He couldn't put up with it. All he wanted was a quiet life—to go to work, come home, and relax in a clean and tidy house with no hassles and the occasional forage out into Bren's bright, exciting life when he felt up to it. He liked everything in its place, even the chaos. He had a feeling this chaos could never be put in any place other than right where it wanted to be.

As he cleaned up the mess, he decided that, as soon as Draven returned, he was going to find out how to get rid of him once and for all. It was bad enough having Bren around the house, but Draven was one step too far.

Chapter Three

By THE TIME he heard Draven's footsteps on the stairs, Keiron had mopped up the worst of the mess and set out two bowls with cereal and milk, two glasses of orange juice, and a bowl of fruit, positioned where Draven wouldn't knock the juice over when he reached for it.

"Oh. I'd have helped you clean up if you'd waited. It was my fault, and I'm supposed to be your slave."

"You're not my—" Keiron glanced up and groaned inwardly. "You're naked again."

"Yes." Draven grinned. "There weren't any more clothes, so I didn't have anything else to wear. I know you said that humans don't, but.... What?"

"Huh?"

"You were staring at me."

"I-I was?" Keiron pulled himself out of his stupor and mentally shook himself. His mind was at serious risk of heading down dangerous roads. Draven was back to his original form and Keiron found it was both a relief and a distraction.

"Yes," Draven said, sitting down and selecting an apple. "You were looking at me as if you'd never seen me before." He finished with his mouth stuffed full of fruit.

"I can't say I've ever seen anything like you before."

"Of course not. That's the point."

"Yes, and coming back to the point, what can I do to get the High Lord, whoever he is, to change his mind about you?"

Draven swallowed and stared at him. "What do you mean?"

"I need him to take back this silly punishment. I just can't have you here for three months. Where can I find him?"

"You can't," Draven said, his voice shaking.

"Well then, you can—"

"I can't," he said, biting his trembling lip.

"But surely there must be some way of talking to him, persuading him to change his mind?"

Draven shook his head. Fat tears were squeezing themselves out from the corners of his eyes. "You can't see him. He won't show himself to you."

"But if he knew why—"

"He won't. He really won't."

"Well then, you—"

"He won't listen to me either."

"How do you know?"

"It's the way things work. The High Lord has made his decision. It is as it is. There's no changing it."

"But there must be some kind of appeal."

"Appeal?"

"A...request for him to change his decision."

"There'd be no point because he doesn't change his decisions. He never changes his decisions. It is as it is." Draven spoke matter-of-factly, spreading his hands in a helpless gesture. Tears were pouring down his face, but his eyes didn't waver, remaining fixed on Keiron's face.

"And there's no way—"

"No." Draven shook his head, chewing his lip to stop it trembling uncontrollably.

"I don't suppose you could just go back home and—"

"For the next three months, I don't have any home but here. If you want, I'll sleep in the garden. I'll stay in the garden. If you don't want me here, I'll try my best not to be, but I think I'll be punished if I do. Although...." He thought for a moment and shrugged. "I suppose, if you order me to, I'll be obeying and that's what slaves do, so he couldn't really punish me for it."

"I'm not going to make you sleep in the garden, Draven."

"You're not?"

Keiron sighed and shook his head. What the hell was he going to do now?

"Well, if that's the way it has to be, I guess I don't have any choice. I'll need to be careful, and of course I'll have to explain to Bren. I've no idea how he's going to take it. You may be in for a bad time with him. He can get very jealous. You really are going to have to stop walking around naked, and you have to be more careful with things."

"Yes," Draven said in a subdued voice, his head bowed, clearly still crying quietly.

"Is it really that bad, Draven? I didn't think you were upset about having to be here. I thought you were enjoying yourself, that you were excited."

"I was," he said very softly, biting his lip hard.

"Draven, what's the matter?" For the first time, Keiron stopped thinking about himself and what an inconvenience Draven was going to be and took note of the pain that radiated from the small man in waves. Keiron realised, with surprise, he could actually feel them as vibrations in the air around him.

It was a strange dichotomy. Draven looked like a child, pain written all over his face, and tears flowing unchecked. Yet, suddenly it was brought home to Keiron that he was also a non-human being and God knows what he was capable of.

"You hate me," he said wretchedly.

"What?"

"You hate me. You want me to go away. You're angry that I have to stay."

"I don't hate you, Draven. How could I hate you?" Keiron found himself moving, against his better judgement, around the table, to crouch beside Draven's chair. Draven turned his head away. Keiron had no idea what to do. It was like trying to be a father to a child that wasn't his or had turned up already a teenager.

Feeling nervous and distraught at Draven's pain, Keiron put a hand on his shoulder. Draven jumped.

"Draven, I don't hate you. I promise I don't hate you. I hate the situation I've been put in. I don't know what to do, and I feel as if my whole life has been turned on its head, but I don't hate you. You're no more at fault for this than I am."

Draven turned his tear-stained face towards him and sniffed. "You...you don't? You really don't hate me."

"No, Draven, I don't hate you." From being distraught, Draven switched instantly to delighted and threw his arms around Keiron's neck. "I don't hate you either. What's next?"

"I think next you eat breakfast."

"Okay," Draven said brightly and picked up his apple, while sniffing in an interested way at the cereal and milk.

Keiron was perplexed. Draven's face was still tear-stained, but he was beaming. Had he been faking it? Pretending to be upset? But it had seemed so genuine. But how could someone switch their emotions on and off that fast? But Draven wasn't human. Who knew what he could do?

After finishing his apple, Draven started on the cereal. "Ooh, this is so good. I like cow's milk. Can I try tomorrow?"

"Try what?"

"Milking the cow," he said, giving Keiron one of his that-was-completely-obvious looks.

Keiron stifled a snort of laughter. "I didn't milk the cow myself, Draven. The milk comes in a bottle."

"It does?" Draven's eyes widened. "How does it get in there?"

"There's a whole process it goes through between the cow and the bottle."

"What process?"

"I...I'm not entirely sure. It's something to do with making it safe to drink."

"Safe?"

"There are a lot of bacteria and...things in the milk when it comes from the cow. It has to be made safe to drink."

"How?"

"I...I'm not sure."

Draven frowned, deep in thought, then pushed his bowl of cereal and glass of milk away from him. "I think I'll stick to oranges, thank you."

Keiron didn't have the heart to tell him the orange juice was processed as well.

When he'd finished, Keiron got to his feet and stretched. A whole Saturday lay ahead of him to do with as he wanted. He'd intended to take a walk in the park on the way to the shops, then relax in the garden or in front of the television with a book and some snacks. Maybe take in a movie in the evening. Now.... He narrowed his eyes. Did he dare take him to the park and the shop?

The thought of Draven in a shop, picking things up and asking questions, balked Keiron. That was a trip for another day. Maybe three months down the line.

"I have to go out this morning," he said. "Try not to break anything while I'm gone."

"I'm not going to break anything," Draven stated with outrage.

"Just be careful," Keiron said, and Draven nodded solemnly.

Not convinced, Keiron left Draven—who'd insisted that, as the slave, he was supposed to clean up breakfast—and took a shower. Usually, he'd have lingered over showering, savouring the feel of the water on his skin, spending time to soap up his hair and maybe take care of other things, not always thinking of Bren when he was doing it.

Today, he was pressured by the thought of Draven downstairs, and what he might be doing. He was intensely surprised, even shocked, to find the table and kitchen clean and the dishes, utensils, cereal boxes, and glasses stacked neatly on the counter. Draven was humming happily as he explored the kitchen, examining the contents of the cupboards. Keiron paused to watch. As frustrating as he was, there was something about Draven, perhaps his complete honesty and innocence that made him achingly endearing.

"I'm going out now."

Draven jumped and spun around. "I wasn't breaking anything. I was just looking...to see where everything goes."

"That's fine. You can look at whatever you want. Just be careful. If you're not sure what something does, don't try it out."

"What do you mean? Things *do* things?" He narrowed his eyes suspiciously at the toaster.

"Only if you switch them on. If something has a button or a switch, don't press or flick it."

"I...okay," Draven said with a sly smile. "Can I play with the television? That has buttons."

"Yes, you can play with the television. I'll show you how it works."

After spending a frustrating ten minutes showing Draven how the remote worked, Keiron was more than ready for a relaxing walk in the sunshine.

"Don't answer the door, don't answer the phone, and don't go outside naked."

"I...um.... If I'm not naked, can I go outside?"

"Of course you can. It's a beautiful day. Why not take a drink into the garden and enjoy the sunshine? You can take a book out too if you want."

"A book?" Draven gazed in open-mouthed wonder. "I can read a book?"

"Sure. There are plenty on the bookshelves. There's bound to be something that takes your fancy."

Draven literally bounced with excitement, and Keiron smiled as he headed out. He had a few moments of blind panic when he locked the front door, but he pushed them aside and began to stroll down the path.

Two hours later, the panic was back as he put the key in the lock and wondered what he would find on the other side.

What he found was...nothing. Everything seemed to be in place in the living room. The television was off and the remote was on the floor. A quick examination of the kitchen showed everything in its place there too. Impressed, he called Draven's name, expecting him to be upstairs. When there was no answer he went to investigate.

The clothes he'd laid out before he left were still untouched on the bed and there was no sign of Draven. Panic began to assert itself again. Where was he? What had happened to him?

Opening the back door, he peered out. Maybe he'd left, gone back to his people. Maybe they'd come for him. A moment's blind hope was followed quickly by a stab of disappointment. But no, Draven had been so sure it wouldn't happen.

On impulse, Keiron walked down to the bottom of the garden and crawled into the space in the bushes. Draven was curled up on the carpet, fast asleep. Smiling, Keiron brushed Draven's hair out of his eyes, calling his name softly. Draven stirred and blinked open sleepy eyes.

"I thought I told you not to go outside without clothes on," Keiron said with a smile rather than a scold.

Draven half smiled, then as if remembering something, he gasped and sprang to his knees. "I'm sorry," he said, his lip trembling. "I'm really, really, really, really sorry. I didn't mean to. I was good. Honestly I was. I didn't touch anything. I just looked. And then I went to play with the television. You said I could," he said defensively, and Keiron nodded encouragingly, wondering with a sinking feeling what had happened.

"I pressed buttons, and there were lots of pictures. Some of them were nice but...there was...there was a horrible one and I-I panicked and pressed lots of buttons and...and I...." His lip trembled even more and tears sprang to his eyes. "I didn't mean to, but I broke it."

"You broke the television? By pressing buttons."

"Yes. I tried to press more to make it stop being black, but it just wouldn't work. The pictures wouldn't come back."

"Draven, you can't break a television just by pressing the buttons. You've just switched it off."

"But it won't work."

"No, not until you switch it back on again."

"Really? It really isn't broken?" Draven sounded as if he didn't believe him.

Keiron smiled. "Come on; I'll show you."

Reluctantly, Draven crawled out of the green cave, following Keiron. They walked back up to the house, with Keiron watching nervously for any of the neighbours who might see Draven and report to Bren that he'd been walking in the garden with a naked man. Fortunately, there was no sign of anyone.

As he'd expected, all Draven had done to the television was press some buttons that had reprogrammed it and switched it off. He'd managed to screw up the programming, but a few minutes of button pressing had it back on track. Draven watched anxiously as Keiron worked and beamed when the picture reappeared.

"I'm sorry," he said, downcast. "I'm a terrible slave. All I do is make things harder for you."

"Harder, but more interesting," Keiron said, earning another of Draven's sudden grins.

"What next?"

"I think we both need a break. How about we just sit a while and get to know each other a little."

"I'd like that."

"Maybe you should get dressed before we do."

"Do I have to?" Draven pouted, but when Keiron narrowed his eyes, he grinned and skipped off towards the stairs. Keiron poured himself a measure of malt whisky. It was a tad early in the day to drink, but he needed it.

When Draven came downstairs, he sniffed. "What's that?"

"What's what? Oh, this?" He held up his glass, and Draven nodded. "It's whisky, just a drop to calm my nerves."

"Your nerves? Why do they need calming?"

"Because... Never mind. Sit down."

Draven sniffed again. "Can I try?"

"I'm not sure you're up to alcohol," Keiron said doubtfully.

"Do you think we don't have any?" Draven asked, outraged. "We have all sorts. I've just never tasted that one."

"Oh," Keiron said. Draven was so childlike, Keiron had begun to look on him as a child. He reminded himself that, although the fiction might be attractive as a means to keep Draven at a distance, it was likely to be dangerous if taken too far. He handed over the glass, and Draven sniffed again before taking a sip.

Keiron expected him to choke, but he simply looked contemplative, then took another sip. "Hmm," he said. "It's a bit harsh, but not bad. We have some fermented spirits that taste similar, but I prefer sweeter things, like mead."

Keiron was shocked. He kept having the rug pulled from under him. It was his own fault. He should stop thinking of Draven as a child. No matter what he looked like or how he behaved, Keiron knew he wasn't. Part of him suggested he was far from it, but Keiron really didn't want to know how far.

"What do you want for lunch?" Keiron asked, distracting himself.

"What's lunch?" Draven asked, curious.

"The meal we have in the middle of the day." Keiron was distracted, thinking what on earth he could give Draven to eat.

"Another one?"

"What?" He turned carelessly. "What do you mean?"

"We've already had one."

"We had breakfast. That's what we have at the start of the day."

"But that wasn't the start of the day."

Now, Keiron was interested, giving Draven his full attention. "It wasn't?"

"No. Dawn is the start of the day."

Keiron laughed. "I suppose so, but who gets up at dawn in the middle of summer?"

"I do," Draven said, surprised. "Don't you?"

"You know I didn't," Keiron said, still smiling.

"No, I don't," Draven said indignantly.

"I was in bed."

Draven put his hands on his hips and frowned at him. "How was I supposed to know that? I didn't come into your room to see what you were doing in there."

"But it's a bedroom. What else would I be doing in there?"

"I don't know. I've never been in there."

Keiron shook his head and sighed. "So you get up at dawn? You were up at four o'clock this morning."

"Yes."

"But, you didn't go to bed until after midnight."

"Yes." Draven seemed confused about the course of the questioning, but he smiled as if he'd resolved that no matter how crazy his new master was he'd humour him.

"So, you had four hours sleep?"

"Yes."

"Aren't you tired?"

"Yes. Will it be time for bed soon?"

"What? Bed? In the middle of the day?"

"Yes, of course."

"I don't understand. You get up at dawn and go to bed at midday?"

"When the days are long, yes. There isn't enough dark, so you have to sleep in the light, and I can't help getting up at dawn, so I have to sleep in the middle of the day. I don't do it when there's much darkness."

"Oh, so you just want to nap?"

"What's that?"

"Sleep for a little while."

Draven grinned. "Yes, for a little while."

"Do you want to eat first?"

"No. I've eaten enough for a while." He yawned widely. "I'm tired now."

"Then go up and sleep as long as you want. Do you want me to save some lunch for you?"

"No, thank you. I'll eat when I feel like it, later."

Keiron watched Draven wander away and shook his head for the umpteenth time that day. He didn't understand Draven at all, not at all.

He carried on not understanding all through lunch and for the hours afterwards when he sat in the garden in the sun, reading a book and drinking homemade lemonade.

At some point, he realised with a jolt that he was actually getting impatient waiting for Draven to get up. When he saw someone move past the window, he put down his book on the seat and hurried across the lawn.

Walking through the kitchen, he asked, "Did you have a nice—" *Oh shit!*

"Baby," Bren cried, throwing himself into Keiron's arms. "I was wondering where you were. Everyone's gone and deserted me. I'm all alone. Make me feel wanted."

Keiron laughed and hugged the temperamental redhead. "You know you're always wanted here. What's happened? I thought you were supposed to be going out with your friends."

Bren flung himself out of Keiron's arms and onto the sofa. He crossed his arms, pouting. "I am, but they're all doing stuff this afternoon and don't want to meet until ten, in town. I have hours to kill." He twinkled at Keiron from under his eyelashes. "I was trying to think what on earth I could do with all that spare time. It's not as if I'm going to have a chance of seeing you for the rest of the weekend, is it? By the time I get up tomorrow morning, my mother will be pounding on the door and I won't get rid of her until Tuesday."

"That's a bit harsh."

Bren grinned. "Not really. You know how much I love her and sis. It's just that they cramp my style. I'm staying at Jack's tonight, just to make sure the house is still relatively tidy when they come. Don't want to clean too much because Mam will do it all over again when she's here anyway."

"That's disgraceful, letting your mother clean your house when she's supposed to be your guest."

Bren shrugged. "What can I say? She's a mother and that's what mothers do. Why fight it?"

Keiron couldn't help but grin. Bren was irascible. He sat with his arms crossed and his feet up on the table like an oversized black-clad leprechaun. His freckles had come out in force in the bright sunlight, scattered across his face like fairy dust. *Fairy? Oh shit.*

"Listen, Bren.... I've got something to tell you. You're not going to believe this but—"

"What's that?"

"Huh?"

"There's someone upstairs."

"Ah...yes, well that's what I was about to talk to you about."

Bren narrowed his eyes and glared at Keiron suspiciously. "Who is it?"

"Well...um...it's not precisely a who, more of a what."

"What do you mean, a what?"

Keiron heard light footsteps on the stairs and opened and closed his mouth, trying to think of something to say that would explain, something that would avert the looming disaster. Ah hell, he really hadn't thought this through. And he certainly should have mentioned it the minute Bren appeared. Now it was going to look—

"What the fuck?" Bren was on his feet, glaring over Keiron's shoulder. "Who the FUCK are you? What the...? What the...?" It wasn't often Bren was speechless, and Keiron didn't think that on this particular occasion it was a good thing.

"Hello," Draven's light voice said pleasantly from behind Keiron. "Who are you?"

"Who am I? Who? Am? I? I.... I.... Who the fuck are you?"

"I'm Draven," he said, coming into view. Keiron groaned. Of course he was naked. Of course he was.

"Draven? What the fuck— What are you doing here? What have you been doing here? Who are you?"

Keiron opened his mouth to stop the terrible thing that was about to happen, but he was too late. "I'm his slave," Draven said happily, "but only for three months."

The best thing Keiron could say about the situation was that Bren was too shocked to speak. He had a window of opportunity before it got violent.

"Bren, I can explain—"

"Explain? Explain? Well, that's going to be an interesting explanation. Go for it. Give it your best shot. Good luck thinking up an explanation I'm going to accept for a naked man turning up in your living room, declaring he's your slave.

"When did this happen?" Bren continued. "When did you start playing this little game? And with...him? What the hell were you thinking of, shacking up with someone like...him?" Bren's voice dripped venom, and he glared at Draven as if he was trying to strike him dead on the spot with his eyes alone.

Draven shrank back and clung to Keiron's arm. Bren was in full flow, his eyes sparking fire and his glowing red hair standing up on his head.

"Go ahead. Explain. Explain what the hell—"

"It's not what you think?"

"Well, this is going to be interesting. Go on then. Try to talk your way out of this one."

"Draven isn't...." Faced with it, Keiron stumbled. What the hell was he going to say? How was he going to explain? How was he going to get Bren to believe him? His sunken heart sank even further.

"Isn't what? Isn't letting you chain him to the bed? Isn't—"

"Human, Bren. He isn't human."

"What?" There wasn't much that could stop Bren in full flow, but that managed it. He stared, first at Draven, who shrank back even further, trying to hide behind Keiron, then at Keiron himself.

"He's not human, Bren. He's a fairy. He let me see him, and he was punished, and...and he...he's supposed to be...." He faltered. He could tell by Bren's face that he wasn't buying any of it. He was silent, but boiling, building up to an almighty explosion. Keiron closed his eyes for a moment, trying to regain his equilibrium. He felt sure he was about to lose his boyfriend. And as difficult as Bren was to live with, the thought of living without him was so much worse.

"Bren," he said imploringly as he opened his eyes.

Bren glared at him. "Don't you 'Bren' me. This is the last straw, Keiron. I've put up with it for too long. I've turned a blind eye, but—"

"Turned a blind eye to what? I've never done anything you needed to turn a blind eye to. I've never so much as looked at another man sexually since we've been together. It's all in your mind. Every time I speak to a man, you think I'm arranging to meet for a blow job. I'm not—"

"All in my mind? You're saying this is all in my mind? A naked man appears from your bedroom and it's all in my mind? How dare you treat me like this! How dare you disrespect me! I've had it, Keiron. How the hell am I ever going to trust you again?"

"But he's not—"

"Human," he sneered. "Yeah, right. He's a bloody fairy, right enough, but I don't see any wings."

"Please, Bren."

"Don't you 'please Bren' me. I've had it. I'm done. I'll call around to get my things and—" He stopped dead. His mouth fell open and his eyes went wide. "I...I...." he stammered, then clamped his hand over his mouth. The colour drained from his face, and for a moment, Keiron thought he was going to faint.

"What's the matter?" he asked anxiously. "Do you feel ill?"

Bren didn't answer. He simply raised a trembling hand and pointed over Keiron's shoulder.

Chapter Four

SLOWLY, KEIRON TURNED and stopped dead. For a long minute, he stared, his brain failing to allow him to acknowledge what he was seeing.

He'd known Draven was a fairy. He could hardly have denied it when he'd changed his form and colour, even if he'd had difficulty before, which, if he admitted it, he hadn't. He couldn't have said exactly what it was, but from the moment he first laid eyes on Draven, he'd had no doubt.

This, though.... This was different. This was....

Draven was still Draven, no doubt about it. He was exactly the same, except...except.... Well, he'd been taller before and his skin hadn't looked as if it had been sprinkled with diamond dust and he certainly hadn't had the diaphanous dragonfly wings that fluttered behind him, raising him a good six inches from the ground.

"Shit," Bren said and sat down suddenly, as his legs gave way. "Shit."

"Draven," Keiron said in wonder. Draven had his head down and his arms wrapped around himself. He was smaller than before, his white hair drifting about him as if there was an invisible breeze.

Draven raised his head. Tears sparkled like crystals on his cheeks. Keiron put a hand on his shoulder. He was cold and shivering. "It's okay, Draven. You can stop now."

Draven's glistening eyes locked with Keiron's, and then he let his feet touch the ground and changed. It was impossible to see how he changed. One moment, he was one thing, and then there was a shimmer around him like a cloud of sparkling dust and he was something else.

"He was angry with you," Draven said simply. "I didn't want him to be angry. He didn't believe you, so...."

"Thank you. I think that was scary for you." Draven nodded, and Keiron smiled. "Thank you," he said again. He turned to Bren. "Say thank you."

Bren blinked. "What? Say thank you? To who? For what?"

"To Draven, for showing you his true form. He hasn't even done that for me, and it scared him."

"Scared him? Scared him. I know it scared the fuck out of me. What the hell am I supposed to say thank you for?"

"For being stopped from making a huge mistake."

"What mistake?"

"You didn't believe me, Bren. You didn't trust me, and you were going to walk out on me."

"Oh. Well. What the hell did you expect? It might have been worth a phone call, or at least you could have told me when you came in from the garden. I saw a naked man walking down your stairs and you tell me he's a fairy and.... For God's sake, Kei, what was I supposed to think?"

"Well...I guess the evidence was damning, but you could have heard me out."

"Heard what? If not for this, what explanation could you have given?"

"I don't know, because it didn't happen.... This did. So now you know. Can we all calm down now, please?" He turned to Draven, who was still shivering and holding tightly to Keiron's hand. "Maybe it would be a good idea if you went upstairs and put some clothes on."

Draven glanced nervously at Bren, then turned and hurried away.

"Fuck, Kei. What the hell is that all about?"

Keiron sank down on the sofa and put his head in his hands. As best he could, he told Bren what had happened. Had it really only been yesterday?

"And he's your slave? For three months? He has to do everything you tell him to?"

Keiron glanced up sharply. He knew that tone and really didn't like the expression on Bren's face. "It's not like that, and it's not going to be like that. Yes, that's why he was sent here but he's.... Well, you'll see. I can't describe it, but in lots of ways, he's like a child. He doesn't understand our world at all. He's never been inside a house and everything's new to him. He's no more a slave than I am. Besides—" He grinned at Bren. "—he's the clumsiest person I've ever met. I think if I let him wait on me, I wouldn't have much of a house left by the time he finished."

Bren smiled, but there was a ferality about it that made Keiron's heart sink.

"Don't even think about it, Bren."

"Think about what?"

"What you're thinking right now. You are not going to use him."

"Depends what you mean by use."

"Bren!"

Bren grinned. "I'm only winding you up. Don't worry. I'll keep my hands off Tinker Bell. And so will you," he added with a snap.

"Bren, you've seen him—and you don't know the half of it. It would be like having sex with a...with a...a kid...or something. He's not human and he's not on the menu. Simple as."

"Hmm," Bren said, frowning thoughtfully.

"Don't, Bren, please."

"Don't what?" Bren was all innocence, but Keiron knew him too well to believe he wasn't cooking schemes, and the last thing he wanted was for Draven to be displayed like an exotic pet to Bren's weird friends.

"I'm stuck with him for three months, and if he has to be here, I'm going to damn well take good care of him. I'm not going to let him be hurt, by you or anyone else."

Bren pouted. "You care a lot about him, don't you?"

"I.... Yes, actually, I do care about him. He's vulnerable, very naïve, and innocent. He doesn't understand us any more than we understand him. He needs protection from the world, and he needs protection from you."

He wasn't entirely sure how Bren would take that and heaved an inward sigh of relief when Bren grinned and shook his head. "No worries here, babe. I wouldn't lay a finger on him. I'd be too afraid of breaking him."

Keiron smiled at him and Bren rose and drifted over to sit on Keiron's lap.

Bren nibbled at his ear and whispered, "He is very pretty, though, don't you think? He'll be a good ornament. Maybe in the bedroom...."

"Don't even think about it."

"Aww, Keiron, you're always so...sensible and serious. Where's the fun? This could be such an opportunity. Does it do magic?"

"What? And don't call him *it*."

"You know. He's a fairy, isn't he? I mean he has wings and he can fly and stuff. He must be able to do magic. Can he give wishes?"

"He's a fairy, not a genie."

"I can," said a voice from the stairs. Both of them turned to stare. Draven was wearing Bren's clothes again and had adjusted his body to fit. Keiron's stomach twisted. Why hadn't he just kept his mouth shut?

"Are those my clothes?"

"What else was he going to wear? I'll get him his own when I can. Would you rather he walk around naked?" Another mistake, Keiron realised.

"It wouldn't be such a bad idea."

"Yes, it would."

Bren grinned at him, mischief flashing in his eyes. He gave him a cheeky wink and turned his attention back to Draven. Narrowing his eyes, Bren looked him up and down.

"You're bigger than you were," he commented coolly. Keiron inwardly sighed again. This was just like Bren. He was so unpredictable. He could easily have been a friend to Draven if he'd wanted to. He could have taken Draven under his wing and taught him so much, more than Keiron could in some ways. Bren was so much more like Draven than he was—he had that same childlike air about him, except his was more careless than naïve.

Unfortunately, Bren was just as capable of being a selfish, spiteful bitch. He could make life very miserable for Draven—for both of them. And that was the road down which they were heading.

"Bren, stop it. It isn't Draven's fault you got upset. It's my fault. I should have told you as soon as I saw you."

"I'm not doing anything, Kei. He's the one who said he can do magic. I just want to know what kind of magic he can do. So, lay it on me, fairy boy. Are you going to wave around your 'magic wand'?"

"No," Draven said miserably, hanging his head.

"Bren, leave him alone."

"Stop being such a party pooper. I'm not hurting it."

"Him."

"Whatever. So. Go on. Show me what you can do."

Draven raised his head and his metallic eyes glittered. Keiron was momentarily scared, and even Bren seemed to take a mental step back. All the things Keiron had heard about fairies being malicious, dangerous, spiteful, without morals— It all came flooding into his head and he was worried.

Draven pointed towards Bren, who cringed away. Suddenly, there was a tinkling sound, like someone had shaken a handful of tiny bells over Bren's head, and a shower of rose petals fell onto him.

Bren gazed upwards as they continued to fall.

"Bloody hell," he said. Then.... "Ouch. They've got thorns." He scrambled to his feet, brushing off the petals and rubbing at his face, which was bleeding from a dozen tiny puncture wounds.

"Roses have thorns," Draven said in a soft singsong voice that sounded light, but Keiron thought with a sinking heart, definitely contained a note of menace.

"Yes, they do," Bren said coldly. "But little good they do them when someone cuts off the stem with a pruning knife."

Draven shrugged. "Do you want to see more?"

"Not at the moment, thank you. You may go," he said imperiously, waving his hand. Draven turned pointedly to Keiron, who nodded. Flashing a look of venom at Bren, Draven turned, tossed his head, and strode out into the kitchen. Keiron heard the back door open and close.

"Don't, Bren," Keiron said, scooping rose petals into the paper bin. He couldn't help but notice there wasn't a single thorn among them.

Bren paced, rubbing at his face. "He made me bleed. The little bitch made me bleed."

"You asked for it."

"I asked for it?" Bren stopped and turned on him, hands on hips. Keiron stifled a smile, remembering Draven had adopted a very similar stance not so long ago. "Whose side are you on?"

"I'm not taking sides. You're my boyfriend. He's a...well, I don't know quite what he is, but I know I don't want to find out exactly what he can do. We were doing fine until you turned up so just—"

"Go? Is that it? You want me to leave you and your freaky little friend to—"

"That's not what I said, Bren," Keiron said in a long-suffering voice. "I don't want you to leave. I just want you to be reasonable and not rock the boat."

"The little bitch scratches the hell out of my face and I'm the one being unreasonable?"

"He wouldn't have done it if you hadn't provoked him."

"Again, taking his side." Bren's eyes flashed dangerously, but he lowered his head and pouted. "Don't you love me anymore?"

Keiron sighed. This was an old argument. "No, Bren, I don't love you. I've told you a hundred times that I'm not like you. I don't say 'I love you' to convey affection, attraction, or even caring. Love is a serious thing."

Bren rolled his eyes and pouted. "So you don't love me. And you do love that...thing."

Sensing a tantrum coming on, Keiron rubbed his temple. "Draven is not a thing, and no..." He held up his hand to stall the storm. "Listen. I don't love Draven. If I *was* going to say 'I love you' to anyone, it would be you. I'm sure that one day I will...if you stop being so jealous and unreasonable."

Bren's lips parted, then closed. He frowned for a second, probably weighing up whether having a strop would get him anywhere. Eventually, to Keiron's enormous relief, he smiled.

"That's okay then," he said smugly.

"Just try not to fight. He's such a child."

"Yeah, a child with a box of matches in his hand."

"Exactly." Keiron sighed. "I have to work on Tuesday. What the hell am I going to do for the next three months? Can I leave him here alone all day? When I went out this morning, I found him hiding in the garden when I came back because he thought he'd broken the television."

"Broken the television?"

"He'd fiddled with the remote and deprogrammed it."

"Oh."

"Bren...please...." Keiron said wearily at the spiteful glee in his voice. "Please don't do this. It's bad enough to suddenly find I have one kid in the house, I don't want to have to deal with two squabbling ones."

"I am not a kid and I do not squabble with anyone." Bren's eyes were blazing with righteous indignation.

"No, but you are perfectly capable of getting into a war with him, sniping at him, provoking him, being spiteful to him. I know how it can go. I know what you can be like."

"Are you suggesting that—"

"Please, Bren. Please don't. I've had enough already. At least you can go home. I'm stuck with him."

"Maybe I could take him with me."

"Maybe not."

Bren threw Keiron a sly, sideward glance. "Do you think the pretty little plaything will be safe down here on his own while we...negotiate?"

Keiron's stomach twitched. "Well...it depends on how open these negotiations are going to be."

"Open? Oh, very. The negotiations are definitely going to be very, very open."

Bren grinned his mischievous grin and ran for the stairs with Keiron close behind.

When they came down, there was no sign of Draven. Bren was disappointed. "I so wanted to say goodbye."

"You'll get your chance. I've a feeling we're both going to be seeing a lot of you over the next three months."

"You say that as if it's a bad thing." Bren pouted, and Keiron smiled. He grabbed Bren around the waist and pulled him into a rough embrace.

"Depends on your definition of bad," he said, kissing Bren soundly.

"Dammit."

"What?" Keiron, still holding Bren tight around the waist, smiling down into his frown.

"I'm going to be tied up the whole weekend. I won't be back until Tuesday."

"I've never seen you so upset at not seeing me before."

"I've never been leaving you alone with a naked fairy before."

"You've seen him, Bren. He's not a love interest, not in any way."

"He can change, Keiron. He can be whatever you want him to be."

Keiron frowned. He'd never thought of that. It was true, of course but... "He could never be you, Bren. You are what I want."

"Right answer," Bren said, standing on his toes to kiss him before dancing out of his arms and opening the front door. "You'd better call me. You'd better call me a lot, or I'll be back here with a shotgun."

"Why do I believe that? Take care. Have a good time tonight and give my love to your mother and sister tomorrow."

Bren grinned. "Maybe I should bring them around here."

Keiron laughed aloud. "I can just see that visit. You remember Keiron, Mam. He's the boyfriend I didn't want to embarrass you with. Now he's living with a fairy, I thought you might want to meet them both."

Bren snorted with laughter at Keiron's terrible attempt at an Irish accent. "You're right. Not a good idea." He sighed. "They're going to be here until Tuesday afternoon. You're working, aren't you?"

"Yes, unfortunately."

"I'll be round after work then. I'm not in until Wednesday. Maybe we could have a takeaway or something and get to know each other."

Keiron knew an olive branch when he saw one, and it wasn't offered that often by Bren. He smiled sweetly and bent to kiss his volatile and unpredictable boyfriend. One thing was for sure—with Bren around, life was never going to be dull.

When he closed the door behind Bren, Keiron turned and pressed his back against it. Things were going from bad to worse, and the whole situation had the feeling of an out-of-control train, collecting speed as it hurtles towards the tree across the line. How could he ever have thought the relationship between Bren and Draven would be anything but conflictual. Bren was insanely jealous, and Draven way too innocent to recognise and avoid it. Or was he?

With a sigh, Keiron went in search of Draven. He found him in the shrubbery. Crawling into the cave, Keiron sat, his head bowed and knees drawn up, as demanded by the cramped space.

"You okay?" he asked. Draven didn't speak or move. He was curled up on the floor, his eyes tightly closed. "I know you're not asleep."

"I wasn't pretending to be asleep." Draven sounded petulant, and Keiron smiled, even as he groaned inwardly. If he'd doubted it before, this certainly reinforced his decision that he just wasn't cut out to be a father.

"You don't want to talk to me?"

"No."

"I get it. I understand if you don't want to talk to me."

"No. I don't not want to talk to you."

Keiron smiled at him, and after frowning for a moment, a slow smile crept over Draven's face and he couldn't help himself. He giggled. Then he sobered.

"I don't like him."

"I'm sorry about that, Draven. It's not Bren's fault. I should have told him about you. I should have called him. He was right to be angry."

"He was nasty and mean and spiteful."

Yet again, Keiron groaned inwardly. "I'm his boyfriend, Draven. He walked in to find me with a naked man in my house. What was he supposed to think?"

"Is it his house?"

"No, it's my house but—"

"If it's not his house, he can't tell you who you can have in it."

"I know that but—" Keiron sighed. "He's my boyfriend."

"What's that? Are you mates?"

"No, not exactly. It's not that.... It's not that...." Keiron struggled to find the right words. "A boyfriend isn't as...committed as a mate. At least I don't think so, if I'm right about what you mean." He quirked a brow at Draven, who frowned in concentration.

"Mates are those who are sworn together for life," Draven supplied.

"Yes, that's what I thought. Boyfriends aren't that committed. They just promise not to be with anyone else."

"Isn't that the same thing?"

"No, because it isn't for life. If...things change, then boyfriends part and—"

"You part?" Draven seemed deeply puzzled, and Keiron searched for the right words to make him understand.

"If we don't love each other anymore."

"But.... If you love, how can you not love?" Draven was evidently even more puzzled. Keiron sighed.

"Love is an elusive thing."

"Yes, yes it is, but...but once you've found it, why would you ever let it go?"

"Things change."

"Love doesn't change."

"It's complicated, Draven, and I've no intention of having an in-depth discussion on the meaning of love in the middle of the shrubbery. Come inside. It's starting to get chilly."

"It's going to rain," Draven said, as if it was a statement of fact.

"All the more reason not to sit under a bush."

Draven smiled and followed Keiron over the lawn.

"Is the shrubbery your safe place? Somewhere to go when things are scary, or hard?"

"Yes. It's...almost like being home. I feel safe." Draven gave a shaky smile, and it suddenly hit Keiron that as hard as it might be for him, it must be so much harder for Draven. He'd been sent from his home into a completely alien world, alone and at the mercy of strangers.

Impulsively, he put one arm around Draven's shoulder and hugged him close. "It's fine. I know this must be scary for you. I'll take care of you, I promise, and you can go to the shrubbery whenever you want. I won't disturb you there. You can take whatever you like—pillows, or...something."

"Why would I want to take—" Draven stopped in the middle of the sentence. He'd looked up and their eyes met. Draven gasped. Keiron felt something...strange. He tried to smile encouragingly, but for some reason, the smile wouldn't come, and he was suddenly very aware of how close they were.

Letting go, Keiron hurried into the house and busied himself putting coffee on to percolate.

Draven sighed. "He has gone, hasn't he?" he asked nervously.

"What? Oh, Bren? Yes, he's gone." Draven beamed. "He'll be back, though."

Draven scowled.

"You have to get used to it, Draven. Bren spends a lot of time here. He has a key, and he treats it as his second home. One way or another, you two are going to have to learn to live with each other. Please don't provoke him."

"I didn't provoke him," Draven said indignantly. "I was nice. He was the one who—"

"It's not nice to shower someone with flower petals laced with thorns," Keiron interrupted sternly.

Draven tried to appear outraged, then contrite, but eventually burst into giggles. "He looked so— The thorns stuck in his face and—"

"Draven, Bren is not your enemy. He's my boyfriend, and he's going to be spending a lot of time here. I want you to promise you'll be nice to him."

"Why should I be nice to him? He wasn't nice to me. I'm not going to let him be mean to me. He scares me, and I'm not going to let him—"

"Draven, I know that Bren can be, er, difficult. He's impulsive and he can be a real bitch, but he means well. He'd never really hurt you, and if you'll just bite your lip and make a proper effort to get on, he'll come round. I promise he will. You can be friends."

"I don't want to be friends with him," Draven said stubbornly. "I don't like him."

"Well, if you're going to stay in this house, you're going to have to do your best to be nice to him," Keiron snapped.

"Yes, Master," Draven sneered.

Keiron sighed. "I don't want you to call me that, Draven. I'm not your master."

"A rose by any other name..." Draven said, trailing off into a sigh. "The fact is," he continued sadly, "whether you want it or not, I am your slave. There's no point pretending I have a choice whether I get on with your boyfriend or not. If you tell me to, I have to. I can't get away from him. I can't hide from him, and you won't protect me from him, so I have no choice but to do my best to make him like me enough to not hurt me."

"Draven...I will protect you. Haven't I promised? I'll take care of you, and I'll make sure Bren doesn't hurt you. He wouldn't hurt you anyway. Bren's hot-headed and, yes, he can be spiteful, but he isn't cruel. You don't have to be afraid of him."

"I'm not afraid of him."

Keiron sighed. "Can we change the subject? We have all weekend before we have to worry about Bren again. Maybe you'll both be a bit more settled by then. Are you hungry?"

Draven considered, then smiled his bright, open smile, all thoughts of Bren gone from his head. "Can I try something new? Can I have some of *your* food?"

"Of course. I usually have a takeaway on a Saturday night. Do you fancy that?"

"Where do you take it away from?"

Keiron laughed. "From a shop. I telephone the shop and they bring it to the door."

"Oh. Oh, I see. I've seen the man come with the box that smells. Was he taking away?"

"Yes. He was bringing pizza. Here—" Keiron slid open one of the drawers in a sideboard and withdrew a brightly coloured pizza menu. Draven squealed with delight at the glossy pictures. He turned it over and over in his hands, examining it from different angles.

"Can I have one?"

"How about we have one to share?"

Draven paused and frowned. "But I want my own. I want a whole round circle just for me. It won't be worth having if I have to share with you."

Keiron stifled a grin. Draven was so serious. "They're a lot bigger than they seem, Draven. Didn't you see the box the delivery man brought?"

Draven shook his head. "It would have been too dangerous. But I smelled it, and I saw the corner of the box. It didn't look very big."

"Well, you can have different sizes. The one I usually have, is this big." He measured out about nine inches with his hands. "But we can get a bigger one. If you want to try out different toppings, we can have a sectioned one."

Draven shook his head. "There's too much to think about. You do it."

"What do you like? Pepperoni? Mushroom? Ham? Pineapple?"

"I know what mushroom is," he said with confusion. Keiron sighed.

"I tell you what, I'll order a sectional. We'll have ham and pineapple, pepperoni, and chicken and mushroom. What do you think?"

Draven regarded him for a moment, then shrugged. "Okay," he said and lost interest.

While Keiron ordered takeaway, Draven wandered around the room again, examining things. He brushed his fingers over the frames of pictures on the walls and photographs on the dresser, then idly picked up ornaments and bits and pieces.

When Keiron turned from the phone, he was carefully examining a DVD, turning it over and over in his fingers with a frown on his face.

"Would you like to watch that?" Keiron asked.

Draven glanced up. "Watch it? Does it do something?" He peered at it again curiously.

"It's a DVD. You put it into the DVD player, and then you watch it on the television."

Draven gazed at the shiny disc in his hand and up at the television. "Why would I want to watch it on the television? Can't I watch it in my hand?"

"No, you don't watch the disc. You watch what's on it. There's a film recorded on the disc. When you put it into the player, it translates the information on the disc into pictures and we watch them on the screen, like we did before."

Draven seemed doubtful, then smiled. He held out the disc. "But you can do it."

Taking the DVD, Keiron glanced at it. "Maybe we'll watch a different one."

"Why?"

"Because this is a horror film and I don't think you'd like it. This one is very gory and pretty scary. There's a lot of blood and violence in it."

Draven considered, then shrugged. "I don't mind."

"But you were scared of—"

"I was not scared. Well, a little. I thought it was real and we were going to get cut down. We couldn't have fought them all. I don't mind watching blood and violence, now I know it's not real. I have been into battle after all."

"You what?"

Draven looked up and smiled, his sweet, innocent smile. "It doesn't happen often, but sometimes there are wars—different clans, races. Sometimes, when there are fights among the vampires or demons, we get involved. I've fought in a few. I don't like fighting, but I can if I have to."

Keiron was utterly astonished. "Have you—Have you ever killed anyone?"

Draven frowned, giving Keiron a level look. "Yes, I have. I didn't enjoy it, but I did what I had to do."

Keiron sat down, his legs suddenly too weak to hold him. He couldn't imagine it. He just couldn't imagine this sweet, innocent child with blood on his hands. Another thought occurred to him. "How old are you?"

"Old?"

"Yes, how many years have you been alive?"

"I don't know. I've never thought about it."

"Well, you must know if you are old or young, among your own kind. There are adults and children and—"

"Not exactly. Time isn't...well, it isn't really the same. It passes differently. We don't age, as such. We are what we are, from beginning to end."

"So, you'll never grow old?"

"No."

"Do you live forever?"

Draven snorted with laughter. "No one lives forever, Keiron."

"Fair enough. Compared to humans, do fairies live long?"

"Compared to humans, just about anything lives long." He thought for a moment. "Except for animals, of course, but they're different."

"So, how do you define *long*? Compared to humans, how long do you live?"

Draven frowned. "I don't know, Keiron. I honestly don't. Like I said, time works differently for us, but I know it's a long time more. Humans get old and die, their children become grandparents, their descendants become ancestors, and fairies remain."

"I understand. Well, no, I don't, but I think I understand as much as I'm going to."

"If it helps, I remember when there used to be a wood here, before the people came. I remember when the horses in the field were used to drive carts, bringing people from the farms. I was already full grown when the very first town rose here."

Keiron blinked. "Not as young as you seem then."

"How young do I seem?" Draven asked with a glowing smile.

"Sometimes older than me, and sometimes about twelve, averaging around sixteen, I think."

Draven laughed. "No," he said, "not sixteen. Not anywhere near sixteen."

When the pizza came, Draven was transported to heaven. He tasted everything, exclaiming over it all. It was clear he'd never tasted anything like it before, and he couldn't get enough. Keiron was content to sit back and watch while he munched, his eyes either wide with excitement or closed with ecstasy. When he finished with one experience, he moved on to the next, leaving Keiron to pick over what was left.

When they'd done, Draven insisted they put the horror film on. They settled on the sofa, Draven snuggled against Keiron's side. Keiron wasn't comfortable with the closeness, but Draven seemed to find it entirely natural to wriggle under Keiron's arm and settle it around his narrow shoulders, before nestling his head against Keiron's chest and slipping a long slender arm across his waist. Keiron froze and stared at it, swallowing hard. Shit. If Bren were to walk in right now....

But Draven didn't seem to mean anything by it. Keiron was learning that Draven seldom meant anything other than precisely what he said or did. He acted entirely on impulse, doing and saying anything that came into his mind. So Keiron allowed himself to relax and enjoy the closeness. Draven was very unlike Bren, who could never sit still and was constantly talking, asking questions, pointing things out, and providing a million and one distractions. If it had been Bren, his hand wouldn't have been resting on his stomach. It would have been considerably lower.

Draven didn't ask any questions or point anything out or chat about anything. He watched avidly, and in particularly scary places, he turned his face into Keiron's shoulder and tightened his grip around his waist.

Towards the end, Keiron noticed that Draven had stopped reacting altogether, and when there was no response to his gentle shake, he realised with fondness that Draven had fallen asleep. Smiling, he looked down at the shiny silver hair and unconsciously tightened his grip around Draven's shoulders. Closing his eyes, he let his head fall back against the sofa and dozed until gathering darkness and the hiss of the television woke him.

Carefully, he stretched and slid out from under Draven, who was fast asleep. He stood for a while, gazing at the sleeping fairy, and shivered. He seemed to be glowing slightly in the gloom, and when he sighed and murmured in his sleep, a thrill shot through Keiron that made him turn hastily away and go about his normal nightly routines.

When he was sure the house was secure, Keiron returned to the living room and attempted, without success, to wake Draven. In the end, he picked up the slight form and carried him to his room. Balking at stripping him, he tucked him under the duvet, fully clothed and, for some reason, bent to kiss him on the forehead before turning and heading for his own room.

Chapter Five

KEIRON WOKE WITH a start. It was pitch dark, and the flashing display of his digital alarm said it was 3:00 a.m. His heart was pounding and his mouth dry. Something had awakened him. There was someone or something downstairs. A particularly painful thump in his chest had him out of bed and pulling on a pair of jeans.

As he stood up, there was a crash and an agonised scream, followed by raucous laughter. Heart pounding even harder, he wrenched open the door and took the stairs two at a time.

"What the fuck—"

He could barely believe the scene awaiting him. Bren and his friends were scattered around the living room, drinking beer and eating various things, from kebabs to sandwiches. They were flushed, clearly very drunk, and laughing at something that was curled up on the floor.

"Draven," Keiron called and ran to him. Draven was curled tightly, moaning and clutching his arm. He flinched away when Keiron touched him. "What the hell have you done to him?"

"Oh that's right," Bren said angrily. "You instantly assume I've done something to it. Taking its side again."

"I told you, Bren—don't call him 'it'. His name is Draven, and you know it."

"Big deal. He's a fucking fairy, whatever you call him."

"Aren't we all, honey," one of his friends chipped in, batting false eyelashes, heavy with silver glitter. Keiron ignored him and bent over Draven.

"What happened?"

"Nothing happened. He stumbled; that's all. I don't know why he even fell over. He was on his way to the kitchen, and the next thing, he's throwing a candlestick at me and writhing around on the floor."

"He threw a candlestick at you?"

Bren bent and picked up the candlestick, which was lying at his feet. "Or do you think it teleported over here?"

"Well, you must have done something. Look at him?"

"I told you; there's nothing wrong with him."

"It's all right," a soft voice said as Draven unwound himself and sat up, bracing himself against Keiron. He was holding his arm against his chest. "He didn't hurt me. Really."

"What's wrong with your arm?"

"Nothing." Draven looked down at it and flexed. "See, it's fine now."

Keiron took his hand and stretched his arm out. It seemed fine. Gently, he stroked the skin. It didn't seem bruised. Draven let out his breath in a sigh, and when Keiron raised his eyes, he was staring at him in a way that made him flush.

"I told you." Bren's voice broke the moment, and for a brief flash, Keiron wanted to punch him until his face was pulp. "The freak's just faking it. He wanted to get out of doing any more tasks."

"Tasks? What tasks? What's he doing out of bed anyway? What are you doing here?"

Bren shrugged. "I just wanted my friends to see the freak. He wants to be a slave, so I figured it was time someone made use of him. I haven't done anything bad to him, haven't hurt him or anything. He just got drinks and food for us, that's all."

Keiron felt his stomach turn and his anger rise. He forced it down to smile gently at Draven. "Are you sure you're not hurt?"

"I'm not hurt. I was, but it's gone now."

"Who hurt you?"

"Not who, what. It was the iron."

"The iron? What iron?"

"Iron? This?" Bren was turning the candlestick over and over in his hand. It was intricately twisted wrought iron.

"Ah hell," Keiron breathed. "I never thought. Draven, why didn't you tell me? I thought it was a myth. I didn't realise it was true, that you really are hurt by iron."

"I didn't know there was any here."

"But there's loads of iron things," one of Bren's friends declared. "There's knives and forks, and the computer and—"

"Not everything metal is made of iron, Rik," Bren said scornfully. "Most of it is steel, which isn't really iron at all." He examined the candlestick and narrowed his eyes. "The candlesticks are probably the only things of actual iron in the whole house."

"Then we'll get rid of them."

"Get rid of them?" Bren was outraged. "Get rid of our nice things because of that?"

"They're my things, Bren, and if I want to get rid of them, for whatever reason, I will."

"But I like these candlesticks."

"Then by all means take them back to your place."

"I.... Fine. I will."

"Now."

"What?"

"Take them back to your house—now."

"You're throwing me out?" Bren gaped at him as if unable to believe his ears.

"For now, yes. No one told you that you could come here tonight. It's three in the morning, and I was fast asleep. If I thought you'd come to see me, it would have been different, but I know damn well why you're here, and I'm not having it. For God's sake, Bren, grow up. It's like having a kid around the place. You're a grown-up now, so act like it."

Bren narrowed his eyes and glared at Draven, who had his head down so he couldn't see the pure venom in the glare. Keiron did.

"All right," Bren said in a soft, dangerous voice. "All right, whatever you say, Kei. I'll see you Tuesday. I'll see you both Tuesday." The *both* was hissed poisonously, and Keiron shook his head. Realising that to make Bren lose more face in front of his friends would make things even worse, he bit his lip and turned away.

"Are you all right?" he asked Draven quietly. Draven looked up at him, his eyes swimming with tears.

"I'm sorry," he said.

"Sorry? What are you sorry about?"

"I didn't mean to get Bren into trouble. It wasn't his fault. I tripped and the metal hurt me. I did throw the iron stick at Bren. I didn't mean to. I wasn't trying to hurt him. I just wanted to get it away from me."

"No one's mad at you for that. Are they, Bren?"

Bren paused on his way to the door. He turned and squinted at Draven in a way that made him cower back.

"I'm not mad, Draven. I'm hunky-dory. See you Tuesday."

"Bren—"

"Goodnight, Keiron," Bren said coldly and disappeared.

"I didn't mean to—"

"It's all right, Draven."

"But I made you mad with him, and I made him mad with you—and me."

"Don't worry about Bren. He'll have calmed down by Tuesday. He knows it was his fault, and he's angry right now because it happened in front of his friends, but he'll cool down and see he's to blame."

"I tried to be good, honest I did. I tried to be a good slave, but the fact is I'm not. I'm terrible. I hate being—"

"Hang on, what do you mean 'tried to be a good slave'? What were you doing down here with Bren and his friends anyway?"

"I'm sorry," Draven said automatically, as Keiron was frowning hard.

"Don't worry. I have a fair idea of the answer, and you're not to blame in the least. Just tell me what happened."

"You won't be mad at me?"

"No."

"You won't be mad at Bren?"

Keiron hesitated. "I can't promise that. Go on. Tell me what happened."

"I was asleep. I didn't hear anyone come in. And then I was awake and..." He frowned. "Well, I'm not sure, but I think it was Bren. He told me to hurry up and get downstairs because it was time to be a good little slave and earn my keep." Draven smiled brightly, although the brightness was rather brittle.

"I was excited. I thought it would be my chance to make up for all the stupid things I've done. I really wanted to be a good slave. I want to," he repeated anxiously, glancing at Keiron, who smiled and nodded for him to continue.

With a sigh, Draven went on. "When I got downstairs, Bren and his friends were here, and they told me to do things."

"What kind of things," Keiron asked darkly.

"All kinds. Getting them drinks and making sandwiches. That one didn't go very well," he said sadly. "I found the stuff but couldn't quite see how it all went together. Bren shouted at me for that."

"He shouted?"

"Well, not very loudly, but he was mad. He said lots of things that weren't very nice."

"What kind of things?"

"Oh," Draven said offhandedly, "only things like I was stupid and clumsy and useless. He was pretty much right, so there wasn't much I could say."

Keiron shook his head and imagined the scene. He growled softly.

Draven carried on as if he'd never been interrupted. "They ate the leftover pizza. I told them they shouldn't do that because we were going to have it for lunch tomorrow, but they said I was only a slave and it wasn't up to me to tell my masters what they could and couldn't do." His eyes flashed as he spoke, and Keiron felt a sinking feeling in the pit of his stomach.

"I told them you're my master and I won't give away your food to...." He trailed off, seeming contrite. "Well, I wasn't very nice at that point either. But"—he hurried on—"they asked for it. I couldn't just let them eat all the food. Of course—" He shrugged. "They ate it anyway, but I didn't give it to them." He peered anxiously at Keiron, who was feeling a little shell-shocked but managed another smile and nod.

"I think they were very drunk because Bren had to keep saying Ssh, so they didn't wake you. I started to get a bit worried about that. I thought, if they were really supposed to be there, they wouldn't have minded if you woke up. I did think about coming to get you but—"

"Why didn't you?" Keiron interrupted.

"Because Bren wouldn't let me. He caught me going upstairs and pushed me back into the room. Then, they all started to push me." Draven pouted, his lip trembling. "I didn't like that. They didn't hurt me, but they wouldn't stop."

"Ah, Draven, I'm so sorry. I—"

"It's okay. I made them stop."

"You did? How?"

"I told them I'd hex them." Draven's face brightened into a wicked grin.

"You did what?" Keiron's heart fluttered. He didn't want to hear, but he had to.

"I said if they didn't stop pushing me, I'd hex them."

"And did they...stop pushing you?"

"Yes."

Keiron heaved a sigh of relief.

"But then they started to demand I show them magic. I kept saying no, but they wouldn't stop and they wouldn't let me leave and I was scared." He flashed his eyes at Keiron, who mentally drew back from the hug he was about to offer. "And I was angry. I know I'm a slave, but I won't be treated like that, not by anyone. So I hexed them." He stated the fact baldly and with a nod of the head.

"You...hexed them?"

"Yes," Draven said proudly.

Keiron groaned. "What did you do? I didn't see anything when I came down."

"Oh, you wouldn't. It hasn't really started yet."

"What do you mean it hasn't started yet?"

"It's a delay-action hex. I thought you wouldn't appreciate it while you were asleep."

"Appreciate what?" His heart was pounding now, and he dreaded to hear the answer, but he had to.

"Well, first they'll start to sneeze and not be able to stop. Then their noses will get really big and run with green snot."

"What! Draven, you have to stop it. You have to take the spell off, right now."

"I can't," Draven said smugly, although with a wary eye on Keiron.

"What do you mean you can't?"

"They're too far away," he said innocently.

Keiron groaned. "I'd better get them back here."

"I won't take the spell off," Draven pronounced stubbornly. "And you can't make me."

"But, Draven, that's— It's just not acceptable."

Draven rolled his eyes. "It's not a problem," he said with an exasperated sigh. "It wears off in a couple of hours."

Before he could think of something to say, Keiron's phone rang. When he answered it, all he could hear was sneezing. Finally, words were spluttered out, in between sneezes.

"What...that...bitch...bitch...done...to us?"

"Don't freak, Bren. It's going to wear off soon."

"Wear...off...I...fucking...kill...."

"It sounds like you asked for it, Bren." Despite everything, Keiron was having a hard time stopping himself from laughing. The image of Bren and his friends sneezing green snot through enormous noses was at the same time frightening and intensely funny.

"Asked...for.... You should...see...Kei...I.... We...." After a particularly explosive sneeze, Bren hung up.

Draven was sniggering.

"It's not funny, Draven. Someone could get seriously hurt. You have to promise me not to use any more hexes while you're here."

"Why? It's just about the only thing in this world I can do well."

"Because it is this world, not your own. People don't do hexes here. There is no magic. People don't understand it. They're afraid of it. And people can get very angry about things they don't understand and are afraid of. They might hurt you."

"I can take care of myself," Draven muttered.

"Against Bren and his friends, yes. But what if they told other people, if many of them came, wanting to hurt you and take you away?"

"I told you," Draven said stubbornly. "I can take care of myself."

Keiron gazed into the small pointed face and smiled at the fierce determination displayed there. "Maybe you can and maybe you can't, but what if someone else got hurt? What if I got hurt?"

Draven looked stricken. "I wouldn't let anyone hurt you. I'd keep you safe."

"You know you can't do that."

"I...." Draven trailed off with a sigh. "If that's what you want, no more hexes."

"Thank you," Keiron said sincerely. "Now, don't you think it's time we both went to bed?"

"There's a terrible mess," Draven said, looking around at the empty bottles and half-eaten sandwiches and pizza.

"We can clean it up in the morning," Keiron said tiredly. "Right now, I'm exhausted and all I want to do is go to bed."

They parted on the landing, and Keiron was very glad of it. Although he was growing fond of Draven, Keiron realised more and more that the little fairy was going to be even harder work than he'd previously thought.

Chaotic thoughts whirled in his head, and it was a long time before he began to sink towards sleep, only to be yanked back again by a hesitant tap on the bedroom door.

With an inward groan, he called, "What is it?"

The door cracked open, and Draven's face appeared, glowing softly in the moonlight.

"Did I wake you?"

"No. Why aren't you asleep?"

"I'm frightened."

"Frightened? What are you frightened of?"

"Dreams."

"You had nightmares?"

Draven nodded and shuddered.

"What about?"

"Lots of things. People chasing me because I did hexes."

Keiron groaned again.

"And...." Draven stopped and stared at Keiron. "I...I dreamed you threw me out. That you didn't want me, and I had to live under the bush for three months. Bad things happened there, and I—"

"Hey." Keiron couldn't bear the tears that were running down Draven's beautiful face or the anguish in his voice or—hang on. Beautiful? When did he start thinking of Draven as beautiful? Of course he'd noticed it. He'd have had to be blind not to but.... "Draven, I'm not going to throw you out, and I'm certainly not going to make you sleep under a bush for three months. Don't worry. I'll figure something out."

"I'm scared."

Keiron sighed and pressed his eyes closed. Some part of his mind was screaming *no,* and he agreed with it. He couldn't believe what he was about to do, but— "Do you want to lie here with me for a while? Until you calm down a bit?"

"Yes, please." The plaintiveness in Draven's voice did a lot to reassure Keiron that he'd done the right thing. It was growing more like having a child all the time, and sometimes children needed to crawl into their parents' bed at night for reassurances after a nightmare. *Yes,* said that traitorously logical part of him mind, *but this isn't really like having a child at all, is it? Children are very different to fully grown naked fairies...who happen to be exquisitely beautiful and smell like—* Keiron battered the voice mercilessly and lifted the covers for Draven to slip under. Thank God he had his underpants on.

Instantly, Draven scooted as close to Keiron as he could and wrapped himself around him, nestling his head into Keiron's shoulder. Taken by surprise, Keiron lay frozen. He had no idea what to do with his hands. Draven didn't seem to have that problem at all. He tucked one hand between his body and Keiron's and curled the other around to rest on Keiron's chest, subconsciously toying with the curling dark hair.

"Mmm." He sighed, snuggling even closer, and Keiron found himself laying his own hand over Draven's. He stroked Draven's hair with his other until the shivering eased as Draven grew warmer and began to relax. What the hell was he doing? Bren would freak if he found them here like this.

Yeah…as if I give a damn what Bren thinks right now.

"Are you okay now?" he asked softly, and Draven sighed, his breath tickling Keiron's chest, ruffling the hair that Draven had stopped playing with.

"Thank you," Draven whispered. "I'm not scared anymore."

It was on the tip of Keiron's tongue to ask him to go back to his own room, but somehow, the words were never spoken and he just kept stroking the long pale hair. Draven's head grew heavy on his chest and the small seemingly frail body relaxed into sleep.

He didn't stop stroking Draven's hair until he was absolutely sure Draven was asleep. Then, he lay staring at the ceiling, hyperaware of the steady rise and fall of Draven's chest against his side, and wondered what it would be like to stroke more than just his hair.

Ah hell, this is starting to get even more complicated and that is not a good thing, not a good thing at all.

When he finally fell asleep, his dreams were full of complications.

OF COURSE, KEIRON woke late in the morning. At first, he had no memory of what had happened the night before, just a vague feeling that something wasn't quite right. As consciousness returned, he first registered a smell. It was fresh and earthy and light, somehow familiar. And then something soft against his cheek and warmth against his chest and— His eyes flew wide.

At some point in the night, they'd moved, so that Keiron was spooning Draven, who was curled up like a child, his silvery hair spread over the pillows and tickling Keiron every time he breathed. Keiron's larger body was wrapped around him, his arm protectively across Draven's chest. The thing that alarmed Keiron most of all was how…right, it felt.

"Are you awake?" Draven's soft voice made him jump, and he regretted it instantly when his morning wood jabbed Draven in the back.

"I'll take that as a yes then."

Keiron froze with horror as Draven uncurled and turned over onto his back. Keiron did the same, fluffing the duvet to cover his embarrassment. Draven grinned at him.

"Don't be embarrassed," Draven said. "My body does the same thing in the morning. I wonder why. Everyone does, even the gnolls. Hmm. Anyway, mine went away ages ago. I've been awake for hours."

"Why didn't you get up?"

"I didn't want to wake you."

"So what have you been doing for all these hours?"

"Thinking."

"Thinking? About what?"

"Lots of things."

"Are you going to share any of them with me?"

"No," Draven said simply.

"Oh," Keiron said, nonplussed. "Do you want some breakfast? I'm starving."

"That's one of the things I was thinking about," Draven said with a grin. "I've been thinking really hard about all the things I've seen and the things I've seen done with them and I think I can work out how to make a sandwich. Or. Or. Or.... I found the toaster and if you push the lever down— You have to press the switch on the wall first or it doesn't work," he announced seriously. "Then you press the lever down and put the bread in and it comes back out all brown and crunchy. Bren showed me, last night."

"Bren showed you how to make toast?" Keiron was shocked. He'd had visions of Bren with a whip in his hand and Draven cowering in the middle of the jeering crowd. It seemed it hadn't gone off quite as he'd thought.

"Yes, he showed me where all the...things...the...um...the things in the drawer that you cut and poke with, and the sharp things that I probably shouldn't play with...and...and...."

"Slow down. I get the message that Bren has been showing you around the kitchen. So, you want to make breakfast?"

"Well...you said breakfast was first food, right? The food you have when you get up."

"Yes."

"And then you have middle food, in the middle of the day?"

"That's right."

"And then end food is the last food."

"Well, unless you're hungry and have supper before you go to bed. What's your point?"

"I don't think we have time for first food, unless you want middle food at the end and end food for supper food."

Keiron blinked. "Could you say that again, more slowly?"

"I've been awake for a long time. The sun was up hours and hours ago. I missed it, but I still woke early. And you didn't. So, if I'd had first food when I woke up, then it would be time for middle food now. But, as you've just woken up, your first food would be the middle food and—"

Keiron dazedly reached for the clock. It was after eleven thirty. He blinked, surprised. "You're right. We've missed breakfast. Do you want to make lunch?"

"Lunch? That's middle food?"

"Yes." Keiron smiled, rubbing at his temple. The mental gymnastics had left him with a slight headache. "So, do you want to make it?"

"Can I?"

"Of course you can."

Draven threw back the bedclothes and bounced out of bed, raising his arms over his head in a bone-cracking stretch. Keiron tried not to stare at the play of defined muscle under the fair skin. Since when had Draven been toned? Was it an illusion he'd created for effect, like when he'd grown to fit the clothes, or had the muscles always been there, covered by Keiron's image of Draven rather than what he actually saw?

Keiron's mouth was suddenly dry as Draven put his hands under his hair and lifted it off his neck, letting it fall in rippling waves over his shoulders and down his back. Had he done that for effect, or was he entirely unaware of the effect he was having on Keiron's reluctant libido?

"Draven," Keiron called as Draven sauntered from the room. Draven turned. "Don't forget to put on some clothes." Draven grinned and disappeared.

Left alone, Keiron groaned and turned over, facing away from the door. He curled up, hugging his chest. What the hell was going on? He had a high-pressure job as an associate at one of the larger accounting firms in the city, and all he wanted when he came home was a quiet life. To be able to close the door on the outside world and know there were going to be no more dramas or crises clamouring for his attention. He wanted to be able to take off his tie, kick off his shoes, have a beer, and drink it with a takeaway pizza while relaxing on his couch. He wanted to enjoy barbecues in his garden. He wanted pressed slacks and loafers. He wanted—

Bren had burst his bubble eighteen months ago, steamrollering into his life at a nightclub he'd been dragged to against his will. The feisty Irishman had wheedled from him a sense of fun and excitement he hadn't even known he had. Suddenly, his life had been filled with colour and more than enough drama. Even that was too much for him. The glitter was wearing off, and it was beginning to feel like everything Bren did annoyed or frustrated him.

It was all complications, all stresses he could do without. Then there was Draven. Had it really only been two days? Less than that. Suddenly all hope of a quiet life had disappeared. Even Bren's drama paled into insignificance next to finding a fairy in your bed. Although....

Letting his mind wander past the throbbing ache between his legs, Keiron had to acknowledge that while Bren's dramas invariably had him gritting his teeth, Draven's made him smile. He let his mind play over the rapidly changing expressions and emotions, the childlike excitement at each new thing, the sweet innocence even when he was saying something outrageous. Even the twinkling mischief that bordered on malice when he felt slighted by Bren.

Unbidden, his thoughts were tugged towards the first confrontation, when he'd seen Bren's frozen gaze and turned to find the little creature with the dragonfly wings that couldn't, just couldn't have been Draven, not his Draven.

Mentally shaking his head, he got out of bed and hurried to take care of business in the bathroom.

Stepping out of the shower twenty minutes later, Keiron felt fresh, clean, and calm. He had two...well, one and a half days of tranquillity remaining until he returned to work—and Bren—on Tuesday. He was going to enjoy it. He'd spend it showing Draven some of his favourite things, maybe even taking him for a walk in the park.

The thought of taking Draven out in public was a scary one, but he wasn't going to be able to keep him cooped up in the house for three months. It might be fun to show him the bandstand. It was Sunday so they'd have someone playing there this afternoon. Yes, that sounded like a good idea. Not even Draven could get into much mischief listening to a band in the park. They'd take a picnic and eat dinner on the grass at the side of the lake. Smiling, he pulled on his clothes and drifted down the stairs to the smell of burned toast.

Chapter Six

WHEN KEIRON TOLD Draven they were going out, Draven got excited and literally bounced around, asking questions. However, as soon as they stepped out of the door, he grabbed onto Keiron's arm and wouldn't let go.

"What's wrong?" Keiron asked.

"It's so...big. I've never been anywhere so big and loud. There are no gates I know of that lead into places like this. That's one of the reasons I got into trouble coming to you. They...they told me there were metal monsters, but I didn't believe them." They reached the main road, and as they waited at the crossing, an enormous eighteen-wheeler rumbled past. Draven jumped so hard, he almost knocked Keiron over.

"Do you want to go home?"

Draven's eyes, when he raised them to Keiron's, were enormous. He'd toned down the colour, at Keiron's suggestion, and now they were pale blue and highly un-Draven-like. His face was even paler than usual. Draven swallowed hard and shook his head—just a short sudden shake. His lips were compressed, trapped between his teeth, giving Keiron the impression he was afraid to open them in case he screamed.

"It'll be a lot quieter at the park. Don't worry. Haven't you ever been into the city before?"

Draven shook his head. His gaze darted everywhere and he pressed so close Keiron that he found it hard to move.

"Lots of people are scared of the city. It's loud and fast and cold. But don't worry. I live here and I'm used to it. I'll take care of you. I promise."

Draven nodded but didn't seem convinced.

Draven didn't relax until they were well into the park, surrounded by trees and greenery. Keiron knew he was feeling better when he started asking questions.

"What's that?" he asked excitedly. "What are they doing?"

Keiron glanced in the direction Draven was indicating. A group of boys were kicking around a ball.

"They're playing football."

"What's football?"

"It's a game."

"Ooh, a game. I like games. Can we play?"

"You need more than two people to play football."

"Well, can we play with them?" Draven, still holding on to Keiron's arm, tugged him towards the group of footballers.

"I don't think so?"

"Why not?"

"I'm not exactly dressed for football, and besides, I haven't played for years."

"I haven't played at all, but I want to try. Please can we try?"

Keiron gazed down into his earnest face. He sighed. "Well...I suppose you can try. Go and ask if you can play. There aren't really that many rules, not in this kind of game. You just kick the ball in the general direction of the other team's goal."

"What's a goal?"

"They'll tell you. If they let you play."

He watched fondly, as Draven scampered across the grass, straight into the group of young footballers. Everyone stopped and stood around in interest. Draven seemed to be talking animatedly, and the others joined in. Once or twice, Draven looked over in his direction and gestured. Suddenly, Keiron's stomach turned over. What was he telling them? Was he telling them he was Keiron's slave? Ah hell.

But no one seemed the slightest bit interested in him. Apart from a brief initial glance, none of them even looked his way. Within five minutes, Draven was tearing around the field, enthusiastically kicking the ball. It was impossible to tell, from where Keiron stood, whether Draven was any good, but he certainly seemed to be getting a lot of ball action.

Eventually, Draven came racing back across the field, paused to wave at the boys, who were all yelling and waving, then preceded Keiron down the path, laughing and literally bouncing. Keiron smiled indulgently but understood less than half of the excited babble coming out of Draven's mouth. The fear was forgotten, and Keiron felt, not for the first time, as if he was the father of a teenager.

"Time to calm down a bit, Draven," Keiron said, after ten minutes of constant chatter. People were staring at the excited young man, and

Keiron grew nervous that they might attract unwanted attention. To be honest, he was beginning to regret ever taking Draven to the park in the first place.

"Sorry, sorry but...but.... There are so many people. There are babies and old people and sweet people and scary people and people running and...what are they doing?" He pointed towards a group of boys who were skateboarding in a very small skate park.

"They're skateboarding, and no, you can't have a go."

"Why not? It looks like fun. There are little wheels on those bits of wood."

"Yes, that's the point. We can watch for a while if you like."

"Yes, yes."

It was only a few minutes before Keiron resigned himself to the inevitability of Draven trying out skateboarding.

"Oh. Right. Go ahead."

Once again, Draven went running across the park to the group of boys. At first, he was treated with caution, if not hostility, but it was a surprisingly short time before someone handed him their board.

Draven kept falling, but he kept getting up. In half an hour, battered, scraped, and bruised, he was taking on the half pipe and earning serious respect from the group. Keiron's heart swelled with pride and affection.

When Draven came running back to Keiron, it was with a huge grin on his face.

"Did you see me? Did you watch me?"

"I saw you. I was very proud."

"It hurt," Draven announced matter-of-factly, rubbing a scrape on his elbow. "But it was fun."

"You're very good at learning new things."

"Am I?" he asked proudly. "I try hard. I was thinking of letting my wings out, but I thought that might be a bad idea, so I didn't."

Keiron swallowed hard. For a time, he'd forgotten. The mere thought that Draven might have transformed here in the park made him shiver.

"Don't do that, Draven. Not out here in front of people."

"That's right. You said." His attention was already diverted to something else. Suddenly, he started to run along the path in a different direction. Startled, Keiron followed. He hadn't even seen the woman fall, but Draven was scrabbling on the ground, chasing oranges. The woman scrambled to her feet, impatiently examining a hole in her tights.

"Dammit," she cursed. "I knew it was a bad idea to walk home through the park. Damn potholes. I'm going to make a complaint to the park commissioner."

Keiron privately thought it wasn't really the fault of the commissioner that she was walking along a rough path wearing six-inch heels, but he didn't say anything.

"I think I got it all," Draven said enthusiastically, handing her a bag full of groceries. "You need to be careful, though, there's a hole in the bag."

The woman snatched the bag, glaring at Draven suspiciously. "Thank you." Her tone was begrudging, and head in the air, she tottered down the path.

"She wasn't very nice, was she?" Draven observed.

"No, not really. Unfortunately, most people are like her, suspicious when a stranger does something nice for them."

"They are?" Draven asked, falling into stride with Keiron as they headed for the bandstand.

"They are. I'm not saying it's right, but so many people take advantage of others that everyone is suspicious."

Draven frowned, thinking deeply. "I don't like it here."

"I thought you were enjoying yourself."

"No, not here. I am enjoying myself in the park. I meant here, generally, in your world. It's cold."

"Yes, sometimes it is. But it's not all like that. Sometimes, we warm up a bit." He smiled, but Draven continued to frown at him.

As they neared the bandstand, they were joined by more people headed in the same direction. The roll of drums rumbled across the grass like distant thunder, and Draven's head went up, an interested expression replacing the melancholy on his face.

"What's that?"

"It's music. That's where we're going. To watch a band perform in the bandstand."

"I know it's music, Keiron. As if I've never heard music. What's a bandstand?"

"You'll see."

A minute or so later, they turned a corner and found themselves at the edge of a fairly steep slope, leading down to a large bandstand where a live band was playing. It wasn't the brass band that used to play there or the indie band that often gigged there. Today, it was a jazz band with electrified cello and bass, along with a very talented sax player and a gravel-voiced jazz singer. Draven was entranced.

They sat down on the soft, springy grass and soaked up the afternoon sunshine along with dozens of others. Children ran around, playing and chasing each other. Lovers stretched out, lying close, their bodies touching. Elderly people unfolded canvas chairs, and a number of people, like Keiron, laid out blankets and picnics on the ground.

Draven sat down, his head swivelling to take in all the activity, the colour, the sounds, the music.

"This is so exciting. So many people. What—"

"Draven," Keiron said drowsily. "Enough with the questions. Just relax and listen to the music."

"I—"

"Relax, Draven."

"All right," Draven said brightly. He leaned back and closed his eyes, tilting his face up to the sun. Keiron allowed himself to relax, letting the waves of music wash over him. He turned to ask Draven if he wanted a cool drink from the chiller, only to find him curled up and fast asleep. Shaking his head with a smile, Keiron popped a beer.

Keiron spent a very pleasant afternoon, people-watching and listening to the band. He'd never been much interested in watching people—the things they did, the way they interacted with each other. He began to find pleasure in small things—the laughter of children, the looks passing between the young lovers, the quality of the music, and the way an elderly couple held hands. They were things he would usually not have noticed, and he realised with a shock after an hour or so that he was beginning to see the world through Draven's eyes. It made him feel warm.

He let Draven sleep for an hour but noticed he was starting to get pink from the sun, so he woke him gently. Draven sat up, sleepily rubbing his eyes and yawning.

"You were going to sleep through the whole afternoon. You've missed most of the band show."

"Sorry. I felt sleepy."

"I'm not really surprised after all the exertion with the football and skateboarding. Are you hungry? I've brought a ton of food, and it'll dry out if we don't eat it soon."

"Mmm, yes. Can I have one of the sandwiches I made?"

"Of course you can. You can have whatever you want."

Sitting back contentedly, munching a sandwich and drinking beer, Draven watched the band and frowned.

"What's wrong?"

"I don't understand it—your world. I don't understand it at all. People can be so mean and cold, but...you're not mean or cold and all these people seem really nice and they obviously like each other. The music players want to make people happy and the children are playing and everyone is smiling. Why isn't it like this all the time?"

"I don't know," Keiron said, frowning. "I really don't know. There are bad people out there, people who hurt others, who just want power and don't care what they do or who they hurt to get it. People lie and steal and hurt other people."

"We get that in our world, too. There are always bad people; bad fairies; bad elves, whatever. But in our world, the good people stick together. We help each other when we can. We make ourselves strong so the bad people can't hurt us so much. We trust each other and take care of each other."

"Maybe in your world it's easier to see who the bad people are."

"Not always. The fairest face can hide the blackest heart."

Keiron looked at Draven in surprise. He seemed sincere, not as if he was reciting something he'd heard or learned. He was still frowning, still eating, somehow distant now, withdrawing from the world he didn't understand. There was suddenly a shadow over the day.

"There's no blackness in your heart," Keiron found himself saying, shocked and horrified that he'd said it, and even more so that he continued, "and your face is one of the fairest I've seen."

Draven turned his head and stared at him with a very strange expression on his face. A smile began to creep through the severe expression. "You think my face is fair?"

For a moment, Keiron was transfixed, and then he broke the connection and glanced away. "You know it is."

Draven was silent for a while, and then he said. "It's true, but it's also true that you've no idea whether or not there's blackness in my heart."

Keiron smiled. "Trust me, Draven, the state of your heart is clear in everything you say and do. There might be darkness there—there is in everyone—but it's not black, that's for sure." He sneaked a glance at

Draven, who looked thoughtful then smiled brightly and lifted his eyes to the band again.

It occurred to Keiron, just as the band was beginning to pack up and the evening chill to descend, that he was happier than he'd been in a long time.

The walk back to the house was just as eventful as the one to the bandstand. Draven almost got run over by a cyclist when he ran across the road to help a little girl who was lost...then got shouted at by her mother. He was also shouted at by a jogger, who fell over him as he was crawling backwards out of a bush. He was so embarrassed that he wouldn't tell Keiron why he'd gone in there in the first place.

Keiron would never have admitted it to anyone, but as they approached the park gates, he was hoping Draven would be as frightened by the noise and pace of the city as when they'd come. He felt guilty about it, but the thought of Draven pressed against his side, clinging to his arm, was so sweet he couldn't push it aside.

As it happened, Draven wasn't as scared, but he was still distinctly nervous of the press of bodies and particularly the heavy traffic. He slipped his arm through Keiron's and held on tight. Keiron smiled and gazed fondly at the top of his silvery head.

By the time they got back to the house, Draven was worn out again and curled up on the sofa, nodding.

"Have you ever tried hot milk with nutmeg?" Keiron asked, and Draven shook his head. "Go upstairs and put on a pair of pyjamas—there are some blue ones in the drawers in your room. They're Bren's, but they'll do. He hardly ever wears them. I don't know why I bought them really. Bren's not the pyjama type. You don't have to change to fit them."

"Why?"

"Why don't you have to change, or why should you wear them?"

"Both."

"Well, there's no need for you to change because it doesn't matter if they're too big or not. No one's going to see you, and you're not going to be jumping around, so—"

"Why do I have to wear anything at all?"

"For the sake of my sanity," Keiron said, only half joking.

Draven frowned, puzzled.

"Don't worry about it. Just go and change while I make the drinks. If you're wearing pyjamas, it won't matter if you fall asleep. I can just carry you up to the bedroom, and I won't have to wake you up...or strip you."

Draven tilted his head to one side and continued to frown at Keiron. "Why don't you want to see my body? Does it displease you that much?"

"Displease me? God no. No, it doesn't displease me, not at all. It's just...." Keiron groped around for words to explain, but there were no words for precisely what he wanted to say, so he made do with what he could. "We—humans that is—we don't show our bodies very much. One of the reasons we wear clothes is to hide our bodies from each other."

"But why?"

"Because...." Keiron suddenly realised that Draven would have no concept of modesty or embarrassment, and he had no idea how to explain it to him. "Nakedness is very much connected to sex."

"It is? Why?"

"Because it is. I can't tell you why it is because I don't know. It is what it is. Sex is a taboo subject."

"What's taboo?" Draven sat forward on the sofa, no longer sleepy but alert and interested.

"It's something people don't talk about."

"You don't talk about sex? Ever?"

"Yes, of course we do. It's just.... It's something that's considered not 'proper', not something that decent people do—talking that is, not doing. It's considered low and crude and improper. Sex is supposed to be something that happens in private, behind closed doors, and not talked about outside. And bodies are only supposed to be revealed during those private times.

"Of course, that's not how it actually happens. There are books and films and pages in newspapers that are devoted to pictures or descriptions of naked bodies and sex, but it's something everyone does, but no one admits to. Do you understand?"

Draven shook his head, and it was clear that he really didn't.

"Well...religion has something to do with it. Religious people, who are in control in most countries, have all kinds of beliefs and constrictions about sex and nudity. A lot of religions teach it's sinful to show your body or to talk, write, or watch anything to do with sex. Religion can have a powerful effect on people's minds.

"The ideal they try to impose is that sex happens for the purpose of having children, and makes people subtly guilty for actually enjoying it. It's supposed to happen only in private between two people; one woman and one man. Anything that diverts from that model is frowned on and sometimes even made illegal."

"Illegal? What's that?"

"It's breaking the law."

"Oh, I know about laws. They're like decrees of the Council, yes?"

"I think so."

"So, if you do things that the religion doesn't like, they'll punish you."

"No. Religions don't make laws. Governments make laws...like your council. The prime minister is, I guess, like your High Lord."

"The High Lord makes rules?"

"Kind of. Let's run with that. I don't really feel like getting into a discussion about politics tonight."

"Politics?"

"Never mind. Anyway, the governments of different countries make different laws and the laws change over time."

"The laws change?"

"Yes, as societies change and develop and grow. Sometimes things that were considered wrong in the past aren't considered wrong anymore."

"Well, were they wrong?"

"They were thought to be at the time, but—"

"Either they were wrong or they weren't wrong." Draven frowned deeply, clearly struggling to understand. He was twirling a strand of hair round and round his finger, distracting Keiron, who was struggling in the face of Draven's blank incomprehension.

"Right and wrong are not absolutes, Draven. They change with the times, with the person, so the laws change to—"

"Change? But how?" Draven frowned deeply, and Keiron could see his lips moving as if he was trying to work through something in his head. Keiron remained silent and allowed him to. "Either something is right or it's wrong. Using dark magic is wrong, unless you're a dark mage. That's a fact. It will never change. Honouring life and not taking it lightly is right. That's a fact. It will never change. The rulings of the council and the decrees of the king and queen are absolutes. They are facts. They never change. They have never changed."

"Are you telling me that your laws are the same now as they were hundreds of years ago?"

"Thousands."

"They've never changed?"

Draven shook his head, putting the strand of hair into his mouth and chewing.

"So, once a decision has been made, once the High Lord or the King or Queen make a decision, it can never be changed?"

"Well yes, it can, sometimes. But only if something very big has happened."

"Like what?" Keiron perched on the edge of the chair, leaning forwards, fascinated by the glimpse of Draven's world.

"Well...." He thought for a while. "Once, my friend was banished for poisoning his brother. Then they found that his brother had been conspiring with dark elves, so they withdrew the banishment."

"Your friend poisoned his brother?"

"Yes, but he was conspiring with dark elves."

"Did your friend know that?"

"I don't know. Does it matter?"

"Um...well...yes. It kind of does."

"I don't know," Draven repeated with a smile and a shrug. He spat out his hair and tucked it behind his ear.

Keiron mentally shook himself...yet again. Yet again, his image of Draven as a sweet young thing was shattered as he sat there and blithely justified poisoning your own brother because of the company he kept. Even though it sounded as if dark elves were bad news.

"Don't you think your friend's brother should have had a trial before a death sentence was passed?"

Draven seemed confused again. "There aren't many trials, Keiron. There is only a trial if the High Lord isn't sure."

"How can he be sure, when he hasn't had a chance to hear evidence and speak to witnesses?"

"He does speak to witnesses. Anyone who has seen or heard or knows anything about it. He speaks to everyone if he thinks he needs to. Then he decides."

Keiron rubbed his temple, feeling a headache coming. "Well...it's very different here. There are laws made by the government and moral laws made by organisations like the church. Those kind of laws are only followed by people who buy into that religion or organisation."

Draven shook his head, his face pained. "So, not only do your laws change, but there are different laws for different people?"

"Yes."

"But how do you know which ones to follow?"

"That's the trick. The problem is that sometimes the wrong kind of people follow the wrong kind of laws."

"Wrong laws? You said that laws change when they're wrong. But now you're saying that some laws are wrong, even when they're not changing."

Keiron thought about it. "Yes, I suppose."

"What kind of laws are wrong? Maybe they're not really wrong, but you just think they are."

"There are so, so, so many laws in so many different countries, Draven. There are some that are thought to be absolutely right in some countries or communities but are wrong in others."

"Like what?"

"Um...." Keiron cast around for an example. "Oh," he said, hitting on a good one. "In some religions, a man having sex with another man is breaking the moral law. In some countries, it's breaking the criminal law. In some places, you can be executed for it."

Draven looked at him blankly. "I don't understand."

"There are people who think it's wrong for a man to have sex with another man. People have been abused, persecuted, or even died for it."

"What? Just for having sex with a man?"

"Yes."

"But you and Bren have sex?"

"Yes." Keiron turned away, suddenly acutely embarrassed.

"You're not going to be hurt, are you?" Draven asked anxiously. He scooted to the edge of the chair and leaned far forward, as if he was about to reach out.

"No. This is not one of the countries where it's illegal to have sex with men."

"Oh. What if you have sex with other things?"

"Other...things?"

"Yes, like...elves and vampires and things. Can you have sex with males who are not men?"

"I can have sex with anyone I want. It's just that some people don't like it."

"What does it have to do with anyone else?"

"That's a big question, Draven. It's something people have been asking for generations. I don't have an answer. Neither do they."

"But what—"

"I'm tired, Draven. Can we have the rest of this discussion another time?"

"But why—?"

"Draven!"

"Oh. Should I put those pinanas on?"

"Pyjamas."

"Whatever."

"Yes, I'll make some hot milk and we can sit...quietly and watch a film."

Chapter Seven

KEIRON WAS LONELY. He'd spent the evening relaxing on the sofa with Draven snuggled in to his side. They'd started at opposite ends, but Draven was a tactile person and craved physical contact, so he'd moved closer and closer until he was cuddled right into Keiron and Keiron had his arm around his shoulders.

For a brief moment, Keiron wondered whether this action was deliberate, but one glance into Draven's face convinced him that his flirtatious manner was entirely innocent.

It wasn't having innocent results, though. When Draven fell fast asleep, Keiron had carried him to bed. As he lifted him into his arms, Draven stirred and wrapped his arms around his neck, nestling his head into Keiron's neck. When he inhaled deeply, smelling Keiron's hair, Keiron started to tremble. He continued doing so long after he'd tucked Draven into bed and, although he knew it was a bad idea, bent over and kissed him on the forehead.

Now, Keiron was lying in bed, feeling it was big and empty, and he was lonely. Memories of the night before, of holding Draven's slender body, were treacherously forcing his mind from the thoughts of Bren he was frantically trying to replace them with. This was ridiculous. Draven was out of bounds. He wasn't even human. And Keiron had Bren. It wasn't going to happen. It just wasn't going to happen. Starting tomorrow, he was going to distance himself from Draven completely. If he had to have a slave, he was going to have to start treating him like one. Draven wouldn't like it but—

The tap on the door made him jump out of his skin. He considered ignoring it and pretending to be asleep, but found himself calling. "Come in, Draven. What's wrong?"

Draven looked dreadful. His eyes were red-rimmed, and he was shaking like a leaf. Keiron was shocked. "What's the matter? Did you have another dream?"

For a moment, Draven gazed at him blankly, then nodded. Again, Keiron groaned inwardly, before pulling back the quilt and tapping the bed in silent invitation. Draven slid in and clung to Keiron, who stroked his back until the shaking eased.

"What's wrong?" Keiron repeated. "What did you dream about?"

"I...don't remember," Draven said. Keiron believed him.

"Then why are you so upset?" Keiron shifted so he could look down into Draven's face.

Unhesitatingly, Draven met his eyes. "I'm alone." His voice was hoarse.

"You're not alone, Draven. You have me."

"I have one person in a world full of people I don't understand. You have so many rules, and they're cruel ones. I'm scared I'll break one without knowing. I'm scared they'll take me away. I...I'm not good with rules, even the ones I understand."

"I've noticed. Don't worry. If you listen to me and don't do anything silly, you'll be fine. It's only for three months, Draven."

"Yes." He seemed even sadder and dropped his head. "I'm tired. Can I sleep now?"

"You feel better?"

"Yes, better." He wasn't convincing, but Keiron left it at that.

Falling naturally into the position they'd started with the night before, Keiron stroked Draven's hair until he relaxed.

"Do you like me?" Draven asked out of the blue, startling Keiron, who'd begun to drift, despite himself.

"Of course I like you. What makes you ask that kind of question? Do you think I don't like you?"

"I did. You were angry about having to put up with me, and I messed up so many times. But today...I thought maybe you like me a little bit now."

"I like you more than a little bit, Draven. I'm growing to be very fond of you." Seeing the puzzlement on Draven's face, Keiron explained. "Fond means you're a very sweet person and I can't help but like you. You're frustrating and annoying, and trouble follows you like a shadow, but despite it all—hell, maybe because of it all—I can't help but like you."

"Good," Draven said. "I like you too." And that was the last he said before falling asleep, leaving Keiron staring into the darkness, feeling like he'd been kicked in the balls.

FOR THE SECOND time, Keiron woke with his body wrapped around Draven and liking it. For the second time, Draven was already awake and well aware of it.

"Can I have another rain bath?" Draven asked quietly as soon as Keiron stirred.

"Rain bath?" he mumbled, still half asleep. "Oh, you mean shower. Of course you can."

"Thank you," Draven said softly and slipped out of bed without turning to look at Keiron. Keiron was left feeling somehow shaken.

Within a few minutes, there was a hesitant tap on the door. "How do I make it start?" Draven called from the other side.

Smiling, Keiron got out of bed and pulled on a robe.

Draven hadn't taken off his pyjamas, so Keiron felt safe to enter the bathroom. He showed Draven how to turn on the shower, and Draven was attentive but cool.

"Is everything all right?"

"Yes."

"Are you sure? You seem upset about something."

"Not upset, no." Draven looked at him with his wide-open stare.

"Then what?"

"I don't want to hurt anyone," Draven said, keeping his gaze steady. "And I don't want Bren to be even madder at me."

"Bren? What has this got to do with Bren?"

"I like you," he said. "Too much. I don't think we should sleep together anymore."

"I don't understand."

Draven put his hands on his hips. "I know you don't like to talk about it, Keiron, but I didn't think you'd be so stupid about it. I like you. I like the way you look. I like the way you smell. I like the way you are. I want to have sex with you, and if I did, Bren would hate me. You'd both hate me, so it would be better if we didn't get so close anymore."

"I.... You.... What?" Keiron stammered, his eyes getting wider and wider as the import of Draven's words sank in.

"You heard what I said. Can you go now, so I can take my rain—my shower?"

"Draven—"

"It's fine. I understand. I'm not going hurt anyone. I won't make trouble with Bren. I won't come into your room again. If you wish, I'll spend my time in the garden. I don't have to come into the house at all."

"I-I'm just a bit shocked at your directness. I'm not used to it. Of course I don't want you to live in the garden. Just-just remember to wear clothes. I think I can manage to keep my hands off you, if you wear clothes."

Keiron was trying to lighten the atmosphere, but it seemed Draven didn't see the funny side. He simply nodded, tight-lipped. "Can I have my...shower please? I promise I'll wear clothes. Would you like me to be less...fair?"

"What? No, no of course not. I don't want you to be anything but yourself. We're going to be together for three months. I'm glad you put everything on the table. We can work with it."

"You confuse me," Draven said and pushed Keiron out the door, closing it firmly in his wake.

Keiron went downstairs into the kitchen and absentmindedly put on a pot of coffee. He didn't know what to think, what to do. It wasn't every day he stood in a bathroom and had a fairy say he wanted to have sex with him. To say he was unsettled would be an understatement of epic proportions.

Automatically, he went through the routines of making coffee and setting out a medley of breakfast things. Then he sat down, waiting and thinking. He honestly didn't know what he felt for Draven. There was an attraction there, for sure. It was different from what he felt for Bren: very different, but it was there nevertheless. When Draven wasn't making him feel like a long-suffering father, he was making him feel something different altogether.

In some ways, Draven reminded Keiron of Bren. He was bright, fiery, inquisitive, exciting, and unpredictable—but he had something Bren didn't have. Keiron couldn't quite put his finger on exactly what that was. For sure, he was more direct and more honest, but it wasn't that. Maybe it was that beautiful innocence, so childlike and pure. Of course, Keiron was aware it was an illusion. No one who could put a sneezing hex on someone or speak calmly about killing could be entirely pure. And as far as he could gather, fey had a different morality, but the feeling was there, nevertheless.

The thing was.... The thing was, there was also something about him that was decidedly not childlike. There was a strength, an unconscious sensuality that had Keiron's pulses racing.

There was only one conclusion to his thoughts—Draven was dangerous, very dangerous, and he had no idea what to do about it.

When Draven came downstairs, the atmosphere was tense. They ate in silence, and Draven avoided Keiron's eyes, even when Keiron was trying to catch his glance. Afterwards, Draven collected the dishes and put them in the sink, managing to drop and smash Keiron's favourite mug.

"Oh, it's no use," Draven cried, sounding distraught. "I'm useless. I don't fit and it doesn't work. I can't do this. I just can't." Before Keiron could say anything, Draven took off out of the door. Keiron had expected something and wasn't far behind. He caught Draven halfway across the lawn and grabbed him by the arm. Draven struggled for a while, then went still, head down.

"It's fine. It's not going to be easy, but we can work through this. We can work it out."

"No. I can't. I'm useless. I can't do anything right, not even...I can't even get my relationship with you right. I've spoiled it. We were supposed to be friends. Just friends. We were supposed to be able to work together and—"

"Draven, stop it. You're not useless. You haven't spoiled anything. I'm flattered and pleased that someone as wonderful as you has feelings for me. It was a shock when you just came out and said it, because it's not something humans do. That doesn't mean it's wrong. I'd rather know. I always know where I am with you. I like that you're so completely honest. I don't want you to live in the garden. I don't want you to run away. I don't want you to feel sad or upset or angry. I want you to be happy. I want...I want...."

Draven raised his head and met Keiron's eyes. The incredible metallic blue was electric in the sunlight and froze him. He couldn't move. He couldn't think. He certainly wasn't thinking when he released his grip on Draven's arm, slipped his hands around his waist, and kissed him.

It was a sweet kiss. At first, Draven was stiff in his arms; then with a sigh, he melted. Draven's lips parted, his arms encircled Keiron, and he moaned softly.

On the brink of getting lost in the kiss, Keiron pulled back. "I can't, Draven. I'm sorry, I—"

Draven's expression changed rapidly from wonder, to shock, to anguish. He tore himself out of Keiron's embrace and fled. By the time Keiron got to the bottom of the garden, he'd vanished.

For a long time, Keiron just stood there, staring at the bushes. He was completely numb. What had he just done? That was way more than a kiss. Dammit. The last thing he'd ever wanted to do was hurt Draven, but by the expression on Draven's face when he ran, that was exactly what he'd done.

What if he didn't come back? Keiron realised it would probably be for the best, that it would solve a lot of problems, but the thought he might never see Draven again hurt so much he groaned with pain and called Draven's name again.

"Please, Draven. Please come back. I didn't mean what you think I meant. Please come back and talk to me. Please, just talk to me." There was nothing.

DRAVEN DIDN'T COME back that day, and Keiron spent an uncomfortable night, trying to convince himself it was for the best. He said it over and over, even aloud, but it rang hollow, and the words fell into a deep emptiness that swallowed them and turned them into lies. Late the next afternoon, Keiron was trying, and failing, to read when he heard the back door open. His heart soared, then sped up and began to hammer in his chest. He'd been doing a lot of thinking and prayed Draven would give him the chance to show him the conclusions he'd drawn.

Draven had his head down when he came into the living room. "I'm sorry. I shouldn't have said what I said, or done what I did. I was wrong and I'm sorry. I-I'll pretend that...that the— I'll pretend...what happened, never happened."

"But I don't want to pretend it never happened," Keiron said softly, getting to his feet. He strode purposefully across the room and held out his hand. Draven looked at it. He stared at it for a long time before he took it. He seemed surprised when, instead of leading him across the room, Keiron drew him into a gentle embrace.

"I have no idea how this could work, if it could work, but when I thought I'd never see you again, it was unbearable. There's a saying among my people that 'you don't know what you've got till it's gone'. It means you don't realise how truly important something is to you until you lose it. That's what happened to me today. I haven't known you for very long, but you've swept into my life and changed it. It's as if you've waved a magic wand and put a spell on me and everything in my life." Keiron drew back a little and gazed down at him. "You haven't have you?"

Draven smiled shyly and shook his head.

"I don't want to lose you, Draven. I don't ever want to lose you. You've made a place for yourself, and I don't want you to leave it ever again."

"Where is it? My place? Where do I fit in? Where do I belong?"

"Here," Keiron said huskily. "Right here in my arms."

Draven's eyes widened. "But what about Bren?"

"Bren and I were never meant to be together for long. We were heading towards the end anyway. He's the wrong person for me, and I think he knows it, which is why he's so jealous. Bren's not the problem."

"He's not? What is the problem?" Draven appeared to be excited now, hopeful but still deeply worried, as if he was afraid something wonderful laid before him might be yanked away again.

"You know what the problem is, Draven. I'm human and you're fey. How would it work?"

Draven shrugged. "I don't know. I guess we'll have to talk to the High Lord."

"Then we should wait until we've done that—and until I've talked to Bren."

"Wait for what? To have sex? Or to be mates?"

Keiron was taken aback. With one of his mercurial shifts of mood, Draven was wildly excited. His eyes were shining, and there was swirling silver stardust scattered over the blue.

"Whoa, hang on. You're moving a bit fast, Draven. No one said anything about being mates. That's a commitment I haven't even given to Bren and we've been together—"

"But Bren wasn't right for you and you've always known he wasn't. You said so yourself. Your heart knows, Keiron. I know humans are very different, but they can't be that different. Maybe you've forgotten how to listen, but your heart knows."

"Maybe, but it's still too soon to be talking about anything like that. Let's just start with—" He swallowed hard. "—sex, and see where we go from there."

Draven grinned. "You paused."

"What?"

"You paused before you said sex. That's really cute."

Keiron smiled and shook his head. "I've got a lot to learn." He raised his hand to brush Draven's shiny white hair out of his eyes. "I just don't want to get our hopes up until we know if we can be together, and I don't want to cheat on Bren. I owe it to him to at least wait until after I've ended it with him."

Draven nodded seriously. "I understand. It's the honourable way. But don't worry about the other things. Love cannot be denied, Keiron. Like a river that wears away rock and changes its course around obstacles, it will always find a way."

"Love is a very strong word, Draven. I'm not making any commitment. I can't say I love you."

"Why not?"

"It's way too early. There's chemistry between us, for sure, but it's going to take time before either of us can know if that's all it is or whether there's something more, something deeper that will turn into love."

"Say what you want, believe it if you must, but I don't tell those lies to myself, Keiron. I'm fey and whatever else the fey might be, they're always honest with themselves. Maybe we'll work and maybe we won't, but I do love you and I will always love you. There's nothing you or your insecurities can do to change that."

Yet again, Keiron found himself stunned by Draven, and it made his head ache. To distract himself, he drew Draven closer, lowered his head, and kissed him gently. Draven responded by teasing his lips with sharp little teeth.

"I thought we weren't going to do this yet," Draven smirked, pulling his head back.

"This isn't sex. It doesn't count."

"You're still cheating on Bren."

"You talk too much."

"No," Draven said firmly, pulling himself out of Keiron's arms. "You said you wanted to wait until you're free and I've spoken with the High Lord. This does count. Either you're honest with yourself, or you're not. Either your morality wants you to wait, or it doesn't. I don't care. I'd lie down with you right now, but I respect your wishes, as long as they're honest."

Keiron frowned. "You're right," he said at last. "I want to do this properly. I don't want any shadows over it. You speak to your High Lord and I'll speak to Bren, and then, when we're completely free with no need to hide or worry about anything, we'll see."

"See what?"

"See what happens."

"You don't know what happens? Surely you must know— You've done it with Bren, right? We're not that much different."

"I didn't mean—" Keiron shook his head and smiled fondly. "I'll speak to Bren tomorrow. When will you speak with the High Lord?"

"At this time of the year, there's a meeting of all the High Lords and Ladies with the King. It's a court that none can miss—or would want to. He'll be gone until after the midsummer festival."

"That's weeks away."

Draven shrugged. "It is as it is."

"And you can't talk to him before then? Isn't there a way to get hold of him? A telephone? Computer?"

Draven grinned. "No, but don't worry, I don't have the same problems as you do. I'm not in a relationship with him and I don't have to wait."

"But what if he says no?"

"Says no to what?"

"To us being together. What if he won't allow us to be together?"

Draven frowned. "I don't understand. What do you mean 'allow'."

"We're not the same, Draven. Your people might not accept us. Your High Lord might not allow us to be together."

Draven let out a peal of tinkling laughter. "You're so funny. You're right. We are very different. We don't put restrictions on who we can love. Of course, if it happens to be a dark elf or other enemy of the fey, you're going to get into trouble, but it's still not forbidden, as such. The only thing we'd have to get his permission for would be for you to live in our world."

"Live? In your world? I-I didn't think...."

Draven grinned again. "Don't worry. I'm not going to make you choose. We'll live wherever you want to live. I'll get used to this place...eventually...I think."

Keiron hugged him close and rested his cheek on Draven's soft, sweet hair.

"I've a feeling that, once I let myself fully feel, completely give myself to you, I'll go wherever you want."

Draven hugged him tightly, pressing his head against his chest.

"There's just one thing," Keiron said. Draven raised his head, enquiry in his eyes. "I've never heard you say my name. You know what it is."

"Keiron."

"Yes. It sounds so good on your lips."

"Keiron?"

"Hmm?"

"Can I sleep with you tonight? Not to have sex, just to lie together and be together. I won't do anything wrong."

Keiron smiled and stroked his hair. "I don't know if I can make the same promise."

KEIRON HAD NEVER found it harder to get up for work as he did on that Tuesday morning. True to their word, they'd done no more than kiss and hold each other, but they'd talked. They'd talked for hours and Keiron discovered a side of Draven he'd never imagined was there. Set aside the childlike wonder and ignorance of the way Keiron's world worked and Draven was witty, clever, and wise.

It was clear the fairy world was very different to the human one. It was not, as Keiron had thought, with a good deal of ignorance, comprised merely of the woods and fields around the outskirts of the city but coexisted in another place altogether. The gateways were situated in secluded places for tactical reason and could only be passed through by the fey.

"It used to be," Draven said nostalgically, "that lots of people would leave parts of their garden to grow wild, and we had lots of places for our gateways. These days everything is so neat. That's why I was fascinated with yours."

"So that's why."

"Why what?"

"My grandmother always used to say we should leave part of the garden to grow wild for the fairies. She never told me it was to create cover for a gateway between worlds."

"Maybe she didn't know. Superstition often continues long after knowledge has been lost."

"True."

They'd touched again on the respective political structures of their peoples but moved swiftly on as it wasn't really a topic for pillow talk. Draven was, however, fascinated, though appalled, that homosexuals were persecuted simply because they fell in love with members of the same rather than the opposite sex.

"And there's absolutely nothing like that in your world?"

"No, nothing at all. We can love whoever we wish. I can't understand why it's not like that here. Why would people hate you for who you love? Why would you let them?"

"Why would I let them? How could I stop them?"

"Not you; not just you. It's a wrong thought. In my home, when people think wrong thoughts, they're made to stop."

"How can you stop people thinking?"

Draven chuckled. "You can't, but you can stop them expressing the thought."

"But who makes the decision about what thoughts are right or wrong?"

"The High Lord."

"What if he's wrong?"

"He's never wrong," Draven stated with absolute certainty.

Keiron propped himself up on one elbow and gazed down into Draven's earnest face, toying with a lock of his hair.

"But what if he is? Is there any means of challenging his decision?"

"We've been through this before. The High Lord's decrees are law. He can't be wrong. We can disagree with what he says, and we can whinge about it, but it's not wrong. It can't be wrong."

"What do you mean 'can't be'?"

"We've been through this before," Draven repeated with a sigh. "The High Lord's word is law. Once the word is made, it can't be wrong because it is his decree and because of that it has to be right."

"I understand the concept, Draven, but I don't...."

"When you speak to him, you'll understand."

"Why would that change things?"

"We aren't human, Keiron." He chuckled and blushed. "I like saying your name, Keiron."

"I like to hear you say it."

Draven's smile turned coy. "We're not human. We're different. The High Lord is more than just a ruler; he's the heart of the people. He is the people. When he speaks, he isn't speaking for us; he's speaking as us."

"I don't understand."

"Of course you don't, but you will when you see him. I promise."

And Keiron had accepted—he'd had to, because at that point Draven kissed him. They'd kissed on and off for the entire time before falling asleep, and both of them had smiles on their faces.

Now it was morning and he had to go to work. Draven, as usual, turned over to smile up at him as soon as he felt Keiron stir.

"Will you be okay on your own today?" Keiron asked, as he tucked a strand of hair behind Draven's ear.

"Bren won't be here, right? Not until after you come home?"

"No, he's with his family today. He'll come by later. I'll be home long before then. Don't worry."

"Then I'll be fine. I'll explore the house and try not to break anything. I found some books in your kitchen with food spells in it. Maybe I can make you something."

"Food spells?"

"Yes. They're in a drawer."

"They're not food spells; they're recipes."

"Same thing, with less magic."

Keiron smiled and kissed him. "Go take a shower, and I'll get you breakfast."

Chapter Eight

"ARE YOU ABSOLUTELY sure you'll be all right on your own?"

"Of course I am. I promise I won't run away, and I'll try not to break anything."

"Don't open the door and don't answer the phone, okay?"

"I...oh, okay, Keiron." He smiled shyly, blushing.

"What?"

"It feels so good to say your name."

Keiron smiled fondly and gathered Draven into his arms to kiss him gently on the lips. "Take care of yourself because I couldn't bear if anything happened to you."

Draven stared at him incredulously. "What do you think is going to happen to me? I'm not a child, you know. I've been a soldier in battle. I've brought a baby out—four actually. I've been attacked by gnomes, kidnapped by dark elves, and almost died under a harvesting machine in a field when I got my foot stuck in a hole. I think I can manage one day in a house."

"If you put it like that," Keiron said with a huge smile. "I'll see you at five o'clock."

"I'll make sure we have something to eat."

"I've left some money with the pizza menu by the phone."

Draven pushed him away and stamped his foot. "You have no faith in me. I can find food and make you a meal. I haven't been very useful yet, but I can be. Have faith."

Draven scowled and it made Keiron laugh. He pulled Draven back into the embrace and kissed him again. "I'll see you tonight. It'll be the longest day I've had to live through."

"Don't worry. I'll have fun."

"That's what I'm worried about."

Draven laughed, and Keiron ducked out the door as Draven reached for something to throw.

KEIRON DIDN'T HEAR the screams until he opened the front door. When he did, they curdled his blood. They weren't like anything he'd ever heard before. They were screams of pain and anguish, flavoured with sobbing breaths. For a moment, he was frozen by them. Then they died into silence and that's when panic kicked in.

"What the fuck's going on?" he demanded as he stepped into the living room, to find Bren and his friends sitting around looking scared. "What the fuck are you doing here? Where's Draven?"

"U-upstairs," Bren said in a shaking voice. His face was chalk white, and he was clearly guilty about something.

"What the fuck have you done?"

"I-I was going to let him go, Keiron. It was only going to be for a bit. I was about to—"

Keiron ignored him entirely as he ran to the stairs and took them two at a time. When he opened the bedroom door, what he saw made him feel sick.

"Oh fuck," Bren said at his shoulder, and Keiron had never felt more like hitting someone. "We only did it for a laugh, Kei—to teach the little bitch a lesson. I mean—you should have seen the mess he made of our noses. I didn't realise—"

"Bren, if I were you, I'd get the fuck out of here before I found myself pinned against the wall by the throat. Take your friends, your stuff, and your fucking attitude, and get the hell out of my house."

"What? What do you mean take my stuff?"

"You heard. I want you out of my house and out of my life. I've had enough of your pettiness and stupid fucked-up dramatics. Just get out."

"You're finishing with me? Over this? He had it coming. He was—"

"No one has this coming, Bren," Keiron said severely as he swallowed hard and circled the bed.

"I told you—I didn't know."

"Oh yes, you did," Keiron said, sliding his arm under the now unconscious Draven, trying to lift him, to ease the pressure on his wrist, which was handcuffed to the bedpost with a pair of cast-iron cuffs. "Where did you get the handcuffs?" Keiron' voice dripped poison.

"I...I...um...."

"You must have spent some time searching for them. They're not exactly your normal, common—or garden cuffs, are they?"

"You'd be surprised. Look, Kei, it was just a—"

"Fucking cruel, that's what it was. There are no other words for it. You wanted to hurt him, and you went looking for something to do it with, something you knew would really hurt him."

"How was I supposed to know this would happen?"

"You know what iron does to him. You saw what happened with the candlestick. I'm not one of your dopey friends, Bren; I know you. You knew this would happen. That's why you did it."

"Yeah, well—I didn't know it was going to be this bad." He glanced at Draven's bloody wrist, which looked as if it had been burned, and at the blood and fluids running down his swollen arm. He squirmed, squeamish and acutely uncomfortable.

"How long?"

"What?"

"How long have you sat downstairs, listening to him screaming?"

"I—"

"How did you get it on him in the first place? He must have struggled."

"He did until—"

"Until what?"

Bren hung his head, biting his lip. "Until Liam hit him and stunned him."

"He did what?"

"We were afraid he'd curse us again, so Liam hit him. Didn't hit him that hard, just enough to take the fight out of him." Some of the fire came back into Bren's voice and eyes as he snapped defiance.

"And what about when it started to hurt him? What happened then?"

"We didn't know it was going to be this bad. He— Well, at first he was swearing and yelling, and he was angry rather than...anything else. So we closed the door and came down. Then he started—" Bren glanced quickly at Keiron and back down. He sighed deeply. "He started to cry and...I thought he was just being a baby. I swear he hadn't been screaming for long and I was going to—"

"I don't want to hear any more. You deliberately set out to hurt him and you have. You're a monster, Bren. I don't want someone like you in my life anymore."

"You're choosing him before me?" Bren gasped, his mouth dropping open.

Keiron gazed down at Draven. His face was pale as paper, puffy, and stained with snot and tears. He stank where he'd vomited over himself, and his hair was tangled and rank. "Yes," he said, "I am."

"But...but you can't. He's not even human."

"He's got more humanity than you have," Keiron spat. "Now, get out." Tears running down a face that was blood red, Bren turned.

"Wait!"

Bren turned back, looking hopeful.

"The key," Keiron said coldly. Bren hesitated. For a moment, it seemed he was going to refuse. Then, he dug into his pocket and threw it. Keiron snatched it out of the air and fumbled with the lock. It wasn't easy, as Draven was a dead weight and his wrist was swollen and slick with blood and pus.

When the lock clicked open, Draven's arm fell, and he whimpered pitifully.

"Hush now. It's over. You're safe. I'm sorry. I'm so sorry I let him hurt you. I knew I shouldn't have left you alone. I knew something was going to happen. I'm sorry. I'm so sorry."

As he spoke, he gently lifted Draven into his arms, ignoring the blood, sick, and snot. Draven's head lolled against his shoulder.

"Draven?" he said softly. "Draven, are you all right?"

Draven's response was a moan.

"I'm going to put you down for a minute. I'm going to get something to clean up your arm." Keiron glanced doubtfully at the misshapen black flesh around his wrist. "If you were human, I'd take you to the hospital, but.... Until you can tell me what to do, I'll just have to do my best."

Making Draven as comfortable as he could on the pillows, Keiron hurried to the bathroom. He glanced around quickly and turned on the shower.

Angry voices and the slamming of the front door heralded the departure of Bren and his friends. Keiron was relieved. At least he didn't have to worry about that. He'd worry about the house key another time.

Back in the bedroom, he stripped off Draven's jeans and pants. He couldn't quite see how to get the T-shirt over his arm, so he found a pair of scissors and cut it off.

When he sat Draven on the floor of the shower, the water started to rouse him. "No," he screamed. "No, no it hurts. Please, please it hurts so much. Don't do this to me. Don't—"

"Draven. Draven, it's me, Keiron. It's over. I'm here."

Draven fought like a demon, forcing Keiron to fight back, trying to avoid hurting his arm. Keiron was afraid if he let him go, he'd hurt it even more with his thrashing.

Eventually, Keiron had Draven pinned against the wall with the water washing over his face. Coughing and retching, Draven opened his eyes and finally recognised who was holding him.

"Keiron?" he choked. "Oh, Keiron, I'm so sorry. I've done it again."

Keiron stopped restraining Draven and slid into the shower, easing himself down next to Draven. Draven gave a great shuddering sigh and leaned against him.

"Sorry? What the hell are you sorry for?"

"I screwed it up, Keiron. I ruined it."

"You didn't ruin anything. Bren's gone. He's gone forever. We can just concentrate on each other. I'll take some time off work and—"

"It was my fault, Keiron. I provoked him, again. I told him I was going to hex him, hex them all if they didn't leave. If I'd just let him in and—"

"There's nothing you could have done, Draven. He came here to hurt you. Those cuffs.... Iron's not what handcuffs are usually made of. He had to go looking for them. He got them just to hurt you. That's why he came early, when he knew I wouldn't be here."

Draven gazed up at him. The water still washed over him, and he spat it out.

"He came here just to do that? He planned it? He...." Draven trailed off, shaking his head.

"You've seen what he's like. He's a mean little—"

"But this.... Why would he do this? He's evil. I'm innocent, Keiron. I've done nothing to him. There's no blood debt, no enemy collaboration. There's no reason. There's no reason for it." Draven seemed to be begging for something, and it hurt Keiron that he couldn't give it.

"I can't answer you, Draven. He's cruel. I wouldn't let myself see it, but looking back, he's always been cruel."

"But there's no reason, Keiron." Draven's voice lost its strength, and he slumped back against the wall, tears mixing with the water streaming over his face, darkening his hair.

"I can't excuse Bren, but it's done now. We have to move on. Tell me what I can do to make it better, to make you better."

"Nothing," Draven whispered, leaning his head back against the wall.

"Draven.... Okay, I understand. We can talk about this later. What can I do right now to make the pain better? Is there anything I—"

"The water will help," Draven murmured. "It will wash away the residue, and it won't hurt so much. Then..." He shook his head and sighed. "You won't have the right things to make medicine for it."

"Then I'll get them. Tell me what I need."

"I don't know. I don't even have the words for them. Fenn made the medicines. I always went to her if I was sick or hurt. I don't know what was in there. This doesn't happen often anymore. We can avoid iron. There isn't so much of it and we don't get...trapped."

"There must be something. Think. Please."

Draven sighed and closed his eyes as Keiron watched him anxiously. "Whisky," he said at last.

"Whisky? Do you need a drink? Will that really do any good?"

"Not to drink," he said with the ghost of a smile, "although, now you mention it, that doesn't sound like such a bad idea."

"Not to drink?"

"Alcohol helps the wound to heal. I guess it doesn't matter, but it might take the pain away a bit."

"I've got some bandages somewhere too. And some antibiotic cream. That might be soothing. Can you stand?"

"Sure I can. It's only my arm right now."

"I know but— Never mind. I'll help you."

Draven climbed awkwardly to his feet, wincing and hissing with pain. When he was upright, he stood with his face raised to the water. He sighed. "This feels good."

"You were sick. It's still in your hair."

"Yes. I remember. It was—" He shook his head, and Keiron took him gently into his arms.

"I'm so sorry, Draven. I'm sorry you went through all that alone. I'm sorry I wasn't here. I'm sorry I didn't protect you."

"I don't need you to protect me. I can take care of myself."

Keiron smiled as the old spark flared again. "Well, I don't know about that. It seems as if every time I turn my back, you get into trouble." He made sure his voice was light and teasing, and Draven responded with a chuckle.

"Help me wash my hair. I want to feel clean."

"Are you sure? You should really lie down."

"I want to be clean."

Keiron rubbed mint-scented shampoo into Draven's hair and worked it through, combing out the knots with his fingers. Draven leaned against the wall and sighed. In other circumstances, it would have been an intimate moment.

As soon as he was reasonably certain Draven's hair was clean, Keiron adjusted the showerhead and massaged Draven's scalp as the water washed out the shampoo, leaving a light, minty smell.

Draven turned in his arms and tilted his face up. "Kiss me, Keiron. Make me feel alive."

"Oh, you're alive, my love. There's no doubt about that. A bit battered and broken, but you're alive."

Draven gave him a pale smile and stretched up until their lips met. Fresh mintiness tickled his nose as Draven teased his lips with the tip of his tongue. Keiron finally relaxed and opened up to him.

Keiron slipped his arms around Draven's slippery body and drew him closer. Automatically, Draven raised his arms and tensed as his bad arm touched Keiron's skin. "Sorry. I forgot."

Keiron chuckled. "I've never met anyone like you, and never will again. I'm so thankful you made a mistake that day and let me see you."

Draven pulled back and smiled at him. "Mistake? What mistake?"

TWO HOURS LATER, Draven was sitting up in Keiron's bed, his arm wrapped in bandages and a dreamy smile on his face. The pain of Keiron's ministrations to his arm had been so great, Keiron had decided it was worth trying Draven with an aspirin. He'd only give him half, but it had gone straight to his head. He'd been practically comatose for half an hour, and he was still high as a kite and not feeling any pain at all.

"What are you smiling about?"

"I don't know," Draven said with a shrug. "It feels good to smile."

"Yes, it does, and it feels even better to see you smile."

"Aww...you're lovely. You're a bit weird, but you're my lovely, snuggly, cuddly Keiron."

"Weird? I'm weird? How come?"

"Well...you live in a house, and I really like your house but it's kind of...stuck. And it has so much...stuff. And you work in a big house with lots of people not actually doing anything. And there are big wheely things and lots of grey and no green. Well, there was a bit of green. We went to the green, didn't we? But it was a long way away. I liked to play with the people, though, and the music, but it's still weird." He sobered and stared at Keiron with a thoughtful expression on his face. "You're really big, aren't you?"

"What?" Keiron asked with a grin.

"You're big. That's one of the things that made me want to see you closer. You're big, big, big. As big as an ogre, as big as a centaur, as big as a...as a...."

"Hey. I do have feelings, you know," Keiron said with a laugh. "I'm not a giant."

"Oh no. Giants are much bigger. Well, ogres are too, but..." He shrugged and giggled. "You are big, though."

"Not among my own people. Just because you're a little thing."

Draven giggled again. "I am not a little thing. I can be big. You can't change, can you? You can't get bigger and littler."

"No, I can't."

"I can." Draven smiled broadly. "Wanna see?"

"I've seen, thank you."

"Oh no, no, no. No, no, no." He chuckled, and suddenly he wasn't there anymore.

"Draven?" Keiron called anxiously. The bandages were empty, but the edges were fluttering and there was a strange squeaking noise. Reaching out with trembling fingers, Keiron picked up the stained strips of cloth and something dropped off the end. Keiron stared in disbelief. Draven waved. He was two inches tall, but Keiron could see his grin. Keiron choked.

"I get the message. Get back up here."

Tiny wings sprouted from the little figure, which fluttered, and he rose until he hovered in front of Keiron's face. Keiron could clearly see the bright grin that lit Draven's tiny face, and his eyes were little chips of sapphire.

"Oh, very funny. You know what I meant."

The tiniest peal of silvery laughter rose in volume as the figure grew, until Draven was kneeling on the bed in front of Keiron, his wings still fluttering at his back.

"Do you want to see me get really big?"

"No, thank you," Keiron said quickly, with visions of the ceiling giving way. "I get the message. I'd be grateful if you lost the wings, too."

Draven frowned. "Lose? I can't lose them, silly. They're part of me."

"I didn't mean that literally. Can you just...do whatever you do to them?"

Draven opened his mouth to say something, then giggled, and the wings shimmered and faded. His eyes twinkled as he reached up and threw his arms around Keiron's neck, pulling him down for a kiss.

"Whoa, hang on. Be careful of your—" Disentangling Draven's arms, Keiron drew them down carefully, trying to protect his bad one...which wasn't nearly as bad anymore. "How...?"

"What? Oh that." Draven frowned. "Yes, it does that."

"Was it transforming? Did getting small kind of...leave it behind?"

"Leave what behind?"

"The wound."

"What? Oh, no. No, it doesn't change anything but my size."

"But then how...?"

"I heal quickly. Well, the outside does."

Gently, Keiron took Draven by the hand and twisted his arm back and forth, examining the cruel red weal around his wrist. Although the skin was still purplish, puffy, and sore, it had stopped weeping and wasn't as hot and swollen as it had been.

"But...."

"Iron has strange effects on us. That's why I couldn't escape." He shrugged. "What else can I say?" Smiling beatifically, his eyes rolled and he fell over backwards.

"Draven? Draven, are you okay?"

Draven lay on the bed, staring up at the ceiling. His eyes were moving as if he was watching something on a screen. He giggled.

"Draven?"

"There are lots of other things that have strange effects on us," Draven said vaguely. "I think I found another one."

Keiron relaxed and smiled. "You're high as a kite, aren't you?"

"No," Draven said with a hiccup. "I'm not high at all. I'm flat on the floor...um...bed." He turned his attention to Keiron. He was totally spaced out. "Would you like me to be? Only you told me to put my wings away. I could—"

"No, no, it's fine. It was just a manner of speaking. What I meant was that you're spaced out, tripping, drugged to the eyeballs."

Draven frowned, thinking hard. His lips moved as if he was working something out. Then his face cleared and he giggled. "Yes."

"Come on. Let's make you more comfortable." Keiron helped Draven get up onto the pillows and settled him down. As he was about to turn away, Draven grabbed him again and pulled him down. This time, his arms were clamped like metal bands and there was no pulling away.

Keiron was glad to surrender and kiss him deeply. He flopped down on the bed and gently cradled Draven in his arms. Draven wound his legs around him and adjusted his position, pressing so close Keiron could feel every line of his body, including the part that was very excited indeed.

"Draven, I don't think—"

"That's right; don't think."

"No, I—"

"Mmm."

Draven was much stronger than he seemed, and even though he struggled, Keiron couldn't break free. In the end, he surrendered and immersed himself in Draven completely.

Before they could move much further than kissing, Draven started to giggle and let his arms fall back onto the bed.

"What's so funny?"

"Bubbles."

"Bubbles?"

"Yes."

"What do you mean, bubbles?"

"Everything's bubbly. My tummy is bubbly and my head is bubbly and your mouth is bubbly and—"

"And you're completely fucked-up, and it wouldn't be fair to take advantage of you."

"Oooh yes, yes. Take advantage of me." Draven flung out his limbs and spread-eagled onto the bed. Keiron swallowed hard. Hell, he was beautiful, his limbs in perfect proportion, his body lithe and slender, and— He swallowed again, so, so, so wanting to...

"I think it might be a good idea if I got some food together. You haven't eaten for hours, and it might sober you up a bit."

"I'm only hungry for you," Draven declared, then dissolved into giggles.

Keiron shook his head. "Wait there. Don't move."

"But what if my nose itches," Draven demanded.

"What if it does?"

"Can I move to scratch it?"

Keiron grinned. "You can scratch anything you want. Just don't leave the bed."

"Yes," Draven agreed. He hiccupped and looked surprised.

Keiron scrabbled to get together a tray of food and, tucking a bottle of lemonade under his arm, practically ran back up the stairs. He breathed a sigh of relief to find Draven still sprawled across the bed in pretty much the same position he'd been when Keiron left. He was humming happily.

"You okay?" he asked, and Draven turned his dreaming eyes on him with a huge smile.

"Uh-huh. Why is there a capital letter here? Nothing itched." He started to hum again, and his eyes drifted back to whatever he'd been watching on the ceiling.

"I've got some stuff together. Nothing fancy. Come on, sit up and eat."

"Not.... Hmm." Draven sighed.

"I don't care if you're hungry or not. You need to eat. It's only a matter of time before you crash completely, and you need something in your stomach."

"Belly, belly, belly, belly, belly," Draven sang, patting his stomach and giggling.

"Here." Keiron held out a cheese sandwich. Draven took it and sniffed at it. Then he peeled off the bread and nibbled at the cheese.

"What's this?" he demanded.

"It's cheese."

"It doesn't taste like cheese, and it has big holes in it."

"It's Dutch cheese."

Draven sniffed and nibbled again. "I like it," he pronounced eventually, stuffing the whole piece of cheese into his mouth and reaching for another sandwich.

"Hey, eat the whole sandwich, not just the cheese."

"Don't want bread," Draven said brightly, flicking the offending part of the sandwich off the bed.

"Draven, don't throw it on the floor."

"Don't throw what on the floor?"

"The bread."

"What bread?" he asked, looking angelic. Keiron shook his head and took the new sandwich out of his hands, pressing it together before touching it to Draven's lips. At first, Draven glared mutinously at him, but eventually he let his lips part and accepted a tiny corner, which he nibbled delicately.

"Don't give me that innocent look, you demon. Eat all your sandwich."

Draven giggled. "It's your fault, you know."

"What's my fault?"

"Me being...making you cross. You drugged me."

"I did not. Well, maybe I did, but...I didn't know how much it was going to drug you. For God's sake, it was only half an aspirin. It would have next to no effect on me."

"I'm not you," Draven announced, as if it was new information.

"Oh boy, do I know that."

Draven giggled again. "What else do you have?" He pulled himself more upright and peered at the tray, exclaiming over the salad bowl. "You have leaves. I love leaves. Are there petals? Do you have any flowers? What are these?" He held up the little cube of a garlic crouton.

"It's a crouton. Toasted bread with garlic and herbs."

Draven studied it suspiciously, sniffing. Then he licked it tentatively with the tip of his tongue and finally popped it into his mouth and crunched. His eyes widened. "I like that." He searched for another, then another.

"Hey, don't steal them all. I like them, too."

"No, no, no. I want them. I want them all." He reached for the bowl, and so did Keiron. They batted at each other's hands, and it turned into a scuffle, during which the bowl was knocked onto the floor and salad scattered. With a cry, Draven made to leap off the bed, but Keiron caught him around the waist and threw him back onto the bed, pouncing on him and pinning him down with his wrists over his head.

"You are so evil, to beat up a poor defenceless, drugged fairy being. And you, such a big clumsy human."

"Ah, yes, but all humans are evil. Didn't you know?"

"I was warned, but I don't take warnings well. I'm a bit headstrong. That's what I keep being told. It's all very unfair. Compared to some, I'm as law-abiding as they come."

"Right. Compared to some."

"You wouldn't believe how lawless some can be, especially those in the wild-lands. Of course I've spent a lot of time there so you can hardly blame me for being a little...wild." He grinned and raised his head, trying to reach Keiron's lips with his own.

Keiron yanked his head away and grinned. "Oh no, you don't, you minx. You deserve punishment for throwing my dinner all over the floor."

"Haven't I been punished enough already?" Draven asked reasonably.

Keiron's playfulness left him and his gaze strayed to the wrists he had trapped in his hand. The swelling had gone down even further, leaving only a raw, red weal.

Keiron let go as if he'd burned his hand. "I'm sorry, I—"

Taking advantage of Keiron releasing his wrists, Draven grabbed him around the neck and flipped him over, landing on top of him. "Now you're my slave," he said, his eyes sparking fire.

Keiron gasped at the intensity of his gaze and went still. Draven lowered his head and teased at Keiron's lips with his teeth.

Keiron moaned and raised his head. "Draven, I—"

"Ssh," Draven whispered and collapsed across him. "I want to have sex with you now. I want you to make me forget."

"Forget what?" Keiron whispered, running his hands over Draven's soft yielding body.

"Everything."

LATER, WHEN THEY were replete, they lay in each other's arms. Keiron felt as drugged as Draven, simply from the pleasure he'd taken from him. Making love to someone whose body could change to accommodate him in every way was an experience Keiron had never had before and was never likely to have again...other than with Draven. He was drunk from it.

Rolling over, he stroked the hair out of Draven's face, unable to resist touching him. Draven, who'd seemed to be asleep, stirred and opened his eyes, smiling brightly. He still seemed dazed and drugged, but completely content.

"Thank you," Keiron murmured, brushing Draven's lips with his.

Draven smiled sleepily.

"That was the most wonderful experience I've ever had. Thank you. You're so beautiful, so very beautiful." He ran the backs of his fingers down Draven's cheek, then traced his lips with a forefinger.

Draven yawned and petted Keiron's cheek. "It was good, Keiron. It was the best. Really. The best ever. I love you so much."

"I...Draven. I...you can't say that."

"Why not? It's true."

"It can't be true. You can't know you love me after only a few days. You don't know me. It takes time for love to grow, time to..."

"Maybe for you. Not for me," Draven said simply. "I know what I know, and I know I love you."

"I can't say it, Draven. I can't say I love you, not yet. If it works out, then one day.... I'm sure that one day soon I'll know it. One day, I'll say it but..."

"One day?" Draven frowned, puzzled. "I don't understand. Either you do, or you don't. I don't see how you say that you might...one day."

"Love isn't that simple."

"Yes, it is."

"Not for me." Keiron shook his head. "I take it seriously."

"And I don't?"

"No, you're different. I can see that. You're different. But I...I can't say that to someone I've only just met. Not yet. I've never told Bren I loved him, and I'm glad of that now. I want us to work, Draven. I want it more than anything and I know that one day..."

"No, Keiron. There is no 'one day'. If you don't say it to me now, you never will."

Keiron scowled and pulled back. He felt as he'd always felt when Bren pushed him on the point. How dare Draven put him in this position after only three days? "That's not fair."

"Fair or not, it's the way it is."

"Will it be worth it? If I say I love you because you force me into it, will it mean anything? Will it be worth it?" Keiron was getting angry. He felt he was being pushed into a corner and didn't like it. He never liked being pushed, especially not when he was being threatened.

"I don't understand what you're saying." Draven seemed confused and hurt, but Keiron wouldn't let that weaken him. He shifted farther away from Draven and sat up, looking down at the dazed and confused fairy.

"You can't force love, Draven. I like you. I like you a lot. And I'm very attracted to you, more than I've ever been attracted to anyone, certainly more than Bren. You're everything I ever wanted and more. I'm sure that, in time I'll grow to love you, but it doesn't happen in an instant."

"There is no time, Keiron. If you love me, you love me, and you have to say it now, because—"

"You can't do that, Draven. You can't blackmail me. You can't make demands of love. I won't say I love you unless I'm absolutely sure I mean it. Giving me ultimatums is not going to help. It's only going to make me angry."

Draven went still and the expression on his face was pained now. "But you have to, Keiron. You have to say it now, or not at all. If you don't say it now, I won't be here and it'll be too late."

"What? What the hell?" Keiron glared down at him. "What are you saying? That if I don't say I love you, you'll leave me? That's not fair."

"No," Draven said, staring at him with such a sad expression in his eyes. "No, it isn't fair. It isn't fair at all."

"Then don't say it. Don't say things like that, not even as a joke."

Draven had gone very still. His eyes were bright and a frown lodged between his brows. "I'm not joking, Keiron. I won't be here. In a few days, I-I won't be here anymore."

"What? But you said...you said you couldn't go back. You said you'd stay. Where else...where would you go?"

"I don't know where I'll go. No one does."

"What are you talking about?"

"The iron."

"What? Draven, I'm confused, and I have to say I'm frustrated and—"

"You don't know?"

"Know what?"

"The iron. Didn't I tell you? It doesn't just hurt us on the outside, Keiron. It's deadly poison to us. It hurts us on the inside, too."

"What?" Something inside Keiron snapped and rose to his throat, choking him. "What do you mean? You said...you said you healed quickly. It's almost gone."

"On the outside, yes. On the inside...." Draven reached up his hand and stroked Keiron's face. "I'm sorry. I thought you knew."

"How the hell would I know that?"

"I...don't know. I—"

Keiron grabbed Draven's shoulders, and Draven winced at the strength of his grip.

"Tell me," Keiron ground out. "Tell me it's a joke. Tell me it's just a sick joke. Tell me you don't mean it. Tell me...."

"I'll tell you whatever you want, Keiron," Draven gasped, wincing with the pain of Keiron's grip on his shoulders. "I'll tell you anything...for as long as I can."

"What's that supposed to mean?"

"I can't talk to you when I'm dead, Keiron."

Chapter Nine

KEIRON FELT AS though he'd been punched and all the air forced from his lungs. "Dead? No. No, I.... How can you say that? How can you be so calm and...? You can't mean it. Please, Draven, don't be so cruel to me. If you want me to say I love you, I'll say it. I'll say anything. Just don't say that."

"Don't say what? Oh, about being dead, you mean? If you don't want me to say it, I won't. I don't want to upset you, but we don't have long. It won't make it stop, you know. Not saying it won't make it stop."

"Then what will? What will make it stop?"

"Nothing. Nothing you have here." Draven smiled, a little shakily, gazing uncertainly into Keiron's face.

"What do you mean 'have here'?"

"Well...there are things back home, of course. There's not so much iron around anymore, but the wise ones still know what to do for it. A few hundred years ago, iron poisoning was common enough."

Keiron's heart leaped. "So there is something we can do. There's something that can save you."

"No."

"But you said... You just said..."

Draven caressed Keiron's face and smiled sadly at him. "I said there's medicine back home, but I can't go back home. It may as well be on the moon."

"Why can't you go?"

"Because I have to be here...for three months, except, of course, I won't be. In three months, I'll be long gone."

"No! No, don't say that. I won't believe it. I won't accept it. You're not going to die. We'll get the medicine. Surely when they know...? If we tell them what happened, they're not going to just turn their backs on you."

Draven shook his head. "Keiron, I'm exiled for three months. The doors are closed to me. I can call, but no one will come."

"Someone has to come."

"No, Keiron." Draven smiled, his fingertips exploring Keiron's face. "We have a few days," he said, then reconsidered. "Well, yes, but not— I won't be.... Well, I won't be...like this for a few days so we—"

"No!" Keiron roughly grabbed each side of Draven's face, holding his head so hard it must have hurt.

Draven gasped.

"I'm not going to let it happen. I'm not going to let you die."

"You can't stop it, Keiron. I don't— Well, I do mind. I do care. I don't want to die, but I can't change it, so it's okay."

"No. It's not okay. I don't see how you can say that. How can you be so calm? How can you...?"

"It's a natural part of life, Keiron. It happens to everyone. I've been alive for a very long time, and I'm not afraid to die. I just wish.... I wish we had more time together."

Keiron shook his head violently, refusing to accept. He wasn't going to lose him, not now, not after everything. He'd find a way. "There has to be a way. There just has to be."

"There's no way, Keiron. Not here, not now."

"But your people. They won't turn their backs on you, surely. Not now. They won't let you die."

"You don't listen, Keiron. I can't go back."

"But—"

"Don't spoil it." Draven raised his hands and drew Keiron's head down. "Don't spoil this time, Keiron. Don't waste what time we have, chasing dreams that won't come true. Hold me. Let me fall asleep in your arms. Tomorrow, we can talk. Tomorrow, we can...we can make love again, and you can show me things and I can tell you things and we...we can spend time together. I don't know how long I have, and I don't want to waste a moment."

"Draven, I—"

"Please, Keiron. Please don't make it harder."

"I-I'll try. I'll try not to. I can't.... It's just.... Why didn't you tell me? Right at the beginning, before I— Why didn't you tell me?"

"I thought you knew."

"How the hell would I know?"

"I don't know." Draven's lips trembled and tears sprang to his eyes. "I'm sorry."

"Now you cry? Now, when I get cross at you? Now, you.... Ah hell." Keiron threw his arms around Draven and pulled him close, holding him tight.

"Just hold me, Keiron. Please. For tonight. Just let me sleep in your arms, knowing you...knowing you care for me."

"I do care for you. I care for you more than I've ever cared for anyone. If there was anything, anything I could do..."

"If I think of something, I'll tell you."

"Yes."

Keiron held on tight, cradling Draven in his arms, resting his cheek on Draven's hair, tears running down his face. To his utter amazement, it didn't take long for Draven to fall asleep. At first, he panicked until he realised it was really just straightforward, peaceful sleep. How could Draven just fall asleep? Initially, he thought it must have been the aspirin, but when he thought about it, he realised it was just Draven. Draven was a creature of emotion. He floated on the tide, letting it take him where it would. When he was angry, the anger flashed like a bolt of lightning, then passed just as quickly. When he was happy, he forgot everything that came before and rejoiced in the simple things, the little things. When he was contented, he curled up like a cat, almost purring, and nothing before or after mattered. He was the most in-the-moment being Keiron had ever met.

Keiron didn't think he'd sleep at all, but he did. He closed his eyes in daylight and opened them again to daylight, but it was a new day. Draven was still fast asleep in his arms.

At first, Keiron felt warm and comfortable. Holding Draven in his arms was so right, so— Memory punched him and was followed very quickly by the realisation that it was late morning and Draven was still asleep. Draven never slept this long. He never— But the aspirin had fucked him up completely. That was why...that was probably why....

"Draven?" he said softly, caressing Draven's cheek. "Draven, wake up. Please wake up." Draven sighed and stirred, his eyelids fluttering. Keiron felt faint with relief.

"Keiron?" Draven murmured sleepily. "Is it morning?"

"Yes, getting late too, I think."

"Is it time to get up?"

"Not if you don't want to." He smiled as Draven opened his eyes and yawned.

Draven moaned and shook his head. "No. Wanna stay right here. Wanna stay with you."

"I need to pee, but when I come back—"

"Don't leave me, Keiron."

Keiron smiled and stroked Draven's hair. "I have to pee."

"I have to.... I—"

"What's wrong?"

Draven stared at him, dazed. "I think... Keiron, I... Don't leave me."

It was rapidly dawning on Keiron that all was not well with Draven. He still appeared drugged, and his words were slow and slurred. "Are you okay?"

"I...yes, I think so. Am I?" Draven frowned.

"Yes. Yes, you are. You're going to be fine."

Draven closed his eyes for a moment, then opened them. They were glazed and dazzled. "I'm not okay, Keiron," he said reproachfully, "I'm dying. I forgot. I think it may be a bit faster than I thought it would be."

"No. No, you're going to be—"

"Are you still doing that?" Draven frowned and shook his head sadly.

"Doing what?"

"Trying to pretend it isn't happening. It's all right, Keiron. It really is. I don't mind. I'm fine."

"Fine? You're not fine, Draven. You're dying and that's not fine."

"But it is. I'm not afraid to die. I've never been afraid to die. I'm a bit sad that it's now, now I've met you but—"

"A bit sad? A bit sad? You're dying, and all you can say is you're a bit sad. Draven, don't you understand what this means?"

"Of course I do. I'm not stupid, Keiron," he snapped. "It's not like I haven't seen people die before." He turned his face away. "Some of them, I killed myself." He turned his face back and there was a clear challenge in his eyes. "Our world is different to yours. In some ways, it's more complex and, in others, much simpler.

"Death isn't the same. Well, it is the same, but I think we feel differently about it. It is as it is. Life. Death. When I die, I'll be free. I'll be part of everything—every leaf, every flower. I'll never leave you. I promise. My breath will be the wind, my tears the rain. My kiss will be the sun on your face, and my love will wrap you in the darkness and make you smile when all you want to do is weep. I won't let you be alone. I won't let you weep for long."

Draven's words dewed Keiron's lashes, and he opened his mouth to speak, but Draven touched his lips and shook his head. "I know about death. I know you can't fight it, that you can waste all the time you have trying to run from it. I just want to enjoy whatever's left. Don't steal it from me."

"I wouldn't steal anything from you, Draven."

"What about a kiss?"

"What?"

Draven smiled at him. "Would you steal a kiss?"

Keiron struggled. Draven was gazing at him with his usual sweet, open expression, his metallic eyes glittering. A few minutes ago, he was talking about dying and now he was teasing about stealing kisses. He didn't understand. He—

Bizarrely, all he could think about was an old film he'd seen as a child. Peter Pan. There was a scene where a fairy—Tinker Bell her name was—was dying and to bring her back to life all the children had to chant. "I do believe in fairies; I do believe in fairies." Well, Keiron believed in fairies. He believed in his fairy. If only that was enough.

"Keiron?" Draven said, frowning.

"I know. I know, and I'm sorry. I'll try. I'll really try."

"Keiron?"

"I mean it, Draven, truly I do. I'll do my absolute best to make sure the time you have left is—"

"Gone," Draven said sadly, his eyes fluttering.

"What? What, I...?"

"It's gone," Draven repeated in a distant breathy voice. "I thought there'd be more but...time...gone...." He faded with the words and went still. For a long, long moment, Keiron stared at him, waiting for him to open his eyes, to give one of his flippant comments or mischievous looks, but there was nothing.

"Draven?" He didn't respond. He was still breathing, his heart still beating, but he was gone so far, far away. "No. This is not happening. This is not going to happen."

Leaping out of bed, Keiron threw on a robe and ran down the stairs and out of the back door. When he got to the bottom of the garden, he stopped. Now what?

"I-I don't know if there's anyone there," he said, feeling foolish. It flashed through his mind that he hoped none of the neighbours were around, and then it flashed right after that he really didn't care. "I don't care who you are, where you are, or what you are. I know you're there. You must be there. Show yourselves. Dammit, show yourselves."

He waited and waited and waited, but there was no sign of movement or life. There was no indication anyone had heard him.

"It's Draven. He's hurt. He's sick, d-dying. My...someone hurt him. They put iron bands around his wrist and poisoned him. He's dying, and I-I can't sit and watch him go. I won't let him go. I know he's supposed to stay here for three months, and he will...but...but.... You can't just let him die. You can't. You have to do something. You have to DO something."

Silence answered him, a deep abiding silence in which he could hear his heartbeat loud in his ears.

"Please. Please, do something. Please. I don't care what you do. I don't care what it costs me. Please don't let him die. For God's sake, don't let him die. Do something. DO something."

He didn't realise he was shouting until a voice came from the door of the neighbour's house. "Keiron? Keiron, is that you? Is everything all right?"

"No. Yes. Yes, everything's fine. I...I lost...I lost my.... I'm taking care of a friend's dog and it got out. I'm calling it, that's all."

"Are you sure? You sounded—"

"I'm panicking a bit. They're coming to get it today. I'm in trouble if I don't find it."

"Well, it can't have gone far. You'll find it."

"I'm sure I will."

"Give me a shout if I can help."

"Will do."

Trembling from the exchange and too scared to yell anymore, he whispered, "Please. Please help me."

When nothing stirred, he turned and walked slowly back to the house. After closing the door, he set his back against it and rubbed his eyes. They were gritty and sore. He wanted to cry so badly. He wanted to sit on the floor and weep, but what good would that do?

With leaden feet, he climbed the stairs. He wanted to be with Draven, but he was afraid, terribly afraid. He'd never been so afraid in all his life.

Draven was lying exactly where Keiron had left him. He seemed peaceful. He was so pale anyway, it was impossible to tell... Taking his courage in both hands, he slid into bed and wrapped Draven in a gentle embrace. Draven sighed and stirred but didn't wake. It was enough to make Keiron weak, shaking as he held him tight against him.

"Draven," he called gently, brushing the hair out of his face, continuing to stroke him—his hair, his face, his beautiful sweet lips. His heart melted as Draven's lashes fluttered and his eyelids rose over rolling eyes.

"Keiron," he whispered, the sound barely audible.

"I'm here."

Draven smiled. "Stay?"

"Yes, I'll stay. I'll stay as long as you want me to."

"To the end?"

"You're going to be fine," Keiron said without conviction. Draven smiled, and then the expression faded from his face and his eyes closed. "Draven?" Keiron called in desperation, but there was no further response, although Draven was still breathing deeply and easily, his eyelids fluttering as if in dreams. "I'll stay," Keiron whispered. "Until the end." He pulled Draven close again and finally gave himself up to weeping.

He was crying so hard, he almost didn't hear the tapping on the back door. When he did, he leaped up as if someone had branded his ass, and after laying Draven down gently on the pillows, pausing to brush the hair from his face, he raced down the stairs, falling down the last three.

When he wrenched open the door, he froze. This time, the fairy standing on the doorstep was a female. She was very slender, very pretty, and most certainly and definitely a fairy. She had long, curly green hair woven with flowers, leaves, and bark, and her skin was a surprisingly attractive bark green. The lightest, clearest green eyes he'd ever seen regarded him coolly.

"I...." he started but found he had no idea what to say.

"I'm Fenn. Take me to Draven before I am discovered and stopped from helping him."

"St-stopped from helping him?"

"You know it is forbidden to show ourselves to you. I will brave the wrath of the High Lord for Draven, but if I am seen, I will be taken away. Will you keep me standing on your doorstep while my soul brother lies dying in your home?"

"I...no...no, of course not. Come in. Please, come in."

Fenn stepped delicately through the door, showing none of Draven's interest in her surroundings. She was much taller than he was, easily as tall as Keiron, if not a shade taller and slightly heavier too.

"Well," she said as Keiron stared open-mouthed at her woody bare breasts and the shimmering wings he could now see were folded down against her back.

"Sorry?"

"Where is he?"

"Oh...oh, of course. This way."

With his heart thundering in his chest, Keiron led Fenn up the stairs and into his bedroom. Draven was as he had been. Fenn sat on the bed and peered into his face.

"Didn't I warn you?" she said softly. "Didn't I warn you you'd get into trouble with this crazy fascination for humans? What have they done to you?"

"I didn't—"

Fenn turned, and Keiron took a step back from the expression in her eyes. "The High Lord entrusted him into your care because he believed you were an honourable man. Draven pleaded that he be allowed to serve his punishment with you. He assured the High Lord he would be safe."

"He...he pleaded? To be with me? Why?"

"Why do you think?"

"I-I don't know."

She turned scornfully back to Draven, leaving him in shock, his mind racing. What did she mean? What was going on?

"Please. I don't understand."

Fenn rummaged in the bag slung over her shoulder. She flicked her gaze up to Keiron. "He's in love with you. He's been in love with you for months. Why do you think he's been watching you, looking through your window?"

Keiron's eyes widened. What the fuck?

Fenn took a bottle out of her bag and worked out the stopper. Sliding her hand under Draven's head, she raised it and put the bottle to his lips.

"Come on, Draven, open your mouth. Drink the medicine."

Keiron watched, as the bark-skinned woman leaned over Draven, her green hair brushing his face. She shook her head, sending petals flying, falling onto his face.

"Please, Draven," Fenn murmured. "Please open your mouth." After a while of pleading, she sat back and turned her face to Keiron. "He won't open his mouth." Her voice was plaintive. For a badass fairy, Keiron thought, she was a bit of a wimp when it came down to it.

"Maybe he can't. Let me try."

Reluctantly, Fenn relinquished her place, and Keiron climbed up onto the bed next to Draven.

"If he won't do it for me, he won't do it for you," Fenn grumbled, but Keiron ignored her.

Carefully, he drew Draven into his arms and tilted his head back so he was looking down into his face. "Draven, it's me, Keiron. You need to drink the medicine now. It's going to make you better, Draven. It's going to make you better so we can be together. Do this for me, please. I can't lose you, not now. Please, Draven. Please try."

If it hadn't been for the steady rise and fall of his chest, there would have been nothing to tell Keiron Draven wasn't already dead. There wasn't the slightest flicker of movement in his face, and Keiron noted with a jolt of fear that his lips had lost all their colour and were pale blue.

"No, oh no, please. Come on, Draven. Come on. Open your mouth and drink the potion." Feeling increasingly desperate, Keiron lightly slapped Draven's face, then pinched his cheeks and gently shook his head from side to side. He was rewarded with the slightest sigh. "Draven? Come on, babe. For me. Just once. Please just once."

Draven drew in a harsh breath and let it out in a long sigh. His eyelids fluttered and rose a little. It was an obvious effort for Draven, but all he revealed was a crescent of white. His lips twitched once.

"Open your mouth, Draven, please. Just open your mouth."

Draven's lips trembled again and then parted. Desperately, Keiron turned and held out his hand. Fenn hesitated.

"Fenn, give it to me. Quick. Give it to me."

Seemingly begrudging, Fenn handed over the bottle and Keiron tipped the contents into Draven's mouth.

"Swallow it," Keiron urged, and Draven's throat contracted weakly. Keiron heaved a sigh of relief. "Oh God, thank you. Thank you, Draven. Thank you."

Draven gasped faintly and his eyes flickered closed. Keiron turned to Fenn. "How long will it take?"

"I don't know. It depends on how bad he is. Maybe a few minutes. Maybe a few hours."

"But it will work? It will save him?"

Fenn shrugged and turned away, looking around the room curiously for the first time. When something crunched underfoot, she glanced down and crouched to pick up a piece of lettuce that still lay on the floor from the scattered salad bowl he hadn't had time to clear up.

"Fenn?" Keiron begged desperately. "Please. I thought...I thought it would.... You said it would make him better."

"I said nothing of the sort. It will help. Whether it makes him better depends on how sick he is and how much he wants to be well."

"He wants it."

"You can't say that. You are not inside his head to be able to convey his thoughts."

"No, I know that. But I do know he wants to be well. I know he wants to be with me."

"Yes," Fenn said without emotion.

Keiron dragged his attention away from Draven and examined Fenn's impassive face and implacable glance. "Why do you hate me?"

"You hurt him," she said simply.

"I didn't...." He sighed. As much as he denied it, he knew in his heart that he was at least partly to blame. He should have handled the situation with Bren better, and he shouldn't have left Draven alone on a day he knew Bren was coming, at least until the whole situation with the hex had been resolved. "I'm sorry. I handled things badly, and I am responsible for this." He was appalled to feel the prickle of tears in his eyes. He was not going to cry in front of this person.

Fenn narrowed her eyes, then turned again to examine things in the room. "You have a strange home."

"It's a home." He ignored her, giving all his attention to Draven. He was cold, so Keiron carefully laid him down, making him comfortable on the pillows, and tugged up the quilt to tuck around him. Draven was so still, so cold, it made Keiron sick to look at him. How could this have happened? How could it have happened now? Holding Draven's hand just made it worse because it hammered home that this creature, who was the most full-of-life, full-of-action being he had ever met was just so, so still.

"Fenn...." he began, turning to her, but before he could say any more, a thunderous hammering on the door made him jump half out of his skin.

Fenn glared at him.

"Just wait here. I'll be back as soon as I can." He laid Draven's hand gently onto the bed and smoothed his hair. "Take care of him."

When Keiron opened the door to find Bren on his doorstep, he was enraged.

"What the fuck are you doing here? You're really lucky I'm not punching you in the face right now. Fuck off, Bren, this is not a good time."

Bren coolly raised an eyebrow, looking Keiron up and down, making Keiron clutch his robe more tightly around him. "I can see that," Bren said with a sneer. "I've come to get my stuff. Liam's waiting in the car."

"I said, it's not a good time."

"But Liam—"

"Get the message, Bren, before I have to beat it into you. Get the fuck out of here."

"Where is he?" Bren spat, glaring at Keiron. "Where's the freak? I've got a message for it."

"Draven's not an *it*."

"Whatever. Where is he?"

"He's upstairs in bed."

Bren paled and growled. "I should have known. You're hardly dressed for work, are you? It didn't take you long to jump into bed with him, did it?"

"I'm not going to tell you again."

"Look, I don't care if you're fucking your little freak or not. He can wait. I want my stuff. You can't stop me. You can't—" Bren broke off as he landed on his bum on the pavement. He rubbed his chin as Keiron slammed the door.

Keiron put his back to the door, breathing hard and trembling. He jumped as Bren hammered on the door again. He ignored him.

"You won't get away with this. This is assault. I'm going to get the police around here, and how do you think they are going to take that freak? I'll tell them it was him. I'll get him hauled away to the station; see how he copes with a night in the cells. I'm going to—"

Keiron wrenched the door open and grabbed Bren by the front of his shirt, dragging him into the house. "You want to see Draven? Well then, come and see him." Dragging Bren after him, Keiron stormed up the stairs.

"What the fuck?" Bren complained. "You've lost it. This time, you've really lost it, and if you think I'm going to just take it, you're crazier than the freak. I'm going to get you for this, I swear. I'm going to—"

By this time, they'd reached the open bedroom door and Keiron literally threw him through it. Bren fell to his knees.

"Are you happy now? This is what you did, Bren. This is your fault."

Bren scrambled to his feet and turned to throw himself at Keiron.

A soft voice stopped him. "Who is this? Why have you brought him here?"

Bren whirled, and when he saw Fenn, his mouth dropped open. "Another one?"

"This is the one who hurt Draven. I want him to see what he's done."

"You? But why? Why did you hurt him like this? He has done nothing to deserve it. He has not wronged you. He does not deserve to die."

"Die? What? What the fuck? I didn't...I didn't hurt him enough.... It was just his wrist. I just chained his wrist." He turned to Keiron, narrowing his eyes suspiciously. "What is this? What are you trying to do?"

"This," Keiron said quietly, "is what happens when fairies get exposed to iron for a long time. You poisoned him."

"I.... What?" Uncertainly, Bren turned again and took in Draven for the first time. He blanched. "What-what's the matter with him?"

"I told you. You poisoned him."

"I didn't...I didn't mean to."

"And that's going to help him, is it? That you didn't mean to? That's going to make him better?"

Bren turned back to Keiron, his face white. "Is he...? He's not going to die...right?"

"I don't know." The anger had left Keiron, leaving him feeling curiously empty and very tired.

"But...but he's...he's not...?"

"I don't know, Bren. He's very sick. I don't know what's going to happen."

"I-I'd better go."

"Yes, you better had."

"I-I'll come for my stuff another day."

"Whatever." Keiron had no energy left to fight. Now he was back in the room, he couldn't take his gaze off Draven. Bren was nothing more than an annoyance, like a large fat bluebottle buzzing around his head. Ignoring him, he drifted back to the bed and stood, gazing down. A few moments later, he heard Bren leave.

"What happens now?" he asked Fenn, who was sitting on the bed.

"We wait," she said. For the first time, her eyes were warm when they met his.

Chapter Ten

THE DAY WORE on, and they waited. Fenn finally seemed to warm to Keiron and started to talk, telling him about Draven. It was obvious she was very fond of him, but when Keiron asked if she was in love with him, she laughed.

"We've had sex now and again, and yes, I do love him, but it's not in the way you love him. Things are different for us. Sex and love are not one. Sex means nothing. Draven is as a brother to me now. He has my back, and I have his. It is as it is."

"Draven says that."

"What?"

"It is as it is. He's said it a couple of times."

"He's right. Sometimes things just are. There is no fighting for change; there is only acceptance. It is as it is."

"But sometimes you need to fight for change."

"Sometimes, yes. It is often difficult to know when to fight and when to accept. Your people seem to have a talent for getting it wrong."

"And you'd know."

"You're right, I don't. I don't know anything about you. I surmise, I assume, I ponder, but I do not know. So tell me, human. Tell me about your people, your world."

Keiron snorted. "Do you have a few years? I wouldn't know where to start. There are so many different kinds of people. Different countries, religions, colours, cultures, and languages. I don't know where to start."

"Then tell me about you, human. Make me understand you. Make me see what Draven sees."

"I've no idea what Draven sees. I've no idea why someone like him would even look twice at someone like me. He's so full of life, so.... He sees everything with new eyes, and he makes me see with new eyes too. He makes me think, and a lot of the time, it's uncomfortable thinking. I have to explain things to him I don't understand myself, or I haven't thought about and—" Keiron shook his head.

"I was half asleep. I was walking through my life half asleep, and Draven woke me up. I thought all there was to life was working, coming home, and chilling in front of the television. After one day with Draven, I saw a new world out there. A world where people actually like each other and where someone can gate-crash groups of strangers and walk away with new friends. He sees everyone as a potential new friend. He looks for the good and finds it, and can't understand the bad, so most of it doesn't touch him. He's beautiful, strong, sexy...wonderful, and I've no idea what he sees in me."

Fenn regarded him silently for a while, then nodded thoughtfully. "You haven't told me much about what he sees in you, but you've told me a lot about what you see in him. You love him."

"I...." Keiron's mind raced, along with his pulse. "No. I-I don't. It's too soon to say I love him. I don't know him well enough. We haven't been together long enough to know if I love him."

Fenn frowned. "I don't understand. If you love him, you love him; if you don't, you don't. What difference does time make?"

"I've had this same conversation with Draven, and it's got my head spinning. I can't answer. I just know I'm not ready to say I love him yet."

Fenn pinched her lip, then shook her head. "I don't understand humans, and I understand less and less why Draven has such a fascination with them...with you."

"I'm with you on that." He smiled at her and sat down on the bed, taking Draven's hand. It was much warmer than it had been.

Draven stirred but still showed no sign of waking up. Keiron noticed a fine sheen of perspiration on Draven's face, and his hair was getting sticky.

"He's feverish," he said to Fenn. "Is that supposed to happen?"

Fenn shrugged, and it made Keiron angry.

"You're supposed to be the expert here. What did you give him? If you don't know what it's supposed to do—"

"I know what it's supposed to do," she said, her voice cold again. "It's supposed to save his life. The medicine acts differently depending on many things—the individual person, the type of iron, the length of exposure, the extent of poisoning, how long after exposure the medicine is given. Draven is strong, but it seems that he was exposed to strong iron for a long time, and you were late calling me."

Keiron was stung by the accusation in her tone. "He didn't tell me," he said defensively. "He didn't tell me he was poisoned. His arm was healing and I thought he was getting better. Draven thought I knew, that I knew about him being poisoned, but I didn't. If I had, I would have called for help yesterday, although I don't know if he would have let me—he was so sure you wouldn't come."

"Draven thought I wouldn't come?" Fenn seemed shocked and hurt, and Keiron mentally backtracked.

"He didn't think you'd be allowed to. He was absolutely adamant that he wasn't allowed to go home and no one was allowed to come to him."

"He should have known," Fenn said. "He should have known I'd come. I would never have left him here alone like this. Not even if the High Lord himself had forbidden me to my face. Not even if he had me put in chains. I would have found a way. He should have known this."

"He wasn't well."

"He should have known it," she repeated stubbornly.

Keiron fell into silence, having no idea what to say to Fenn. Draven whimpered, and Keiron lost all interest in her.

"Ssh," Keiron crooned, hooking damp strands of hair off his face.

Draven moaned and turned his head away.

"I'm here, Draven, just like I promised. I'm here, and so is Fenn. We'll stay with you." Glancing at Fenn for confirmation, he received a terse nod. "We'll both stay right here until you're better. Try to rest. I'll take care of you."

There was no indication Draven had heard him. He moaned again and slowly turned his head from side to side. His eyes were open just a crack, and the light glittered on the slivers of white.

"What should I do?" Keiron looked to Fenn, his heart thudding.

"Wait," she replied calmly.

"But I have to do something. I have to do something."

Fenn sighed. "You humans are so impatient. You're always wanting to *do* and never to *be*." She rummaged in her bag and brought out a packet of something that looked like grass. "Steep a pinch in boiling water for two minutes. Then put it in a bowl with enough cold water to make it warm but not hot. Bring it with a cloth. It will make him more comfortable if you bathe his face and hands."

"Is there nothing more?"

"There is nothing more. Take this, or do nothing."

With a sigh, Keiron took the bag and hurried downstairs. Whatever the herb was, it smelled vile and turned the water a muddy brown colour. While it was steeping, he found a mixing bowl and a soft hand towel. On a whim, he buttered some bread rolls and put them in a bag with fruit and mixed nuts. It was a poor meal to offer a guest, but he couldn't bear to be away from Draven long enough to cook anything more substantial.

Struggling with the bowl, the towel, and the bag, he hurried up the stairs.

"I have some bread, fruit, and nuts. I'm sorry it's not a better meal, but I didn't have time to cook."

Taking the bag, Fenn peered into it and her face lit up. "Thank you, human. It looks good. I was beginning to wonder if you were trying to starve me."

Ignoring her, Keiron set the bowl on the nightstand and sat down. Draven was even more feverish, tossing restlessly and shivering. Keiron wanted to ask Fenn if everything was okay, but he knew what she'd say, and was too proud.

Carefully, he dipped the towel into the bowl and squeezed most of the moisture from it before dabbing it onto Draven's face. It stank, but if it helped, he was prepared to do anything.

Draven moaned and turned his head, arching his back as Keiron worked carefully down over his body, then along his arms and even between his fingers. The revolting stuff dyed Draven's skin faintly green but didn't seem to be doing any good.

"It's not doing anything," he snapped at Fenn.

"I never said it would."

"You did. You said it would make him feel more comfortable."

"Do you know that it has not? It has not reduced his fever, but you don't know how he is feeling."

Keiron gnashed his teeth. "Dammit, Fenn—" With some effort, he controlled himself and sighed deeply, reining in his temper. He dropping his head into his hands and rubbed at his eyes. They stung from the mystery liquid that covered his hands.

"Keiron." Draven's voice hovered between a whisper and a groan.

"Draven." Keiron bent over him and stroked his face and hair. "I'm here. I've been here all along. Fenn's here too. She's given you medicine."

Draven blinked his eyes very slowly. "Fenn," he said in a cracked whisper.

Keiron was rather hurt that Draven wanted Fenn and not him, but he bit it back. He was just so glad Draven was awake and talking.

And then Fenn was there and she was in Draven's arms, and the hurt threatened to drown him.

"I'll go and make some breakfast then, shall I?" he said coldly.

Draven pushed Fenn away and reached for him. "No, Keiron, please no. Don't leave me. Please don't leave me."

Pain turned to guilt at the expression of fear on Draven's face, Fenn's too. He sank back onto the bed and took Draven into his arms, gently. Draven was shivering and his hug was weak.

"I'm not going anywhere. Look at you, you're shivering. Come on. Let me tuck you in. I'm staying right here, baby. Right here. Just like I have been all along."

"You have?"

Draven seemed to be drifting. Keiron stroked his cheek. "Yes, I have. Go to sleep now. Get your strength back."

"Fenn?" Draven asked, his eyes flicking to her. Fenn nodded and smiled, and all the tension went out of Draven. He smiled his old sweet smile. "I'm going to be fine," he said happily, slurring. Then he sighed and was instantly asleep.

Keiron was startled and not a little scared.

Fenn laughed at him. "Haven't you noticed?" she said in an amused voice.

"Noticed what?"

"That's what he does. He never drifts off or sinks into sleep or all those other things people say. Draven has a switch; it's either on or off. He does it all the time, and you're not the first to get scared by it."

"Wow. Yes, thinking about it like that makes sense. He's going to be okay now, right?"

Fenn smiled. "Yes." She got to her feet and rummaged in her bag. "It's time for me to go. Give him one of these when he wakes." She held out a small cloth bag. "And one every hour for the first day. They will make him sleep so do not be alarmed. By this time tomorrow, he will be well again."

"He will? That quickly?" He sounded doubtful and Fenn glared at him.

"Draven is not human, Keiron," she said reproachfully, as if that explained everything.

"I know, but—"

"Make sure he eats. Just a little between each dose of medicine. Meat would be good. Tomorrow, when he is well, call me and I will come to check him."

"I.... Whatever you say." Dumbly, he followed her to the back door where they hovered, not knowing what to say to each other. "Thank you, for helping Draven."

"He is my soul brother. There was nothing else I could have done."

"Will you get into trouble?"

"That is my problem."

"Not entirely. I called you. If there's anything I can do...."

Fenn stepped over the threshold and laughed lightly, her wings shimmering. "Anything you say will only make things worse. Call me tomorrow." And then she was gone. Between one breath and another, one shimmer and another, she was simply gone.

Hurriedly, Keiron fried sausages. He made himself a sandwich and put the rest in a box, which he took upstairs. Draven was still sleeping. Keiron sank into a chair, munched on his sandwiches and pondered. Could he ever feel confident to leave Draven alone in the house? He knew it wasn't his fault that Bren came and Draven had been hurt, but the thought he might be hurt like this again was unbearable. Maybe Draven should go home. But that was unbearable, too.

"Keiron?" Draven's voice was soft and sleepy, but it dragged Keiron out of his daydream.

"Hello, babe," he said, kneeling at the side of the bed. "How are you feeling?"

"Sick. Where's Fenn?"

"She had to leave."

Draven's face fell and tears sprang to his eyes, but he shook his head impatiently. "Of course. She probably wasn't supposed to be here at all." He sighed, then smiled brightly. "But you are here. Come lie with me."

"You need to have something to eat."

"I'm not hungry."

"I don't care. I have strict orders from Fenn."

Draven pouted, but Keiron just smiled. He took a sausage out of the box and handed it to Draven as he climbed up onto the bed. Draven sniffed at the sausage and nibbled hesitantly.

"Mmm, tastes good."

"Yes, it does. Here, have some milk, too."

"From cows?" he asked dreamily, still nibbling.

"Yes, cows."

"Hmm." Draven put down the sausage and drank deeply of the milk. He wiped his mouth with the back of his hand and held out the glass.

"Had enough?" Keiron asked.

"Yes. My stomach feels weird."

"What do you mean weird?"

"All fluttery."

"Then you should eat more to settle it."

"Don't want to." Draven pouted and snuggled in to Keiron.

Keiron revelled in the feel of Draven in his arms and rested his cheek on Draven's soft hair. He almost drowsed until he remembered Fenn's pills.

"Oh, I almost forgot. Fenn said you have to take her medicine every hour."

"Oh. Well, if she said, I suppose I do." Obediently, he took the pill and swallowed it with the milk. "What does it do?"

"Make you better. She said you'd be better by tomorrow and she's coming to check on you."

"Fenn's coming? Tomorrow?"

"Yes, so you'd better rest and get better."

"She shouldn't have come. She'll get into trouble."

"I'm sure she knows what she's doing."

"But—"

"Ssh," Keiron said and kissed Draven's cheek. "She can take care of herself."

"But I care for her too."

"I know. You care for everyone, and that's one of the reasons I love you so much." As soon as the words left his mouth, he gasped. Shit. He'd made a real slip there. "Draven, I-I didn't mean...." But Draven was asleep.

Religiously, Keiron woke Draven every hour all day and night, forcing him to eat and take another pill. Every time, it was a fight. The pills clearly drugged him heavily, and Keiron struggled to keep him awake long enough to eat a few bites of sausage. In the end, he had a brainwave and liquidised the sausage with milk and made him drink it. That was more successful, but messier.

"Come on, babe, just one more sip. Just one more." It was three o'clock in the morning, and Keiron was exhausted. Draven was draped over his arm, his head lolling against Keiron's shoulder. Milk dribbled from the corner of his mouth, and he stared at nothing. "Draven, please."

Clearly struggling, Draven forced himself to swallow and choked weakly, spraying sausage-flavoured milk all over the bed.

"Fuck it, Draven. Can't you just try? Just—"

Draven coughed again, then forced his eyes to focus on Keiron. "S...s...orry," he slurred, and Keiron felt evil.

"Ah, babe, don't be sorry. I'm sorry. I'm so sorry. Just rest. You can eat in the morning."

"Mor...ning," Draven murmured and was asleep again.

Keiron lay down, gazing at Draven. He was so sweet, so trusting, so beautiful. Keiron smiled, brushed Draven's cheek, then succumbed to the lure of sleep.

Chapter Eleven

KEIRON WOKE TO the sound of hammering on the back door. He jerked upright, shocked out of deep sleep. Draven stirred and moaned, and Keiron took time to soothe him back to sleep before he got out of bed, realised he was still dressed, and hurried down to the kitchen.

Fenn wasn't happy. "I've been standing here for many minutes."

"I'm sorry; I was asleep."

"You were supposed to be taking care of Draven," she scolded.

"Well, fairies may be able to stay awake for forty-eight hours straight, but I can assure you humans can't. I did my best, but—"

Fenn waved off his explanation and hurried up the stairs in front of him.

"Please come in," he grumbled, following in her wake. "Make yourself at home."

Fenn went straight to the bedroom and sat on the bed.

Draven stirred and opened his eyes. When he saw Fenn, he threw himself into her arms and hugged her tightly. "Fenn. I've missed you so much. Thank you for saving me. Thank you. Thank you."

Keiron almost fainted on the spot. He was still deathly pale and sounded weak, but he was so much better. Relief stole the strength from Keiron's legs and he had to sit down or fall down. Sitting in the chair and watching Fenn and Draven hug, Keiron felt strange. Not so much unwanted as unneeded. They were speaking together—over each other, under each other, around each other, but somehow understanding and responding to each other.

Maybe.... Maybe Draven shouldn't be with him. He'd never fit in with this life, this world. He'd get hurt again. It was inevitable. He should go back with Fenn. It would kill Keiron to say it, but he was going to have to. It was best for Draven, and what was best for Draven was best for him—even though it would tear out his heart to see him go.

"Keiron," Draven's voice drew him out of his gloomy contemplation. He smiled to see Draven sitting up, propped against the pillows, holding out his arms. Wearily, he got to his feet, and willingly, he went to them.

It was more than good to feel Draven's arms around him, more than great. It was heavenly. "Thank you, Keiron," Draven whispered, nestling his head on Keiron's shoulder. "Thank you so much. You saved me. You found Fenn and brought her to me, and you saved me." Draven beamed, and the ice that had formed around Keiron's heart thawed a little.

"I didn't do anything, Draven. Fenn saved you. Without her, I'd have sat here and watched you die."

"But you did, Keiron; you did do something. You could have sat here and done nothing, but you didn't. You went searching for help, and you found it. You found Fenn. Without you, she wouldn't have known. Without you, she wouldn't have come."

"True, I suppose, but—"

"Ssh." Draven lifted his head and smiled. "It doesn't matter. All that matters is that it's over."

"Yes. Over now. Everything's—"

"I think," Fenn said coolly, "that if you've finished, you might want to think about getting Draven something to eat. He needs to build up his strength now."

"Oh, I'm sorry. I'm sorry, Draven. Are you hungry? What would you like?"

"I'm not hungry."

"You should eat to get strong again."

"Later. Just hold me, Keiron. I just need you to hold me."

"Okay," Keiron said, a little anxious, adjusting his position to make both of them more comfortable. "Are you feeling all right?"

"Of course he's not, and he isn't going to until he gets his strength back. And he's not going to get his strength back if you don't feed him."

"But he's not hungry."

"No, he's not hungry, but that doesn't mean he shouldn't eat," Fenn snapped.

"But...." Draven began, subsiding when Fenn gave him a hard stare. He sighed and smiled at Keiron. "I suppose I had better eat something or Fenn will be cross with me. Can I have some more milk, please? They have milk from cows, Fenn," he added, as if imparting an important piece of information.

"Of course they do," she said in the kind of voice that suggested it was just another line on a list of strange and stupid things humans did.

"I don't suppose you'll be wanting any then?" Keiron said dryly to Fenn. She narrowed her eyes, then smiled the smile of a cat about to pounce.

"Yes, thank you, Keiron, I'd love to try some."

Growling under his breath, feeling tired and grouchy and pushed out of his own bedroom, Keiron stamped down the stairs and pulled together a hurried meal of sandwiches, crisps, chocolate biscuits, and milk. He was going to need to do either some shopping or some cooking very soon.

As he climbed the stairs, voices and Draven's laughter floated from the bedroom. He paused for a moment to savour it. It seemed like a very, very long time since he'd heard Draven laugh.

Keiron opened the bedroom door with his bottom, carefully manoeuvring the tray so as not to dump its contents on the floor. Fenn didn't make a move to help and held Draven back when he would have leaped from the bed to grab the falling milk bottle.

"Oh no you don't, sunshine. You stay put. You're not well enough to get up yet."

"Yes, I am. I feel fine now. I need to help Keiron."

"You are not well enough yet, Draven," she repeated in a voice that brooked no arguing.

Fortunately, the milk bottle was plastic and didn't break when it hit the floor. Thank goodness he hadn't poured it into glasses yet. After setting the tray down on the bed between Draven and Fenn, Keiron pulled up a chair.

"Why don't you sit with me," Draven asked, pouting.

"Because there isn't room. The bed's not that big."

"But if you put the tray on the table, you can come here, between me and Fenn." He smiled hopefully. Keiron met Fenn's eye. Not a fucking chance was he going to sit next to her.

"I'm fine over here. It's not as if I'm far away."

"But...but you're not touching me," Draven said plaintively, and Keiron could swear he saw tears glisten in his eyes. After having so nearly lost him, he wasn't about to deny Draven anything, especially when it involved holding him in his arms. If it hadn't been for Fenn, he wouldn't have thought twice. With a sigh, he picked up the tray and put it on the bedside table, where it perched rather precariously. Draven scooted back, sitting against the pillows with his knees drawn up, making room for Keiron. Actually, it wasn't so bad because, to face Draven, he had to turn his back on Fenn, and that suited him fine.

"Oh, but I can't see Fenn now," Draven complained.

"Then Fenn can sit in the chair," Keiron suggested, and after a moment thought, Draven grinned.

"No. You come here." He patted the other side of the bed, next to him. "Fenn can stay where she is and we'll all be together."

"When you have quite finished giving your orders, Your Majesty," Fenn said severely but with a smile in her voice, "maybe we can all have something to eat. I am rather hungry."

"Sorry, Fenn," Draven said with a grin that indicated he really wasn't sorry at all. "Hand me a sandwich."

"Yes, Your Majesty," Fenn said and reached across to the table to select a ham sandwich, which she passed to Draven. "Would you like some milk with that, my lord?" She inclined her head to him, and he giggled, leaning back. He cuddled into Keiron's arms, which automatically went round him.

"Yes, please. Can you get Keiron a sandwich too?"

"Keiron is perfectly capable of getting his own sandwich."

"No, he's not. He's got his hands full...of me." Draven chuckled. Keiron met Fenn's eyes over the top of his head and raised an eyebrow.

She frowned and threw a sandwich at Keiron. It fell onto the bed next to Draven, spilling lettuce.

"Don't do that, Fenn," Draven scolded and there was something in his voice that made Keiron think he understood far more than Keiron had previously thought he did.

"No, my lord," Fenn said dryly, handing him a glass of milk. "Should I pour one for Keiron too?"

"Not if you're going to throw it at him." Fenn pursed her lips. "Don't worry, he can share mine."

"You need to drink all yours yourself."

"Don't worry," Keiron interjected. "I'm good."

"Yes, you are," Draven purred, tipping back his head to look up at him in a blatantly flirtatious way that shocked him.

"You're feeling better," he blurted, and Draven laughed.

"Much," he said.

"What did I tell you?" Fenn smirked at him. "Draven is not human. He is fey. We do not take weeks to recover from the slightest thing, as humans do."

"Fenn," Draven said sharply. "Stop it. Why don't you like Keiron?"

"Who says I don't like him?"

"You do, with your voice and your eyes and your actions. I know you too well to be fooled by your words."

"It's not that I don't like him," she said, turning her head away and munching her sandwich.

"But?" Draven prompted when she didn't speak again.

"But what?"

"You said, it's not that you don't like him...but...?"

Fenn sighed. "I miss you. I want you to come home."

"I can't go home," Draven said with a sigh.

"Don't be ridiculous," she snapped. "Of course you can come home."

"I'm banished for three months."

"Only because you wanted to be."

"Shush," he said, glaring at her, with a glance back at Keiron.

"It's too late. I've already told him."

"You have?" Draven turned in Keiron's arms to gaze into his face. "Are you angry with me?"

"Angry? For what?"

"Because I asked to be sent here. Because I chose this to be my punishment and I lied when I told you I hadn't."

"It makes no difference to me why you were sent here. Especially not now." Draven smiled a beautiful smile that tugged at Keiron's heart. "Although I'm confused about why you didn't go back when you knew you were sick."

"I can't go back," Draven said, shaking his head. "I chose the punishment, but that doesn't mean it isn't a punishment. I was sent to you for three months, and I have to stay for three months. It's the decree of the High Lord."

"And you know as well as I do that if you asked he'd take you back."

"I don't care. He sent me here and here I will stay. I'll show him that I can follow through, and I can be committed, and I can—"

"You'd die to prove a point?"

"Well.... No.... I— It was more than just to prove a point."

"Really?" Fenn raised her eyebrows and glared at him.

"Yes," he said firmly. "It was. If I'd gone back, I'd have had to stay. I wouldn't have been able to come here again, not ever. He'd have seen to that. This is my one chance. He only let me come because he was sure I wouldn't stay, that as soon as I had a taste of this place I'd want to go home, forget all about humans, about Keiron. And I wasn't going to do that. I'm not going to do that. I'd rather die here with Keiron than live a hundred years back home without him."

He sounded so fierce, so proud, so...sure. Keiron almost choked on his sandwich. The expression on Fenn's face was priceless, too. She wasn't at all happy at what Draven had said.

"Don't be so silly, Draven. You don't mean that. You're not yourself and—"

"Fenn," Draven said softly. "I love Keiron. You knew that. You all knew that when you let me come. Don't expect me to give up just because of a few hiccups."

"A few hiccups? I don't consider getting severe iron poisoning a 'hiccup'. And it's still only your first week."

"Is it? A week? Just a week? Hmm." Putting down his sandwich, Draven leaned back into Keiron and sighed. "I'll get used to it soon. I know what to look out for and—"

"And you don't really know anything at all, Draven," Keiron broke in. "You don't know what to look out for. You don't know the dangers and pitfalls...and I can't be at your side all the time. On Monday, I have to go back to work, and I'd be so scared of leaving you here on your own. Maybe it would be better if you went back with Fenn."

"You want me to go back with Fenn? You're sending me away? You don't want me?" Draven sounded so heartbroken, Keiron wanted to rip out his tongue.

"It's not that I don't want you, Draven; you know that. It's just that...I'm scared for you. There are so many things here that can hurt you. And I can't be with you—"

"Will you two please stop treating me like a child? I'm not a child. It's been a long time since I was a child. I'm perfectly capable of recognising and assessing risks, and making decisions. I've made my decision. I'm staying." He crossed his arms stubbornly.

"Draven, can I speak to you alone for a minute?" Fenn said.

"What?" he snapped. "Why?"

"There's something I need to discuss with you," Fenn replied calmly.

"You can talk to me in front of Keiron. I don't have any secrets from him."

"Don't you?" She gave him a hard stare.

"Don't, Fenn, just don't. I'm not feeling up to it."

"No, you're not. That's why I need to talk to you."

"It's all right, Draven. I've a few things to take care of. I'll be back in a little while. You'll be okay with Fenn."

"Of course I will, but don't be long."

Draven seemed so sad, it was hard for Keiron to let go of him, let alone leave the room. He glared at Fenn. "Call me when you've finished," he said, and she nodded once, her face grave. At the door, he paused and glanced back. Draven was watching him with a strange expression on his face. It was very sad and kind of hungry. It made Keiron smile. He knew for sure now that Draven wanted him more than Fenn. The thought shocked him. Since when had it been a competition? Oh, who was he kidding? He was jealous of Fenn and she was jealous of him. It was most certainly a competition, and he was winning.

Humming, he floated down the stairs, and his good mood lasted right up until he called his boss at work. One very uncomfortable conversation later, he found himself with the choice of returning to work after the weekend or not returning at all. Great. Just great.

He was sitting brooding at the kitchen table when Fenn appeared.

"Leaving? So soon?" he asked with barely concealed relief and not at all concealed sarcasm.

"Yes, and you'll be glad to hear I won't be back anytime soon." She was clearly upset, in a pissed off kind of way, and curiosity got the better of him.

"You don't have to— I mean...yeah, I admit I haven't been entirely comfortable with you, but I wouldn't want you to think you're not welcome to visit Draven."

"No. If I wanted to and he wanted to, I would visit. He doesn't want me to come here anymore, although I'm sure that's just the spoiled brat in him talking, and of course he doesn't want me telling you things he doesn't want you to know."

"What kind of things?"

"Things I have promised not to talk about." She turned to him, drawing very close. "Take better care of him this time, and for his sake, don't delay too long in calling me back. He'll fight you on that one, but don't listen."

"What do you mean?"

"I can't say, but I hope I've done enough by giving you the warning. Take very good care of him. He won't be strong. He needs taking care of and he won't let you. Make him."

"I can't make Draven do anything he doesn't want to do."

"Then accept the consequences. You've been warned." She sailed through the door with her head in the air.

"Warned? Warned about what?"

Fenn turned, a haughty expression on her face. "Do not forget that the High Lord's anger is a terrible thing, and he is not someone you want to be on the wrong side of. To see one of his children hurt in this way has angered him, although he accepts, this time, it was not your fault. To see him hurt again would not be tolerated and you would bear the consequences of his anger."

"His ch...children?"

Fenn gave him a strange look. "To one degree or another, we are all the High Lord's children. And we are all, to one degree or another, children of the king...and queen."

Keiron had the strangest feeling she was trying to tell him something but couldn't work out what it was, other than a warning he'd better take better care of Draven in the future. "Don't worry. I'll take much better care of him from now on."

"See that you do. Stay vigilant, human."

With a toss of her head and flutter of her wings, she disappeared. Keiron stared after her and shook his head. She was the strangest creature he'd ever met. He caught himself and smiled...no, the second strangest.

By the time he got back upstairs, Draven was asleep again. He'd eaten half a sandwich and drunk half a glass of milk. Better than nothing, but not good enough. Leaving him to sleep, Keiron gathered up all the rubbish and dirty dishes and put them on the tray, which he carried downstairs. After a thorough search of the kitchen, he found the necessary ingredients, most of them frozen, to make a nourishing meat stew.

Chapter Twelve

KEIRON WAS PUTTING the finishing touches to the soup when he heard footsteps padding over the kitchen carpet. He sighed and shook his head.

"You're supposed to be in bed," Keiron said without looking over his shoulder.

"I was lonely." Draven trotted up behind Keiron and put his arms around his waist, resting his head on Keiron's back.

"I won't be much longer. Go back to bed, and I'll bring this up when it's—"

"No. I want to go in the...shower and be clean."

"Oh. Have a shower, and then—"

"I want to go in the shower with you." Draven's voice was more of a purr, and he rubbed himself against Keiron, who was suddenly very aware that he was naked.

"Draven, you should...you should go back to bed." He swallowed hard. "I-I don't think it would be appropriate."

"Please, Keiron. I just want to be close to you. You don't even have to fuck me...if you don't want to."

"Draven...." Keiron turned carefully and took Draven into his arms, resting his head on top of Draven's. Draven really did need to take a shower. That strange stuff Fenn had Keiron paint on him stank, and his hair was stuck to his head and shoulders in places.

"I'm tired, Keiron," Draven said, gazing up into Keiron's face. "I want to shower, but I'm really tired. Please, help me."

Keiron scoured Draven's face for guile but found none. He brushed some of the sticky strands off his face and stroked his cheek. "Are you really tired? You look tired."

"Yes. Tired but stinky. I need a shower really, really bad, but I-I want...I want you to help me." Draven stuck out his bottom lip and pouted at him, gazing up through his eyelashes. It didn't have quite the same effect with his eyelashes stuck together in clumps and his hair hanging in sickly green ropes.

"Come on; let's shower."

Turning down the stew, Keiron took Draven's hand and led him up the stairs. He couldn't help but notice that Draven wasn't entirely steady on his feet. Maybe it wasn't all about flirting after all.

Draven stood, leaning against the wall, and watched Keiron prepare the shower. His eyes were dull but started to twinkle as soon as Keiron was naked. He grinned when Keiron reached out his hand to him. With a flutter of his eyelashes, Draven took it and stepped into the shower, immediately wrapping his arms around Keiron and resting his head on Keiron's chest.

"You okay?"

Draven sighed. "I'm very tired. Maybe a little weak. I'll get better soon. I will." He spoke the final words with a curious certainty, as if he was trying to convince himself. Keiron smiled and gently enfolded Draven, pressing him close.

"I'm here for you, Draven. I'll take care of you and make sure you get well again. Fenn was very sure you'd be better soon."

"Was she?" Again a strange tone in his voice. It would have worried Keiron if he'd dwelled on it.

"She was, and I trust her." He rested his cheek on Draven's hair, so glad to have him in his arms again, he didn't even care about the smell of that godawful herb.

Draven sighed. "I want to be clean."

"I agree with you there, dear. Fenn had me bathe you with some horrible smelly herb stuff when you had a fever."

Draven sniffed. "Yes, I stink. She must have had a reason."

"Everything she did had a reason. It was to make you better. That's all either of us cared about."

"Really?" Draven dropped his head back and smiled up at Keiron. "You were worried about me?"

"Worried? I was frantic. I thought you were dying, Draven. I was insane with worry."

"You saved me," Draven breathed, rubbing himself against Keiron in a blatantly seductive way.

"You can't help yourself, can you?" Keiron laughed and hugged him. "And for the record, it was Fenn who saved you. I've already told you that."

"Yes, yes, you have. And I've already told you I don't agree. Will you help me wash my hair, please? I don't like it like this."

Draven wriggled as Keiron massaged his scalp and ran his fingers through Draven's long white hair. "Mmmm," he hummed and rubbed himself against Keiron.

"Stop doing that, Draven. I can't concentrate on your hair."

"But it's not my hair I want you to concentrate on, Keiron. I want you to touch me. I want you to touch me all over."

"Behave yourself." Keiron tried to stop him turning in his arms, but he was slippery and Keiron just couldn't hold on to him. "You're not well enough yet," he mumbled as Draven rubbed against him, and pressed his lips to Keiron's in a hot kiss. "Stop it. I.... You're not well."

Draven drew away and frowned. "Does my sickness disgust you?" He sniffed at his hair and skin. "I'm clean now. I don't stink."

"Oh God no, Draven. You could never disgust me, even when you do stink. I just... I don't want to hurt you. I don't want to take advantage of you."

"Ah...but Keiron, I'm the one who wants to take advantage of you." Draven pressed against Keiron so hard Keiron stumbled backwards, his back hitting the wall.

"You said...you said you wouldn't...."

"I lied," Draven purred and wound his arms around Keiron's neck, rotating his hips in a way that made Keiron feel positively unhinged.

"Mmm" was the only defence he was able to raise as Draven rubbed his soapy body over Keiron, making him stand to attention in more ways than one.

"Oh God, Draven," Keiron moaned, when Draven finally released his lips. The strange blue on blue eyes twinkled into his, and although Draven's face was still impossibly pale, a faint pink tinge over his cheekbones gave away his excitement.

When Draven sank to his knees, Keiron thought he was fainting, but his cry of concern changed to something quite different when Draven laid his head on Keiron's stomach and started licking moisture from his skin.

"No, Draven. You're not.... You can't...." His words ended in a long moan as Draven flicked him with his tongue.

"Let me. I want to. I need to." Draven looked up at him, water cascading off his face. There was something in his eyes that made Keiron pause, smile, and then let his head fall back against the wall. He thrust his hips forward and allowed Draven to have his head.

Draven drew a shuddering orgasm out of Keiron, then remained on his knees, his head against Keiron's stomach. Draven made a strange humming, purring sound that vibrated through Keiron's belly and earned another shudder and twitch.

"You sound happy," Keiron said in a hoarse whisper. Draven stopped purring and rubbed his cheek on Keiron's skin with a sigh. Keiron massaged Draven's scalp and felt him relax.

Draven tilted his head up again, and Keiron smiled at him. Draven didn't smile back. "Keiron," he said in a thoughtful, sincere voice. "That was good but...I think I might.... Hmm. Yes. I'm definitely going to"—his voice faded—"faint," Draven murmured as he passed out cold.

"Goddamn it, you stubborn son of a bitch," Keiron growled as he stepped over Draven to get out of the shower. Draven was weightless as he scooped him up in his arms and carried him to the bedroom. He took a quick glance around his bedroom and wrinkled his nose at the smell and the mess, and then he strode across the landing to lay Draven on the spare room's bed.

For a long time, Keiron stood gazing down at the little fairy sleeping so peacefully, a tiny smile on his face and his ridiculously thick lashes fluttering with dreams. Then he made up his mind and strolled purposefully down the stairs.

After his phone call, he stripped his bed, put the sheets in the washer, re-made the bed with fresh linen, and cleaned the room until everything was back as it had been...apart from the smell of the strange herbs, which seemed to cling to everything. He had to throw the bowl and towel away. He opened the window and left it.

Draven was still fast asleep, and as he looked at him, Keiron felt a dragging weariness gnawing at his bones. It seemed to have been a very long time since he'd last had a long peaceful sleep. With a deep sigh, he stripped and climbed into bed. As soon as he pulled the covers over them, as if he'd sensed him or felt his body heat, Draven nestled into Keiron's side, throwing an arm over Keiron's waist. Keiron covered Draven's hand and moved it, until both rested over his heart. After a few moments of feeling utterly *right*, Keiron fell asleep.

Keiron woke when something patted his cheek. It was still patting him when he opened his eyes, to find Draven's face very close. Keiron smiled. "Hey." He carefully drew Draven into his arms, and Draven wriggled until he was half on top of him, his leg hooked around Keiron's. Keiron groaned. "Oh God, you're not looking for sex again, are you? I don't think I could—"

"No," Draven breathed, "too sleepy. I just woke up. Just want to feel you."

"I'm not complaining." Gently, Keiron stroked Draven's hair and kissed his cheek. "I'm so glad you're feeling better. I've been so scared. I truly thought you were going to die."

"So did I." Draven shrugged, not appearing to be too concerned about it.

"Were you scared?"

"A little. I was sad I had to say goodbye to you."

"That's all? A little scared and sad?"

"Yes. Why? Was that wrong?" Draven murmured, his breath tickling Keiron chest, ruffling the fine hairs.

"Wrong?" Keiron mused. "No, not wrong. Just...different."

Draven sighed. "Everything about me is different."

"That's one of the things I like most about you."

"Thank you," Draven said, sounding somewhat unconvinced.

"Hey, don't start with that. You're my angel, Draven, and I don't care how different you are. You're the same in all the important ways and your strangeness is sweet and fresh and beautiful."

"I'm not an angel," Draven said, but with a smile. "I'm a fairy. Angels are bigger and scarier and don't like humans very much."

Keiron smiled. Would there ever come a time when the things Draven said stopped surprising him? He hoped not.

Draven patted Keiron's face and kissed him softly, and then he curled up again, snuggling into the warmth of Keiron's body. Keiron realised Draven felt chilled. "Are you cold?"

"Mmm. Cuddle me," he demanded, and Keiron obliged.

"Are you hungry," Keiron asked after a while. "I made stew."

"Stew," Draven asked with a smile. "What kind of stew?"

"Beef stew with potatoes, carrots, onions, herbs, and gravy."

Draven sniffed delicately. "What's beef? I know the rest."

"Beef? It's meat."

"Meat? What kind of meat?" Draven was genuinely curious, his eyes shining as he raised himself to gaze down at Keiron, his small icy hand resting on his chest. "Is it from a bird or an animal?"

"A cow."

"Cow? You milk them and you eat them."

"Yes. Have you never tasted beef?"

Draven shook his head, causing his long fine hair to tickle Keiron's skin. "I don't usually eat such big animals. I didn't know you ate cows. Do you eat horses too?"

"God, no. No, we don't eat horses."

"Why not? If you eat cows, why don't you eat horses?"

Keiron frowned. That was a difficult one. "Because we...well...we ride horses."

"And you don't ride cows?"

"No, cows are...there's not much else you can do with cows."

Draven frowned. "So you use animals if you can, and if you can't, you eat them."

"Um.... Hmm.... When you put it that way, it doesn't sound very nice, does it?" Keiron shifted uncomfortably, his cheeks beginning to heat.

"No, it doesn't. It isn't."

"But you eat meat," Keiron said on the defensive.

"Yes, but I don't only hunt things that are useless. I hunt things I need to eat. I hunt small animals if I'm alone and larger animals when I have companions. I hunt what's there, but only what we need when we need it."

"Do you hunt cats?" Keiron's eyes widened as he remembered what Draven had said about milking them."

Draven gawped at him as if he was utterly insane. "Of course I don't hunt cats. Why would I hunt cats? You don't think I'd eat a cat...do you?"

"Absolutely not," Keiron said with less conviction than relief.

"Good. I hunt with cats sometimes; they wouldn't be happy at all if I started to eat them. It would be like eating...Fenn."

Keiron almost choked at the image. "There are some places where they eat cats."

"What?" Draven sat up, his eyes like saucers. "They eat...? Cats?"

"I... In some countries, yes."

"Would they eat me?" He seemed genuinely scared, crouched on his hands and knees, almost as if he was set to run.

"No, they wouldn't eat you. You're a person, a—"

"A human being? But I'm not."

"Don't be silly. They still wouldn't eat you."

"Cats are people too," he said, lying down again, still suspicious. "Sometimes they let us ride them."

"You ride cats?"

"Sometimes."

"You never cease to amaze me."

"Do I?" He sounded pleased, and that made Keiron warm inside. He lay for a few minutes, enjoying holding and being held by Draven. But Draven was so cold. He needed feeding. "I'm going to get some stew."

"I'll come." Draven bounced out of bed, then stumbled and grabbed at Keiron to steady himself. "Oops," he said with a sad little smile. "Not all better yet."

"You should go back to bed. I'll bring your stew up here."

"No. I'm bored. I want to come downstairs and watch a film again. I want to watch one that will make me smile. I promise I'll be good. I promise I'll lie down and be quiet...and I'll eat all the stew." He smiled a brilliant smile, and Keiron just couldn't say no.

"Come on then, superhero." Before they left the room, Keiron insisted Draven put on some pyjamas. Draven grumbled but complied. While he was getting dressed, Keiron took a quilt from the bed and made a cosy nest on the sofa. Then he put his arm around Draven's waist to support him as they slowly descended the stairs.

"Know what?" Draven said when they got to the bottom. "That was much more difficult than if you'd let me go by myself. I'm not that sick anymore."

"Draven, yesterday I didn't know if you were going to live or die. Give me a couple of days to get used to the idea you're not and let me nurse you in between."

"Nurse me? What does that mean?"

"Take care of you. Make you feel better."

"Just being here with you makes me feel better," Draven said, patting Keiron's face with that small cold hand that made Keiron want to capture it and hold on tight.

"Come on," Keiron said softly and tucked Draven up on the sofa with a soft pillow under his head. Draven beamed up at him and a warm, cosy feeling settled around Keiron's heart. He sat down and took Draven's hand. He just held it, gazing at him and feeling...right.

"Did you make stew?" Draven asked at last, after his stomach growled loudly.

Keiron laughed. "I'll be right back."

When he brought the bowls of steaming stew and hunks of bread back into the living room, Draven was asleep. As loath as he was to wake him, Draven really did need to eat.

"Draven. Draven, sweetheart. Time to eat." Fortunately, as soon as he waved the bowl of soup under Draven's twitching nose, he opened his eyes and patted his stomach.

"Mmm, smells good."

With some of his former bounce, Draven sat up, still with the quilt tucked around him, and took the bowl. Closing his eyes, he sniffed at the stew. "Mmm," he murmured, then dipped in his spoon and started to eat. At every mouthful, he stopped and chewed thoughtfully, then swallowed and took another. Keiron watched him with a smile on his face. It was obvious Draven appreciated the meal, and it had been a long time since anyone had eaten something he'd cooked with such enthusiastic enjoyment. Bren had never been much for compliments, and he wouldn't have dreamed of saying thank you no matter how much he'd enjoyed.

"Cows taste good," Draven announced from nowhere, halfway through his bowl of stew.

"I'm glad you're enjoying it."

Keiron watched with amusement as Draven ate. From his outward appearance, Keiron might have thought he would be neat and delicate when he ate, but that was anything but true. Draven threw himself at his food in much the same way he threw himself at life, with a considerable amount of enthusiasm. He spooned chunks of stew into his mouth and chewed each mouthful thoroughly, his expressions clearly revealing his enjoyment.

"Well, I've never tasted anything like it before, but it isn't bad. In fact, it's really good. I mean, the cow is weird, but in a good way." With a yawn, Draven leaned forward and placed his bowl on the coffee table. "Can we watch a film now?"

"You haven't finished your dinner."

He patted his stomach and grinned at Keiron. "I've had enough. The cow was very filling. I'm only little, you know."

Keiron shook his head and laughed. He took both bowls out into the kitchen, then flipped on the entertainment centre. "What kind of film would you like?"

"The kind with people in it."

"All of them have people in it. Do you want something funny, scary, or romantic?"

"What's romantic?"

"A love story."

"Ooh yes," Draven said, his eyes lighting up. "I want to see stories about love."

"No, not stories; just one."

Smiling, Keiron selected a film and inserted it into the DVD player. He was about to return to the chair, but Draven held out his hand. "Come sit with me."

Keiron sat down on the sofa and settled Draven against him, his back to Keiron's chest. Draven still felt cold, so Keiron tucked the quilt around him. "Comfortable?"

"Mmm."

"Warm enough?"

"Mmm," Draven said, snuggling further. "Thank you, Keiron." He rubbed his cheek on Keiron's chest. He was so beautiful, so sweet. Keiron couldn't help himself and had to touch Draven, stroking his hair as they relaxed together. They weren't even ten minutes into the film before Keiron realised Draven had fallen asleep.

Chapter Thirteen

THE NEXT DAY, Saturday, Keiron woke with Draven in his arms and the sun in his eyes. It was late and he felt well rested and full of energy. Today was going to be a good day, he could feel it. A little surprised that Draven was still asleep, he gazed down at his sleeping angel and gently brushed Draven's cheek with his fingertips.

"Mmm." Draven stirred and snuggled into Keiron's side with sleepy noises that made Keiron's heart twinge. With a catlike stretch and a yawn, Draven opened his eyes and smiled. Reaching up, he patted Keiron's cheek. It was a gesture Draven seemed to have adopted since they'd...connected.

"I like it when you pat my cheek."

"Of course you do," Draven stated and yawned again. Keiron smiled, as mystified as ever, and returned the favour, gently patting Draven's cheek. Draven closed his eyes and practically purred. "Thank you," he murmured contentedly.

"For what?" Keiron asked with another pat.

"For telling me you love me."

"What? But I...I didn't.... Oh." He snatched his hand back as if Draven's face burned him. "It's that, isn't it? That patting thing. It's a way of saying—"

"Yes."

"You know I didn't know that. You know I didn't mean—"

"Oh yes, you did." Draven patted him again. "You don't need to tell me you love me for me to know you do."

"But—"

Ignoring him, Draven slipped out of bed and stretched, his slender body swaying as he raised his hands, lifting his hair off his shoulders. "I want to go outside today."

"Yes, it seems like a nice day. I'll make us breakfast and we can eat it in the garden."

"I don't want to go to the garden; I want to go to the park. I want lots and lots of trees and grass...a big place."

"Would you be able to walk that far?" Keiron asked doubtfully. "It's not just getting there. It's getting back and walking around."

"I need it, Keiron. I need something big and green and...and trees and water and life."

"Water and trees, huh? Well, how about instead of going to the park I take you out into the countryside a little? I know a place where there's a stream that runs down from the mountain. There's a kind of beach along the banks and it's on the edge of a wood. Nothing but water and trees and grass as far as you can see."

"Oh yes, yes." Draven bounced and clapped his hand in a curiously childlike way. His face was so full of joy and excitement, Keiron would have promised him anything just to keep it there.

"Let me get you some clothes. It looks like it's a warm day. I'll find you some shorts so you can paddle in the water."

"What's paddle?" Draven followed close to Keiron as he searched through drawers and selected a pair of long shorts and a T-shirt. It was blue and had a wavelike design on the front. It suited him perfectly. The only problem was that it enhanced a blue tint in his hair and accented his eyes, making them both more prominent and Draven more alien.

"It means to walk in the water. Maybe not that T-shirt."

"But why? I like it."

"I know, but it makes you too...blue."

"What do you mean?" Draven held the shirt against him and peered at himself in the mirror. "Oh. I see."

With that strange shimmer in the air Keiron had noticed when Draven changed before, the blue tint disappeared from his hair, and although his eyes retained their remarkable colour, they seemed more...human. Keiron walked up behind him and put his hands on Draven's shoulders, bending down to kiss his hair.

"Thank you, baby."

Draven caught his eyes in the mirror and grinned at him, the newly human eyes glowing. "I'd do anything for you."

Keiron hugged him. "I'd do anything for you, too."

"Except say you love me."

"I will, Draven, I'm sure I will...when I know. When I really know."

Draven sighed and turned in his arms. He reached up and patted Keiron's cheek. "I know right now, and I'm going to keep telling you all the time until you get the message." He smiled gently and pushed Keiron away so he could dress in his new clothes.

After a truly bittersweet moment, Keiron went back to his rummaging, to find a similar outfit for himself. When he'd found it and pulled it on, he turned to find Draven twisting around, examining himself closely in the mirror.

"What are you doing?"

"Liking the way I look in these clothes. They make me feel good so I wanted to see if they make me look good."

Keiron let his eyes rove appreciatively over Draven's compact body. "And do they?"

"Well, you can see that, can't you?" Draven tilted his head to one side and gazed thoughtfully at himself.

"Yes, I can see it. I was just wondering what you see."

"I see me looking pretty good." He grinned, and Keiron hugged him.

"Yes, you do look pretty good. Come on. Let's get this show on the road."

Draven bounced along beside him as he gathered together a quick picnic, two fold-up chairs, and as an afterthought, some sun lotion. No one as pale as Draven could fail to burn in the hot sun. All the time, Draven chattered excitedly, and eventually Keiron blanked it out. It was impossible to answer Draven's questions when he moved on to the next before Keiron'd answered the last. Smiling as he went, he moved methodically through his preparations, delighting in Draven's excitement.

When at last they were ready and Keiron had forced Draven to eat some breakfast, struggling to get him to stop talking for long enough to put the food in his mouth, they went down to the garage where Draven stopped dead.

"What's wrong?"

"It's one of them," Draven whispered, shrinking back. "One of those things out there. The ones that roar and make the air taste bad."

"It's a car. If we want to go all the way to my special place, we have to go in the car."

"In? We have to let it swallow us?"

"It's not going to swallow us, Draven. It's not alive. It's a machine, just bits of metal put together that can travel very fast. We can sit inside and travel long distances much, much quicker than we can walk."

"And it won't bite me?"

"It doesn't have any teeth, Draven."

"Oh. It won't hurt me?"

"I promise it won't hurt you."

"Will we be going out there with all the other metal boxes, the big ones?"

"To begin with. When we start to get out into the countryside, there'll be much fewer."

Draven seemed doubtful, but he reluctantly walked forward, and when Keiron opened the door, he ducked his head and peeped inside, then clambered into the passenger seat. Keiron got in beside him.

"You need to put your seat belt on."

"My what."

"See? This." Keiron put his own belt on to show Draven how it worked.

"I have to tie myself up? I-I don't know...." He sounded very nervous.

"It's not tying yourself up. It's just making yourself safe. If we have an accident, you might go through the window if you don't have a seat belt on." Keiron realised his mistake as soon as the words were out of his mouth.

"Accident? Window? I-I don't think I want to—"

Keiron covered Draven's hand with his own. "It's all right. It's very safe, Draven, very safe. The seat belt is just a precaution."

"Do I...? Do I have to?"

"Yes, I'm afraid you do. It's the law."

Draven huffed. "The law again. Your laws make no sense."

"You're right. Many of them don't. Are you ready to go?"

"Umm. Yes." With trembling fingers, Draven put on the seat belt, allowing Keiron to help him. Draven whimpered when the car started and again when the garage door opened. When Keiron pulled out onto the road, Draven squealed and tore off his seat belt, trying to crawl into the footwell. Keiron swerved and quickly pulled in to the side of the road.

"Draven, you can't do that. It's dangerous. Just sit back and relax. Close your eyes if you want to."

Uncertainly, Draven sat back in the seat and allowed Keiron to strap him in. As they drew off, he looked out of the window, then whimpered and shut his eyes tightly. Reaching over, he grabbed Keiron's hand.

"Draven, I can't hold your hand. I need both of mine on the wheel to be able to drive."

Draven opened his eyes and stared at him, his lip trembling. "Okay," he whispered and turned towards Keiron, away from the window, curling up and squeezing his eyes tightly closed.

"Draven, if you're this scared, maybe we shouldn't go."

Draven shook his head, his eyes still closed. "I want to go to the trees and water. I want quiet grass and big spaces. I'll be all right."

Keiron stared at him for a long moment, then shook his head. "Tell me if you're not doing well, okay?"

"Yes," he whispered again. Shockingly, when Keiron glanced at him again a few minutes later, he was fast asleep. He wondered if this was normal, then laughed. Nothing about Draven was normal.

Draven slept for the whole two-hour journey, and Keiron had to wake him when they pulled into the deserted car park.

"Draven, come on, babe, wake up. We're here. Come on, wake up." He shook Draven gently. Draven yawned and opened his sleepy eyes. The smile he gave washed over Keiron like a ray of golden sunshine, and he felt warm right through.

Sitting up, Draven looked out of the window, and when he saw the open fields and big blue sky, he turned to Keiron, his eyes wide with wonder. "Keiron," he gasped.

"Do you like it here? It's very beautiful."

Draven leaned over and kissed him. "Yes, it is and so are you. Thank you, beautiful Keiron."

Before Keiron could say a word, Draven released himself from the car and ran across the grass. Keiron got out and sat on the bonnet, smiling as he watched Draven run. It was like setting free a pony and watching it gambol in the fields.

Then something amazing happened. Where Draven had been running was only a shimmer on the grass and Keiron blinked, scared for a moment that he'd fallen. He jumped off the bonnet and was about to run to the field, when he glanced up and saw the little figure soaring and dipping against the sun.

"Oh, God."

It was breathtaking, terrifying, dizzying. He stared and stared. There was something about the sheer joy of Draven's dance that touched his heart. He hadn't realised how...confined Draven had been. A strange melancholy fell over him. This was where Draven belonged. He deserved to be free to soar.

Draven touched down running and threw himself at Keiron, slamming him back against the car bonnet. Draven bounced off and tumbled over to sit down hard. He looked up at Keiron with shining eyes.

"Are you okay?" Keiron asked, holding out his hands. Draven took them and bounced lightly to his feet. He hugged Keiron tightly, and Keiron could feel the energy thrumming through him.

"It's a wonderful place, Keiron. It tastes so good."

"Tastes?"

"Yes, yes." Bouncing away, Draven grabbed Keiron's hand and began to drag him across the field. "There's water over here," he said excitedly.

"I know," Keiron responded with a smile.

Keiron allowed himself to be towed into the wood. His feet slipped on the mulch of a steep slope, but Draven seemed to float across the ground as sure footed as a mountain goat. Keiron wondered if he was even in touch with the ground.

Skidding on the last steep slope, they arrived at a leafy beach bordering a fast-paced stream. Without pausing, Draven kicked off his shoes and splashed into the water, an expression of ecstasy on his face.

He turned to Keiron and held out his hands. "Come on, Keiron. It's wonderful. Come in with me."

"Oh, I don't know. I'm not much for paddling, and it's cold, and—"

He was answered by a face-full of icy water. "What? What? You," he spluttered and, tearing off his shoes and socks, plunged into the water, which rose to midcalf. It was so cold it made his teeth chatter, even in the heat of the summer afternoon.

Laughing, Draven dodged away and scooped up more water, throwing it all over Keiron. "Stop it, you little demon," Keiron said, half amused and half annoyed. Draven's response was to throw more water and then more. "Draven, I'm not kidding. Stop it. It's cold."

But Draven didn't stop it. He kept on throwing water until Keiron had cycled through irritation, annoyance, blazing anger, and back to amusement. He started to fight back, and soon they were both laughing and soaking wet. Keiron was much wetter than Draven, because Draven was lightning fast, never there when Keiron threw his water and always well positioned to catch Keiron, usually in the face.

And then, while Keiron was shaking water from his eyes, Draven threw himself on him and knocked him over backwards, landing him on his bottom in the water. "Ow," Keiron moaned, his tail bone having struck a rock. His feet were already bruised and sore from the rocks on the stream bottom. He forgot the pain quickly, though, when Draven threw cold, wet arms around him and kissed him. It was the wildest, most joyful, and sweetest kiss he'd ever had, and it took his breath away far more than the icy water ever had.

Keiron put his arms around Draven's slight figure and poured the tumultuous emotions that filled him into the kiss. Draven pulled back and frowned at him with a puzzled expression. Then he shrugged, grinned, and then threw himself into the kiss again.

Five minutes later, they were both shivering and turning blue. The water washed over them in bubbling little waves, and silvery fish tickled their bare skin. A few hundred yards downstream, a heron observed them suspiciously, and overhead, birds swooped and called, obliterating the trail of an aeroplane way overhead. It seemed alien, as if it had no place in this magical world that belonged only to them.

"Maybe we'd better get warm," Keiron suggested through chattering teeth. Draven gazed into his eyes with an expression that took his breath away. There was something so...pure about the joy and so open about the love, it made him feel distinctly uncomfortable. Draven had no boundaries, and the fact that he loved and trusted Keiron so unconditionally was frightening.

Draven leaped up and held out his hand to Keiron, who took it gladly, and Draven towed him through the trees to the field. Once they were out on the grass, the dry, wild shoots and hidden tussocks further bruised Keiron's feet but didn't seem to bother Draven at all as he swayed and leaped and danced, taking Keiron with him, his arm around his waist. Despite the discomfort, Keiron had to laugh and join in with the wild joy Draven spun around him like magic.

Eventually, Draven collapsed into Keiron's arms and rested his head against Keiron's chest, gasping for breath. He grinned. "That was fun," he said with a beatific smile. "I'm hungry now."

Walking back to the car, arm in arm, Keiron was as happy as he'd ever been, despite the gnawing uncertainty and sense of doom hanging over him. Everything that had happened since Draven arrived on the doorstep had taken him further and further from his comfort zone, but he found he was beginning to enjoy the feeling of never knowing quite what was going to happen next.

Pulling out the food basket, cool box, and blanket from the boot of the car, Draven and Keiron carried them down to the edge of the river and, still watched by the heron, laid out the food and drink. They sat in companionable silence while they consumed it.

"You've completely turned my life on its head," Keiron said at last after watching Draven munching a sandwich with obvious relish and sharing some of it with the river. "Nothing is the same."

Draven turned to look at him, his eyes anxious. "Is that a bad thing?"

"No, it's not a bad thing." Keiron reached out and tucked a long strand of Draven's blue/white hair behind his ear. It was completely dry and as sleek as ever, shining in the sunlight, catching shimmering glints of silver from light reflected on the river. Draven grinned, delighted, and was immediately distracted by something on the far side of the river.

"Look," he said breathlessly. Keiron followed his pointing finger, and at first saw nothing. Then a flash of brilliant blue and another of bright orange caught his eye and he saw, shy and hesitant among the leaves of an overhanging tree, the breathtaking beauty of a kingfisher. Beside him, Draven made a strange little sound, and the kingfisher hopped out onto a bare branch that leaned right over the water. Another chirrup brought the bird skimming over the stream to alight on Draven's outstretched hand. Keiron held his breath as Draven stroked the bird's belly with the back of one finger.

The kingfisher twisted its head from side to side, seeming for all the world as if he was listening to Draven's chirping, then gave a sweet little call and fluttered up from Draven's finger. The dazzling bird swooped over the water, dived, and rose with one of the silver fish in its mouth. After circling them once, it disappeared, leaving Keiron feeling overwhelmed.

A rustling in the foliage behind them heralded the arrival of a pair of squirrels, who sniffed at the basket and accepted titbits of fruit from Draven's fingers. Keiron watched in open-mouthed astonishment as they played around Draven, running up his arm and around his neck so fast Keiron could barely follow them. Soon they were joined by other animals, from tiny voles to a large brown rabbit.

"What the hell...?" he gasped.

Draven glanced up, an expression of total joy on his face. "I'm sorry, Keiron. It must be because I'm not well yet. I only meant to call the bird, but I've accidentally called them all. You're not cross, are you?" he asked, looking anxious. What could Keiron say?

"Of course I don't mind. Anything that makes you happy, precious. I was just a bit...a bit surprised."

Draven grinned again, the clouds disappearing from his face. He held out his hand, offering a shy mouse that sat on his palm. Keiron reluctantly accepted the tiny creature. Its questing whiskers tickled his hand, and then it ran up his arm to investigate the pocket of his shirt, where it soon settled happily and curled up to sleep.

As if it was a signal, Keiron was included in the strange animal party, and soon he had a baby rabbit curled asleep in his lap and the pair of squirrels running up and down his back, their sharp claws scratching his skin as they found purchase in his shirt.

"Fuck," he gasped. "What the fuck?"

Draven grinned at him. "They seem to like you."

"Yeah...um...yeah. It feels...weird."

"Haven't you ever done it before?"

"No, of course not."

Draven's face fell. "What do you mean, of course? Don't humans do this when they come here? Don't they share with the animals?"

Keiron laughed ruefully. They seemed to have shared half their picnic with them. "No. Most of the time, animals don't show themselves to humans at all."

"They don't?" Draven tilted his head to one side. "I wonder why not."

"I don't have to wonder, Draven. It's because, by and large, humans aren't very nice to them. I think most humans, faced with this kind of behaviour, would either try to hurt the animals or run away."

"Hurt them? Why would they hurt them?"

"I honestly don't know. I suppose for the same reason they hurt each other."

Draven frowned and it appeared he was going to say something but instead went back to watching a butterfly that had landed on his knee and was shaking out its jewel-bright wings.

"Draven," Keiron gasped sharply. "Stay still."

"What?" Draven glanced up, surprised and alarmed.

"There's a snake. Just by your hand. Stay still and.... Draven, no."

To his absolute horror, Draven held out his hand to the snake, which raised itself into the air, tasting him with its flicking tongue. Apparently satisfied, the snake slid over Draven's hand, and began to curl itself around his arm.

"Draven, that's—" Keiron gasped.

"It's all right, Keiron. It won't bite me."

"But Draven, it's—"

"Are you afraid?"

"I.... No, of course I.... Yes, Draven, I'm afraid. You're so...sweet and all this is.... But fuck it, that's a snake, and it's not a garter snake or any of the non-poisonous ones. It's—"

"I know," Draven said quietly. He seemed suddenly sad. "It won't hurt you unless you threaten it, Keiron. Snakes don't like to bite things unless they're really hungry or they're threatened. Just like everything else, they like to just get on with their lives in peace."

Draven bent his head close to the snake. Keiron was utterly horrified when he blew gently on the snake, and it reared in front of his face. The tongue flicked out over Draven's lips, and Keiron held his breath. If it struck now.... If it bit Draven, he'd—

Draven raised his head and the snake uncurled itself. Bright scales flashing in the sun, it slid into the grass, heading away from them, back into the woods. Draven regarded Keiron thoughtfully.

"You were afraid of the snake," he said after a while.

"Yes, I was afraid of it. It's poisonous. It could have hurt you."

"Yes, it could have but.... Lots of things could hurt me, Keiron. You could hurt me. Should I be afraid of you?"

"No, of course not. I'd never hurt you, Draven. You know that."

Draven stared at him, then nodded slowly. "Yes, I know that...and I know the snake wouldn't hurt me either, even though it could."

Keiron smiled, totally believing him, totally believing that no one and nothing could hurt this beautiful, magical creature.

"I believe it. I believe it totally. No one could hurt you."

"Bren did," Draven said matter-of-factly, bringing a cloud across their sunshine.

"Yes," he said grimly. "Bren did. I don't know how to say how sorry I am for that."

"Sorry? You? Why would you say sorry? It wasn't you who hurt me. You helped me. You nursed me and took care of me. You didn't make him do it, Keiron."

"No, but I didn't stop him either."

Draven laughed. "You're so funny."

"I am?"

"Why do you want to control everything?"

"I don't," Keiron responded automatically and defensively.

"Yes, you do. You want to control everything, even other people, like Bren, and you take responsibility for the things they do."

"I...I...." He floundered. Draven didn't understand. How could he understand? He had no idea what it was like to live in his world. He had no idea how different it was to live in the city, among people. He had no concept of the games, the expectations, the...hypocrisy, the unreasonableness. "Maybe I do, but it's the way you have to be to survive back there in the city."

"Is it? Then why do you live there?"

"Because...because it's where my home is. Where I feel...comfortable."

"Are you scared of this world, Keiron? The sky and the sun and the trees and the grass and the water?"

"No...no, not scared, just...."

"Are you scared of the animals—the spiders and the snakes and the birds and beasts?"

"I...maybe a little."

"There are dangerous things in the city too, much more dangerous things. And everything there is dark and fake and poisoned. It's all poisoned, Keiron, and it poisons you, too. It makes you stiff and scared and...different."

"It's my world, Draven," Keiron said defensively. "It's what I know, where I feel comfortable."

"I know," Draven said sadly. "Do you want to go back now?"

Keiron found he was stiff and sore. The squirrel claws had scratched his back, and he was pretty sure the mouse had peed in his pocket. He squirmed uncomfortably. "Yes, I do. Do you mind?"

Draven gazed at him with such a sad expression on his face that Keiron knew he did mind, but Draven nodded and carefully sent the animals back into the forest before he stood up and brushed himself down. Carefully, he began to pack away the picnic things, making sure there were no small animals trapped inside, occasionally chasing off a bee or ant and rescuing a vole from the salad box.

Keiron didn't have it so easy. The rabbit wasn't happy to be disturbed and scratched him fiercely with its back claws before it hopped off into the undergrowth. The mouse bit his finger as he fished it out of his pocket. Sucking his finger, he threw the rest of the things into the basket and flung the blanket over his shoulder.

"Don't, Keiron, be careful. You might—" He took one look at Keiron's face, then dropped his eyes and meekly took the blanket from him, carefully shaking it out before folding it and putting it on top of the basket.

"The bloody mouse bit me."

"Here, let me take a look." Draven took his finger and examined it. He drew Keiron down to the river and thrust his hand into the running water.

"That's not going to do any good if the bloody thing infects my finger."

"It wasn't the mouse's fault. You probably hurt it when you were getting it out of your pocket."

"I did not.... Well, I didn't try to hurt it. It shouldn't have gone in there in the first place."

With a sigh, Draven nodded as if he was too tired to argue. When he took Keiron's finger out of the water, he kissed in gently, then walked away without another word, to pick up the basket. Keiron collected the cool box, automatically checking it for stray animals, and followed Draven to the car.

Chapter Fourteen

DRAVEN PACKED AWAY the things and got into the car without a word or a glance at Keiron. Uncertain, Keiron got into the car. "Do you want to play in the field again?"

Draven shook his head.

"Do you want me to drive to the lake? It's a lovely place. We can get a boat and—"

"No, thank you. I'm tired. Can we go home now?"

"Are you angry with me?"

Draven turned his head and his eyes were sad, not accusing. For some reason, it made Keiron mad.

When Draven shook his head, Keiron snapped. "Look, we're very different. Maybe your way's right, more natural, more respectful, more...whatever, but it's not my way. I like to come to places like this for the day. I loved playing in the water and running in the field, but it's not where I live, Draven. I was born and bred in the city, and that's where my life is. That's where I'm comfortable. That's my world."

Draven nodded. "I know," he said sadly.

"And there's no need to be so superior about it. So you can summon animals like some kind of Snow White, but that doesn't make you better than me. That doesn't mean your way is better than mine."

"I know," Draven said again, still sad.

"And it's not fair to make me feel guilty about it. It's not fair to make me choose."

"Fair?" Draven asked, seeming perplexed. "I don't understand. What's not fair? I haven't said anything to make you feel guilty. I haven't said there's anything wrong with your world or asked you to choose anything. Why are you so angry with me? What have I done?"

The tears in his eyes made Keiron angrier than ever. "You obviously feel more at home here. You've shown me things I never thought possible, and you were so happy. I was happy for you. But all you could do was throw in my face how much better everything is here than in the city...at least to you. We're different, Draven, very different, and yes, I like to come here, but this is not where I belong and you knew that. You've known that from the first, and you've done nothing but rub in my face how much you'd prefer to be here than to be in the city with me. Well, if you hate the city so much, if you want to be here so much, why don't you just get out the car and stay here. Let me go back to the poisonous city alone."

The moment the words were out of his mouth, he regretted them. Draven seemed stricken. "You...you want to leave me here? You want to leave without me?"

"No...no, that's not what I want. That's not what I want at all."

"But—"

"Draven...I suppose it's just made me realise how different we are. I can't live like this, Draven. I just can't. I don't feel comfortable here. This isn't my world. I just can't."

"I-I know. I never asked you to."

"Didn't you? You were trying to send me on a guilt trip, Draven, to manipulate me."

"I wasn't. I would never do that. I wasn't trying to make you think anything. I was just...I wanted you to see my world, Keiron. I just wanted you to understand, to see. I didn't mean to make you so angry. I really didn't. I don't...I don't understand." And he began to sob in earnest.

For a moment, Keiron stared at him and anger bubbled in him. How dare he make him feel guilty? How dare he manipulate him like this, make him feel so...so.... But he wasn't, was he? Suddenly, things became crystal clear in his mind. None of this had come from Draven. Draven hadn't said a single word to make him feel guilty—the guilt had all come from inside himself. He'd seen how Draven shone in this environment, and he felt guilty that the river and the stream and the animals had given him so much more than Keiron could, that Draven was happier here than Keiron could ever make him back home in the city. And, as well as feeling guilty, he'd felt scared.

"I'm sorry, Draven. I'm so sorry. I didn't mean it. I didn't mean any of it. I was just.... I'm so sorry. Please forgive me." He took the sobbing Draven into his arms as best he could over the console, and petted him, kissing his hair and stroking his back.

Eventually, Draven calmed and looked at him, sniffing. "I'm sorry, Keiron. I-I don't know what I did, but I'm sorry."

"You didn't do anything, Draven. It was never you. I just.... I feel so guilty that I can't make you as happy at home as you are here. I can't live here like this. I can't give you what you want, what you need. I—"

"But I don't want you to live here. I don't want to take you away from your home. I never said I did. And you do make me happy, truly you do. If you can.... If I can.... If you can just bring me here sometimes, I'll be happy, I swear. I don't want to be here without you."

"Of course I'll bring you here...whenever you want. Whenever I can. There's a place, further on, where you can rent cabins. We can stay here for a whole week if you want to, or for a few days over the weekend or—"

"I can? You will? Oh, Keiron, thank you. Thank you so much." Draven threw his arms around Keiron's neck and his anger disappeared. Not so the fear, unfortunately.

Draven slept most of the way back, and Keiron had the feeling that when he woke he would have completely forgotten the argument, which he'd never understood in the first place. He felt guilty that he'd hurt him so much, and that part of it was deliberate. He'd been angry that Draven had liked the fields and the river more than he liked home, and that was stupid. Draven couldn't help what he was any more than Keiron could help what he was. He'd known that. He'd known it, but he hadn't *felt* it. Now he did feel it, he was scared the difference was too much, that they'd never be able to learn to live together.

Could he be happy living in the country, spending every day watching Draven play in the fields, sharing his home with animals, and living on hunted meat and fish? Did it have to be that stark a change? Maybe he could find a nice house in the countryside, with all the mod cons, and a job he could do from home. He was intending to do that anyway, now he'd resigned from his job. He had some savings, but they wouldn't last forever. He needed a new job, something he could do at home, so he wouldn't have to leave Draven alone. Would it matter where that home was?

The truth was, it did matter. He loved his house—the sound of the traffic passing by, lulling him to sleep at night, the wail of sirens, the calls of people rolling out of the clubs, the general hustle and bustle of life in the city. He liked the busy shops, the strange assortment of people he came across. Hell, he liked people. He loved to stop and chat to the characters he passed every day on the way to work—the flower shop owner, who spent more time standing on the doorstep and smelling the air than inside serving customers, the old man who always sat outside the Italian pavement café being waited on by what were obviously his sons. And then there were the people he knew in the park, that he nodded comfortably to when he walked through to the supermarket.

He loved everything about living in the city. Could he really give all that up for the deep silence of a cottage in the country with no one around for miles? There'd be no sounds in the deep darkness of the night, except maybe the hoot of an owl to raise the hairs on the back of his neck. There'd be no one calling greeting when he picked up the morning paper and milk. There'd be no morning paper and milk. There'd only be him...and Draven. Would that be enough? No, no it wouldn't.

Back home, Draven was silent and thoughtful as they unpacked the car. When they got inside, he put the basket in the kitchen and went straight out into the garden, disappearing into the shrubbery.

With a sigh, Keiron emptied the basket, washed the dishes, and put everything away. Then he poured and drank a glass of whisky before wandering down the garden.

Draven was curled in the "cave", staring into the distance. He started when Keiron approached.

"Are you okay?" Keiron asked.

"Yes," Draven said simply, with a smile. "I just wanted to give you some time to think. I know I made you mad. I don't quite know why, but I understand you're upset about me liking to be out there in the openness. I was trying to work out if I should pretend I don't want to go there anymore, but I can't, Keiron, I can't pretend that, because I do want to go, and I do feel happy there. It's not that I don't feel happy here...with you, but...."

Keiron, horrified, took Draven into his arms and lay pressed against him, his heart beating fast and hard. "Please don't think like that, Draven. Don't ever think you have to hide the way you feel from me. That's one of the things I love most about you, that you don't hide anything. I don't want that to change, not for anything. I want you to always show me what you feel, always, even if you think I won't like it. Even if you think it will make me sad or angry or anything else, because if I am it's my problem, not yours."

"But I don't want to make you sad and angry."

"I know you don't, and I know you would never do that deliberately. But I don't want to change you, not for anything. I want you to always be just as you are now. I want to see your face light up when something amuses you. I want to see your eyes fill with tears the minute you see something sad or feel emotional about something. I want to see them flash when you're angry. Most of all, I want to see the way you look at me just before you kiss me. I want to see that expression of love and happiness without any clouds spoiling it."

Draven lifted his eyes and smiled at him shyly. "Really? You mean that? You really love me?"

"What? When did I say that?"

"With every word, Keiron, with every word." Leaving Keiron feeling as if he was standing on shifting sands, Draven hugged him with the expression he loved so much in his eyes, and then he kissed him and the sand shifted again and poured away, leaving him floating in the air with nothing but Draven's arms anchoring him to the world.

They ate dinner late, after having spent most of the evening in the cave. Draven made love as he did everything else, sweetly and gently and strangely. Cold fingers explored every inch of Keiron's body, closely followed by lips and tongue. He sniffed and touched and tasted as if he had to wring every last iota of experience his senses would allow.

Keiron lay stunned and still as Draven completed his exploration, then tipped Draven on his back and carried out a thorough examination of his own. Draven squirmed and giggled and gasped and allowed himself to fully ride and express everything his body experienced. He wasn't loud. Everything was soft and gentle, expressed in sighs and sweet moans. Even when he came, he rode the waves of pleasure in silence with such wild joy on his face that Keiron couldn't have held back his own release if his life had depended on it.

When they were spent, Draven curled against his side like a contented cat and fell asleep. Against all the odds, Keiron followed him quickly.

By the time dinner was over, the light was beginning to take on the unreal quality that announced the approach of the end of the day. On an impulse, Keiron took Draven's hand and led him to the park. Draven was reluctant, especially when they were out among the traffic, but he kept close to Keiron's side and followed obediently wherever he was led, apparently believing Keiron when he said it would be worth it.

In the park, Draven relaxed, although he didn't show the same excitement he had on the last visit. Indeed, he seemed strangely subdued.

"What's wrong?" Keiron asked.

"I'm very tired, that's all."

"I'm sorry, Draven. I shouldn't have brought you. I should have let you rest. I forget that you're not well yet."

"I'm fine." Draven smiled, then tucked his arm into Keiron's and matched their steps. "Where are we going?"

"Not too much further. See that little hill? Just on top."

"Oh. Why?"

"You'll see when we get there."

The park was deceptive. Because the rise was so gradual, it was easy to forget that the highest point in the park was the highest point in the city. It afforded a view over all but the tallest buildings, out over the city to the hills beyond.

The hill was already busy. A number of couples stood or sat around, all facing in the same direction. "What is this, Keiron? Why are all these people here? Why have you brought me here?"

"It's a surprise," Keiron said. He put his arm around Draven and pulled him close to his side.

"I don't like it," Draven said, a pout in his voice.

"You don't? Why?"

"There's poison in the air."

"What? What do you mean?"

Draven pointed down at the city, spread out before them, its lights beginning to come on—a patchwork of dark and darker sprinkled with glitter. "All the poison in the air down there rises up and it's horrible here. Can't you smell it? Can't you see it? Can't you feel it?"

"Don't be silly. There's no poison in the air, Draven. Come and sit over here." Keiron led him to a spot where a large flat rock protruded from the earth, forming a natural bench. He sat down and drew Draven down beside him. Draven shivered and leaned it to Keiron's side, resting his head on his shoulder.

"I don't like it, Keiron," he whispered, but it was a hopeless plea, as if he already knew it would be brushed aside.

"Ssh. Just bear with me. It'll be worth it in a minute."

"But it.... It's making me—"

"Look," Keiron said excitedly, pointing to where the sun, which had seemed to be hanging in the air, touched the top of the mountains and the sky turned golden. The underside of the clouds lit up with an almost unearthly light. As the sky darkened, it took on a purple hue. Fingers of lilac, violet, and pink shot across the horizon. Slowly the whole sky changed to an artist's canvas of bold strokes and glowing colours.

"Isn't it beautiful?" Keiron whispered as the breathtaking display unfolded. There was silence on the hill as each couple became lost in their own worlds, their own feelings, watching the sunset and drawing closer. Keiron didn't feel that closeness at all. In fact, he began to believe the longer they sat there, the more distant Draven became. It started to irritate him. "Don't you think it's beautiful, Draven?"

Draven shrugged, his head heavy on Keiron's shoulder. Keiron sighed and tried to find the deep peace he usually found when he came here, for sunrise or sunset. Even Bren had grown soft and silent here. Even Bren had appreciated the magic. Dammit, Draven was supposed to be magic. How could he not be deeply affected by the beauty, the enchantment?

"What's the matter with you? I brought you here because I thought you'd appreciate the magic. You showed me your magic this afternoon, and I wanted to show you mine. I wanted to show you there can be beauty and enchantment in the city too. Why are you determined to spoil it?"

"I'm not," Draven whispered. "I'm trying."

"No, you're not," Keiron said angrily. "I wanted to do something nice for you. I brought you here to share something beautiful, and you're spoiling it. I made an effort for you. I took you to the river because I knew you'd like it. I let you splash me with water, drag me around a field, and get crawled all over by animals, but you won't make any effort at all to do this one thing for me. You have to spoil it."

"I...didn't mean to. I-I am trying. I...stayed."

"Oh big deal. You stayed. Thanks for that."

Draven's eyes were huge and bright in the darkness. "I...don't know what else to do."

Keiron sighed. "Don't bother. Let's go home."

"You're angry with me again."

"No. Yes, I'm angry. You're so...selfish. When you're doing things that interest you, please you, and excite you, you're full of bounce and enthusiasm, but when things don't interest you, you're like a flat bottle of pop. This was important to me, and okay, maybe you weren't enjoying it, but you could have tried, you could have made an effort...for me. We're here. We're together in a beautiful place at a beautiful time. I wanted it to be special. Why couldn't you at least have tried to appreciate it, to— Oh, I don't know what I wanted you to do."

"But I-I stayed."

"Yeah. Right. You stayed."

"You...you said that as if it's a bad thing."

"No, Draven, that's not a bad thing. I'm just disappointed that's all you did."

"It wasn't enough?" Draven looked astonished, hurt, and Keiron shook his head in exasperation.

"Come on," he said. "Let's go home."

"Yes," Draven said with obvious relief, and it made Keiron unaccountably angry, as if his attempt to make things up to Draven had been thrown back in his face. He got up and pulled Draven roughly off the stone. Draven stumbled to his knees, and Keiron was contrite. He immediately stooped to help him to his feet. Draven was crying quietly, and Keiron thrust aside his frustration to pull him close.

"Come on, let's get you home. Clearly, I made a mistake. I'm sorry. I shouldn't have brought you here." He put his arm around Draven's waist and snuggled him into his side. Keiron was even more contrite when he realised how much Draven was shivering. "Are you cold?" Not waiting for an answer, Keiron slipped out of his jacket and wrapped it around Draven's shoulders. "Better?" Draven gazed up at him with glittering sad eyes and shook his head. Keiron sighed.

Draven clung to him as they moved across the grass towards the path that wound down the hill. Suddenly, he stopped.

"What's wrong?"

"Nothing," Draven said in a tiny, tearful voice and rested his head on Keiron's shoulder.

"Are you that upset? Draven, I'm sorry I was angry. I was the one who was being selfish. Please don't be upset."

Draven lifted his head, as if it was an effort. "I-I don't think I can do it, Keiron."

"Do what?" Keiron asked, truly puzzled.

"I...shouldn't have stayed."

"What? I said I'm sorry, what else—?" He stopped at Draven's bleak expression. Draven shook his head.

"You didn't listen," he said. "I...I tried. I...I...." His lips continued to form the shape of words for a moment after his voice ran out, and then his eyes rolled and he collapsed against Keiron.

"Shit. Shit, Draven. What the fuck? What's wrong?" He lowered Draven to the ground, propping him against a tree stump. A woman who'd been walking past with her boyfriend hurried over and crouched down.

"Is he all right? What happened?"

"I don't know. I think he fainted."

"Do you want me to call for help? For an ambulance or something?"

"No. No. thank you. I think...I think he'll be okay." Draven was already stirring and his beautiful eyes fluttered open. The woman drew back a bit. Keiron vaguely wondered why. He'd got so used to Draven's eyes he didn't think about how strange they were anymore. "He's been ill," he said, hoping the woman would go away. "I shouldn't have brought him. I think it was too much for him."

"Poor thing. You should get him home. Take those contacts out and get him into bed."

"Contacts?" He stared at her blankly for a moment, and then it clicked. "Oh. Oh right. Yes, I will. We'll be fine." With a last, slightly suspicious look, the woman straightened and, collecting her boyfriend on the way, disappeared down the hill.

"Draven?" Keiron asked anxiously, stroking Draven's cheek. Draven sighed and his eyes fluttered.

Draven blinked, clearly dazed. "What happened?"

"You passed out."

Looking very confused, Draven struggled to sit up. "I shouldn't have stayed," he murmured, then passed out again. Truly alarmed, Keiron scooped Draven up in his arms and practically ran all the way home.

As soon as he got through the door, he lay Draven on the sofa and grabbed a blanket to tuck around him. He wondered if he should call Fenn.

"Keiron?"

Keiron threw himself to his knees next to the sofa and stroked Draven's forehead. "I'm here. Are you feeling better now?"

Draven looked around. "It...it's better here," he said with a sigh.

"What's better here?"

"The...the poison."

"What? What poison? Are you delirious?"

"I...told you, Keiron. That...that place." Draven shuddered. "The air was poisoned."

"What? The hill? You mean...? You were being serious? When you said all the poison from the city rose to the hill? You really meant actual poison? It poisoned you?"

"Yes."

"Then why in God's name didn't you tell me?"

"I tried."

"You— Ah shit...you did. You did try to tell me, and I didn't listen. I thought...I was so sure you'd appreciate the sunset I steamrollered you. I'm so sorry. But...if you knew the air up there was poisoning you, why the hell did you stay there?"

"You wanted me to. You wanted it so much."

"You stayed for me?" Draven nodded. "You hung around somewhere you knew was making you sick, just to please me?"

"I....You.... You were so angry and upset. And then you were excited and I-I wanted to make you happy. I thought I could.... I thought it would be all right. But it got worse and worse, and I really tried, I really did, but I...and then it just...and I-I couldn't." He ended with a sigh and closed his eyes.

"Should I get Fenn?"

"No, I'll be fine."

"You're obviously not fine, Draven."

Draven opened his eyes and raised his hand to touch Keiron's face. "No, but I will be. Just let me sleep for a while."

"Are you sure?"

"Yes. It's not so bad here. It'll wear off now I'm not in it anymore."

"Do you want to go to bed?"

"No. Just...here. I need.... Stay with me."

"Of course I will. Draven, are you sure you're going to be okay?"

"Sure. Absolutely...." His voice died out as he faded.

"Oh shit," Keiron said and sat down to wait.

Chapter Fifteen

WHEN KEIRON WOKE, he was curled on his side on the floor. The blanket he'd put over Draven was wrapped around him and there was a pillow under his head. Disoriented, he blinked and sat up. Someone was singing softly in the kitchen. The light coming through the window was misty—either dawn or dusk. Had he slept through the night?

"Draven," he cried and leaped to his feet.

"I'm here," Draven sang out from the kitchen, then appeared in the doorway. He was naked, as usual, and had something brown smeared on his nose. "I was hoping I could make breakfast to surprise you before you woke up."

"You...making breakfast? But.... But you were...."

"All better now," he said, maybe a shade too brightly. "Come and eat. I'm almost done."

The kitchen was a mess. Draven had made toast and there were crumbs all over the counter. There was a milk spill on the other counter over by the fridge, mixing with an even larger spill of orange juice.

"I'm sorry about the spills, Keiron. I couldn't work out how to open the cartons, and I kind of squidged them. There was plenty to fill the glasses...although I had to use smaller ones for the milk because I had to put some on the cereal. Oh, and you need more cereal because I kind of had an accident with the box."

"I can see," Keiron said with a grin, looking pointedly at the little pile of cereal in the sink where it must have been swept off the counter.

"I had a bit of trouble with the jam, too, although—" Draven glanced up with a grin of triumph. "—I didn't make as much of a mess as I did last time, because I used a knife." True, he hadn't made a mess as he had before, although there was still plenty of jam on his face and in his hair, even a generous smear on his belly. "And I found some of this brown stuff. I didn't know what it was, but I figured if it was in a jar in the fridge it must be eatable so I tried it and it's sweet."

"Yes, it's chocolate spread."

"Chocolate. I've heard of that. It tastes good." Draven grinned triumphantly and swept his hand over the organised chaos. "Come and have breakfast. You need to make the coffee. I didn't know how."

Grinning, Keiron sat at the table and contemplated his bowl full of soggy cereal. Not having the heart to tell Draven the milk was supposed to go on just before it was eaten, he dipped his spoon into the gloop. It wasn't bad actually, and it was fun watching Draven enthusiastically attacking both cereal and jammy toast at the same time. Draven glanced up and beamed.

"Do you like it, Keiron? Do you like the breakfast I made for you?"

"I love it. And even more than I love the breakfast, I love that you made it for me."

Draven frowned, working it out, then beamed even more.

"Thank you, Keiron. I wanted you to love it. That's why I did it. I want you to love what I do for you, because I want you to love me."

"I know. It's so sweet of you and—"

Draven narrowed his eyes.

Keiron sighed and shook his head. "Draven, I—"

"Haven't we been through it enough yet? Haven't you learned how to say it?"

"I can say it. I just don't.... I'm not sure...."

Draven smiled softly and patted his hand, leaving sticky jammy fingerprints. "I don't have to hear it to know it."

"Draven, I don't want you to misunderstand me. I don't want you to build your hopes and—"

The little fairy shook his head with the sweetest smile on his face. It was somewhat spoiled by the jam and chocolate spread. "I'm not misunderstanding, Keiron. Don't worry. I'm patient. I'll wait. I'll wait forever if I have to because then you'll have to admit it."

Keiron opened his mouth to say something, then closed it and grinned. "Deal. If we make it to forever, I'll say it."

Giggling, Draven flicked jam across the table, hitting Keiron square in the eye.

"Now, don't start that," Keiron said sternly. "I know where it's going to lead."

"You do?" Draven asked innocently.

"Oh yes. It'll lead to you in the shower for half an hour and me cleaning up the kitchen."

"Not in my head," Draven said, his voice full of mischief.

"Oh, and what's going on in your head, then?"

"Both of us in the shower, and to hell with the kitchen." Draven laughed and got to his feet. Running round the table, Draven grabbed a piece of jammy toast, and when Keiron covered his face, he rubbed it in his hair and fled.

Keiron caught him in the bathroom and pulled him into an embrace, rubbing their sticky faces together to smear the jam and chocolate, then started to lick sweet mix off Draven's nose. Draven giggled and sucked Keiron's chin until Keiron pulled away and took Draven's face between his hands, gazing into his eyes.

"Are you feeling better now?"

"Yes, thank you, Keiron. I'm better now."

"What happened?"

"I told you. All the poison from the city rose up and made the air bad. I didn't like it there." Draven frowned with the memory. "Please don't make me go there again."

"Never," Keiron promised, pulling him close. "You stayed there for me. You stayed, even though you knew it was making you sick...just for me."

"Of course I did. It was important to you."

"I was an idiot, Draven. It was important to me because I wanted it to be good for you. It was so twisted up it's unbelievable. Don't do that again. If anything like that ever happens again, don't let it go on. I may need to be beaten over the head, but I truly don't want anything bad to happen to you, and if you tell me it is or that you're not happy or don't like it, I'll stop. Just make me listen."

"Make you?"

"Absolutely."

Draven frowned. "I don't think that's a good idea, Keiron. It's not a good thing to make people do things."

Keiron laughed. "Strongly encourage me?"

"That'll work." Draven beamed. "Can I get destickyfied now?"

"Destickyfied? What kind of word is that?"

"My kind of word," Draven said with a smile that melted Keiron's heart completely.

"Go sit in the kitchen," Keiron said a little too harshly. It was not the tone he'd aimed for at all.

"What? Why? Don't you want me to shower with you anymore? What did I say?"

Keiron laughed and lifted Draven off the floor, kissing him soundly. "You've said nothing at all that wasn't wonderful and sweet and as lovely as you are. I want to surprise you, that's all. Go down to the kitchen until I call you, and try not to make too much mess."

"A surprise?" Draven cried excitedly. "Oooh, what is it?"

"If I told you, it wouldn't be a surprise. Now will you please just turn around and get your cute little arse out of here?"

Giggling, Draven turned and walked from the room, swaying his hips to make his bottom wriggle in a way that almost had Keiron chasing after him right there and then. He controlled himself, however, and when Draven closed the bathroom door behind him, he quickly went to the bath and turned on the taps.

The bath was a big corner one, built for two. He and Bren had shared many glorious times— No, this wasn't the time to think of Bren. He quickly opened and closed cupboard doors, digging out candles, bath oils, rose petals, incense. He lit the candles and pulled down the blinds, plunging the bathroom into blackness lit with the warm glow of the flickering flames. A few scatterings of petals and lighting of incense sticks had the room perfumed just right. After finishing off with two of his best Egyptian cotton towels on the warming rack, he looked around at the magical wonderland he'd created and shivered with anticipation.

Creeping downstairs, he found Draven up to his elbows in suds in the sink. He was singing to himself, and his body swayed as if he was restraining himself from dancing around the room.

"Aargh!" Draven jumped almost out of his skin when Keiron slipped his arms around him. "I didn't hear you coming. You could have given me a heart attack."

"Perish the thought." With a smile, Keiron scooped Draven up in his arms.

Draven squealed. "What are you doing? Put me down."

"Patience," Keiron purred and hugged Draven close. Draven stopped wriggling and nuzzled into Keiron's shoulder, making his legs almost too weak to walk up the stairs.

When Keiron nudged open the bathroom door with his backside and carried Draven inside, Draven gasped. "Oh, Keiron, it's beautiful. It's magic. I love it. What's that smell?"

"There are dried rose petals in the water and incense burning."

"It tickles my nose," Draven said, wrinkling it, "but I like it."

"Good."

Gently, Keiron lowered Draven into the water and he slid right under, closing his eyes and letting his hair float around him. The candlelight, reflecting off the surface of the water, made his face and hair shimmer with an unearthly glow. He'd never looked more beautiful or less human. Keiron stared, frozen.

Abruptly, Draven sat up, shattering the surface and the illusion. "What's the matter?" he asked, shaking his head like a dog and scattering water everywhere, soaking Keiron and putting out some of the candles with a hiss and a sizzle.

"Hey, be careful. It took ages to light all those candles, and you soaked me."

"You should have got naked faster then, shouldn't you?" Draven said with a cheeky grin. Matching it, Keiron threw off his clothes and stepped into the water, sighing as its warm embrace enfolded him. He closed his eyes and leaned back, resting his head against the cool enamel.

A small splash preceded the touch of Draven's body as it slid up to rest on his. He opened his eyes to find Draven only inches away, smiling broadly. "Thank you."

"For what?" Keiron smiled and took Draven's face between his hands.

"For this." Draven rolled his eyes, indicating the room. "For everything."

"It's my pleasure, all my pleasure. You're the best thing that ever happened to me. I want to show you that every day of our lives."

Draven all but purred and laid his head on Keiron's wet chest. Keiron stroked his hair affectionately and closed his eyes. It was perfect, just perfect.

"I love you, Keiron," Draven murmured.

"I know you do," Keiron responded, stroking Draven's back. Draven tickled him under the water as his fingers ran over his ribs. Unlike Bren, he wasn't instantly "on heat" as Keiron laughingly used to call Bren's insatiable desire for sex. Everything was about sensuality for Bren, who immersed himself in decadence at every possibility. Nakedness, especially with skin touching skin, inevitably meant sex.

Draven was just as sensual, but his sensuality was all about experiencing life to its fullest, and although sex was part of it, it was only a part and not the whole. He was quite sure Draven would be more than happy to simply lie there until the water went cold, then get out with Keiron and move on to whatever experience life might hand him next.

The knowledge that Draven was with him just to be with him, not because he wanted something from him was like a refreshing shower of rain after a drought. It made Keiron smile and unconsciously tighten his arms around Draven.

"What's wrong?" Draven asked, raising his head.

"Nothing's wrong. Nothing's the slightest bit wrong. Everything is a lot more right than it has ever been before."

"You're weird," Draven announced and lowered his head to rub his cheek against Keiron's partly submerged chest. He kissed Keiron's skin, then blew bubbles in the water that tickled and made Keiron laugh even more and hug Draven even harder.

Slowly, Keiron explored Draven's back, rubbing and tracing, ticking and stroking. The skin under his fingers was as soft as a rose petal and had the same velvety feel. There was something subtly different to human skin, something softer, finer. It sent delicious shivers through his fingers and up his arms.

Not that it was all perfect. There were tiny imperfections, faint lines that could only be seen on close inspection. Keiron hadn't asked what they were but assumed they were scars from his battles or hunting or whatever. He bent his head to lick and kiss one of the scars on the curve between his shoulder and neck.

Draven lay so still he thought he'd fallen asleep. It didn't make the slightest difference. Eventually, Draven gave a deep sigh and raised his head. He looked sleepy and utterly calm and at peace.

"You make me feel good," he said simply and kissed Keiron with such a sweet kiss it brought a brief but powerful urge to cry.

Rising to his knees, sloughing water like a merman, Draven stretched his arms over his head. "I'm getting all wrinkly," he said, examining his fingers. "I'm cold, too."

"Do you want me to put in some more hot water, or do you want to get out now?"

"Oh, make it hot again, make it hot again, and make love to me in the water." Letting himself fall backwards, Draven hit the water and most of the water hit the floor, putting out more candles.

"Draven," Keiron scolded, laughing, and Draven, rubbing water out of his eyes, laughed back at him.

When the bath was again full and about as hot as they could stand it, Keiron moved carefully to the other side of the tub and supported himself on his arms. He gazed down at Draven, who smiled at him drowsily and raised his hands to draw pictures on Keiron's chest.

"My God, you're the most beautiful creature I've ever laid eyes on. I've never seen anything to compare in all my life."

Draven's smile broadened, and he laid his palms flat, running them over Keiron's wet skin. "Wash me," he said, his smile expanding into a grin. "Wash me with lots of soap and bubbles."

"Yes, Master," Keiron joked as Draven stretched his arms over the sides of the bath, offering his body to Keiron. Keiron sat back on his knees and stared at him, running his fingers lightly over Draven's chest. Draven closed his eyes and sighed. The low light deepened the blue in his hair and the candle flames danced across his skin, raising flecks of gold. Keiron swallowed hard.

"I'm not feeling any soap," Draven said in a voice that tried to be stern but utterly failed, especially after the giggle at the end.

"Oh well, if it's soap you want, Master." Keiron poured liquid soap onto his hands and started rubbing it onto Draven's chest. Draven sighed again and let his head fall back into the water, exposing his throat.

Slowly, Keiron worked his way over Draven's chest and down his arms, carefully working each finger. "Mmm," Draven sighed in appreciation.

"Is this enough soap, Master?"

"Right soap, wrong bits."

"Bits? Bits of what?"

"Bits of me."

"Oh. So what bits would you prefer? This one." He slid his hands over Draven's soapy sides to his hips.

"Nope. Not that bit."

"Well, what about these bits?" He moved down to the outsides of Draven's thighs, sliding round to underneath and making Draven squirm.

"Closer, but still not quite right."

"Aha."

Brushing his thumbs over the top of Draven's thighs, he moved up towards his groin, then slid his thumbs around the inside. Draven squeaked. "Yes, yes, that's it. More. More."

Leaning forward, Keiron lowered himself onto Draven, supporting himself on one arm as he used the other hand to soap up Draven's genitals. Draven gasped and panted, raising his hips. "Ohhh," he sighed and licked his lips.

Keiron lowered his head and kissed Draven deeply, feeling his body buck and writhe under his hand. "Oh yeah, you like that, don't you?" he murmured, lifting his head from the kiss but plunging right back in without giving Draven a chance to respond. He was rewarded with a whimper.

There were lots more whimpers as Keiron kissed, licked, nibbled, and stroked until Draven was weeping and begging when Keiron redoubled his efforts and brought him to an explosive climax, which left him shuddering and moaning.

Keiron continued to stroke his chest and stomach until he calmed down.

"Are you all right," he asked, teasing Draven's lips with his own.

"Yes," Draven sighed. "Oh, yes." He gazed at Keiron with shining eyes, full of adoration. It made Keiron smile. Clearing the wet hair out of Draven's face, Keiron stroked his cheek and Draven shivered. "I like that."

"I know you do. That's why I do it."

"What do you like me to do to you?"

Keiron laughed. "Everything. I like everything you do to me. Most of all, I like it when you smile. That's all I want, Draven. I just want your smile."

"I have lots of smiles for you, Keiron," Draven said, giving him one. Then he sighed and closed his eyes. "I like being here, like this, with you, but...I'm cold and wrinkly. Would you mind if we got out now?"

"Of course I wouldn't mind. You're right; it is getting cold." Keiron got out of the bath and held his hand out to Draven.

Draven looked at it. "I'm tired. Carry me."

Keiron laughed. "You're full of demands today, aren't you? Wait there."

He gathered up one of the huge fluffy towels and laid it out on the side of the bath, then scooped Draven out of the water and sat him on the towel. After wrapping him up in the towel, he picked him up again and carried him into the bedroom. Draven snuggled his head into Keiron's shoulder and sighed.

"You're very snuggly today."

"Yes. I feel like snuggling."

"I'm not unhappy with that," Keiron said, smiling.

In the bedroom, Keiron laid Draven on the bed and rubbed him dry with the towel, while Draven giggled and squirmed. When he was done, Keiron went into the other room to fetch some clean clothes for Draven. By the time he got back, Draven was fast asleep.

"I guess you really were tired," he said with a smile. Carefully, he lifted Draven, threw the towel on the floor, and tucked him up in bed. Unable to resist, he wiped himself quickly and slipped under the covers, snuggling close to Draven. Draven sighed and wriggled back into his arms.

Chapter Sixteen

KEIRON WAS SURPRISED to find they'd slept for hours, and then he remembered that he'd spent the previous night on the floor. Draven stirred in his arms, and Keiron nuzzled into his neck, burying his face in the now-dry white hair. Draven stirred again and hummed.

"I like that," he said sleepily.

"Mmm, so do I. Are you hungry?"

Draven yawned. "Yes. We didn't really have breakfast, did we?"

"Not really, no. "Would you like to go out to eat?"

"Out?"

"To a diner or restaurant...even a sandwich in the park. I just want to take you out of the house. Start getting you used to the outside world, if you're going to stay in it."

"Stay in it? Am I going to stay in it? I thought...I thought we were going to ask the High Lord about you coming back with me to my world."

"Draven, I can't do that. We can go visit whenever you want and you can spend time there, but.... You saw what I was like with the countryside thing. I'm a city man. I can't live without the noise and the hustle bustle and.... Draven, I'm sorry." He truly ached at Draven's pained expression, but he knew he couldn't do it. There was no way he'd be happy living in the world Draven left. "I'm really sorry."

"It...it's all right, Keiron. I kinda knew. I told Fenn...."

"You talked to Fenn about it? When?"

"Oh, just a bit. She wanted me to go back until I was...better."

"But you are better."

"No, not really. Not like I was." Draven lowered his head and jutted his lower lip.

"I'm sorry, Draven. I-I thought.... Dammit, I'm an idiot. No wonder you were sick last night. You didn't say."

"I didn't want you to worry." Sucking in his pouting lower lip, Draven chewed on it and peeped up at Keiron through his lashes, which was an achievement as he was lying on his back.

"You're not.... I mean you're not still...?"

"No, I'm not dying. I'll get stronger. I'm just tired and...not as strong."

"But you will get better."

"Better...yes. Yes, I will get better." Draven smiled, and Keiron reached for him, relief making him weak.

"Don't scare me like that, Draven."

"I'm sorry. I didn't mean to. I.... Are you mad with me?"

"Mad with you? Of course I'm not mad with you." Keiron held Draven close. "It's just that I love you so much and the thought of losing you drives me crazy, especially after what happened. I couldn't bear it, Draven."

Draven smiled and kissed him warmly. "I'm not going anywhere, Keiron. I'm not going to leave you, and I'm not going to die."

"I'm very glad to hear that."

"Are you going to take me outside now? I think I would like to see more of outside."

"Do you want to go to the park again?"

Draven shook his head quickly. "No, thank you."

"I won't take you up the hill."

"No, I don't feel like the park today. Can we go somewhere I don't have to walk too far?"

"I could drive us."

"No." He shook his head. "Not the car."

"All right, I have another idea. Get dressed and meet me downstairs."

Draven smiled at him. "Where are we going?"

"It's a surprise."

"It's not another scary one, is it? It's not going to poison me or—"

"Draven, I promise you. I absolutely promise you that you'll love this surprise."

"Hmm." Draven grinned and bounced out of bed, making Keiron shiver. His body was slender and pale and.... Oh God, so beautiful. "Keiron," Draven said as he got out of bed. "You said you love me."

"Did I? I guess if I said it, I must have meant it, huh?"

Draven grinned and kissed him.

Hurrying down the stairs, Keiron pulled out his phone and made a few calls, then poured himself a coffee and waited. Draven seemed to take a long time, but eventually he came bouncing down the stairs, looking excited.

"What have you been doing?"

"Had a tricky moment with the shoes," he said, frowning down at the sneakers. "I forgot how to tie them. Most of the knots I know didn't look right and took ages to undo. I think they're fixed now."

Keiron examined them and pronounced them adequately done.

"Come on. It's all arranged."

Gazing at Keiron quizzically, Draven allowed himself to be led by the hand through the back door and down to the bottom of the garden. Right at the very end, on the opposite side to the shrubbery, was a gate that led into a back lane. They followed the lane past other garden gates, all in high walls that tended to make the lane feel a little claustrophobic. They strolled hand in hand, and Draven seemed so happy and content, the fresh fear that had surrounded Keiron's heart a short time before began to disperse again. He couldn't help but notice now, though, that there wasn't quite as much bounce in Draven's step, and there were still dark shadows under his eyes. That worried him and made him feel suddenly very protective.

At the end of the lane, the path led along a shady suburban street, then turned to the right and went downhill towards a river that cut through the outskirts of the city.

"I can smell water," Draven said, his eyes glowing.

"It's not as pretty as the one I took you to before, and it's still inside the city but...well, wait and see."

Draven was skipping by the time they reached the banks of the river. It was wide enough to have a proper bridge. Keiron didn't take them over the bridge, though. He led them along the bank. After a few hundred yards, small trees and shrubs began to appear, and in five minutes, they were encased in a green colonnade that made it feel as if there was nothing beyond except woods and fields and hills.

The river was a gentle companion. While not sparkling and crystal clear like the mountain stream they'd paddled in, it was clean enough to have fish and, here and there, fishermen had set up their station to try their luck.

Small boats and barges slid or bobbed past, and with the sounds of the city muted in the distance, it was a lovely escape.

It was strange. This river, this path, this surprise had always been here, and yet Keiron had hardly ever taken advantage of them. He'd had neither the time nor the inclination to walk along the banks of the river on a path that led nowhere, just for the sake of the walk. Yet, when he'd wanted to do something nice for Draven, it was the first place he'd thought of, and now, walking hand in hand with him, seeing his eyes dart here and there, watching the emotions dance over his face and barely being contained within, it was the most pleasant thing in the world and he couldn't believe he hadn't done it far more often.

"This is such a beautiful place, Keiron. Can I come here when you're in work? I won't get into trouble, I promise. I'll just walk and sit. Please."

"Well, I'm not going to work anymore, Draven. I quit my job when you were ill. I'll be freelancing, working from home. But you can come here whenever you like, alone or with me."

Draven frowned. "You gave up your job? Because of me?"

"No. Yes. Partly. I hated it anyway."

"But you gave it up because of me, because you couldn't trust me to be on my own." Draven seemed so sad the last thing Keiron would ever have done would be to admit the truth in that.

"I gave it up because I'd been so scared I was going to lose you that I didn't want to spend one minute I didn't have to away from you. I want to be here with you, right here, by your side, all the time. I know that's not possible, not every minute, and it wouldn't be right—you need your space and so do I, but…I just want to be with you, Draven."

Typically, Draven went from sad to excited in moments. "I want to be with you too…all the time, every minute…except when I want to be by myself, which I do sometimes." He seemed doubtful. "You don't mind, do you? That I want to be on my own sometimes."

"Everyone needs to be on their own sometimes," Keiron said and bent to kiss Draven. "Now come on, hurry, your surprise awaits."

"This isn't it?" Draven asked in astonishment.

"No, this isn't it. Well, a tiny bit of it."

Skipping again, Draven danced beside Keiron, making him once more feel like the guardian of a playful teen. He was sure that's the way some of the people they passed saw it. They all smiled broadly at them, and Draven invariably smiled back.

Eventually, after a sharp curve in the river, they came to a small jetty where boats were moored. Some were rowing boats, some a little larger. One, in particular, stood out. It was snow white and hung with twinkling lights. A cheerful man standing on the dock beside her waved to Keiron, and Keiron led Draven towards it. Draven stopped and stared.

"Are we going on a boat, Keiron? Really? On a boat?"

"Only if you want to," Keiron said nervously. The owner of the boat was a friend of Keiron's, but even so, he'd pulled off far more than Keiron had expected and must have worked bloody hard in the time he had. He'd feel bad if they just turned around and walked away.

"Want to? Keiron, it's the best thing anyone's ever done for me. I've seen them, like big birds on the water, and I've always wondered. Of course, I've sailed on leaves and things, but I think this will be a lot different."

"Oh yes, I think I can safely say this will be a lot different than sailing on a leaf."

Draven instantly had the captain eating out of the palm of his hand, and as they pulled off, he explained everything to Draven and let him stand next to him at the helm while he explained the banks of switches and dials, even letting Draven steer the boat for a few minutes when they were on an even course.

Keiron waited on the deck, where a table had been laid out with sandwiches, cheeses, sliced meats, fruit, and bread. He smiled as he picked at the food and watched Draven, feeling warm inside. Every now and again, the captain would glance up and wink at him. It was clear he was enjoying the jaunt as much as Draven.

Finally, Draven came bounding back to him like an excited puppy and stood for a moment, letting the wind blow through his hair. He was breathtaking. Even though he made an effort to change his eyes and bleach the colour out of his hair when they were around other humans, Draven could not help but look otherworldly and ephemeral. Keiron wondered what other people saw. How could they not know what he was? Did they? Did they care? Or did they not see it because they didn't want to see it...just like he had at the beginning.

"This looks nice," Draven said, throwing himself down and picking at the fruit. "If I have a sandwich, will I have to eat the bread?"

"Every bit of it."

Pouting, Draven stuffed cheese into his mouth and grinned around it. Keiron had to laugh. He laughed even more when Draven turned the whole meal into a contest as to who could pull the funniest face while having their mouths stuffed full of food. Of course Draven won.

After lunch, they sat, side by side, watching the world slide past and just enjoying being together. Draven rested his head on Keiron's shoulder, and Keiron snuggled him into his side, relishing his touch, his voice, incessantly questioning everything, and his smell of freshness and magic.

As the sun began to go down, the boat pulled in to a jetty outside the city, where a bar-restaurant opened directly onto the bridle path, its garden sloping gently towards the river. There were other boats and a barge moored here, and the sound of lively conversation and laughter drifted to them from inside.

Mooring the boat, the captain strode off straight into the bar, leaving Draven and Keiron to follow at a more leisurely pace.

"Will we go back in the boat?" Draven asked, and Keiron smiled, drawing him close.

"We sure will. Won't the lights be pretty in the dark?"

"Do I have to go in there?" Draven asked nervously, pointing at the rowdy bar.

"No. Come over here." Keiron led Draven around the side of the bar where a much quieter patio held a number of tables with colourful umbrellas over them. Potted plants and patio heaters gave it a rather Mediterranean feel, and it was far more relaxed than the bar behind it. A few of the tables were occupied but mostly with couples who spoke in quiet voices when they weren't gazing into each other's eyes.

"Oh, I love it, Keiron. It's so beautiful." Sinking into one of the wooden chairs, Draven gazed upwards. Keiron wondered whether he was looking at the parasol or the stars.

"I thought we'd have dinner here. Are you hungry?"

"No. I'm still full from the cheese and meat. Can we just sit for a while?"

"Of course."

"What's that?" Draven asked after a short while. It was way too much to expect of Draven to sit in silence for any length of time. He was pointing at the barge. "It's a strange kind of boat. I haven't seen one like that before."

"It's a barge. They used to be used for taking goods up and down the river to the sea. Part of the reason the city grew up here was because it was a trading post for the barges. In the old days, horses would pull them, walking along the bridle path."

"Oh yes, I remember," Draven said, distracted. "Can I go see?"

"Well, I don't suppose it would hurt to take a peep. But you can't go aboard, and you can't touch because that's someone's home."

"Oh, okay. I won't, I promise."

Keiron followed as Draven skipped down to the barge and stood, hands on hips staring at the bright paint and intricate patterns. It was a traditional barge, painted in bright greens and reds with painted milk churns and buckets decorating the deck. Keiron could tell Draven was itching to touch. He was such a tactile creature. All the fixtures were glowing either silver or copper and the whole thing seemed fresh and new.

Draven was drawn closer and closer to the bright shiny boat, until Keiron had to pull him back before he fell into the river.

"Draven, you're going to drown yourself. I told you, you could only look."

"I know," he said with a sigh, "but it's so pretty."

"Yes, it is pretty."

"Can I—" Draven stood on tiptoe to whisper in Keiron's ear. "Can I change so I can peep in the window?"

"No. No, you can't. People will see."

"I'll hide to change, and I'll go really, really small. No one will see me, Keiron, I promise."

"No, Draven. Absolutely not. No."

"But—"

"Please, Draven. I.... You're a grown-up, and I can't forbid you to do it. I don't have the right. But please, please don't."

"Why not?"

"I'm afraid you'll get caught, or hurt, or lost, or—"

"It's not as if I'm not used to it, Keiron. I do it all the time...well, I did before I came here, to you."

"But you are here with me now and I'd never forgive myself if something happened to you when I'm here."

Draven smiled up into his face and sighed. "I like being taken care of, Keiron."

"And I like taking care of you," Keiron said, brushing hair out of Draven's face so he could look into his eyes properly. "You're so very beautiful," he murmured, gazing into Draven's eyes.

"You're beautiful, too, my Keiron, my human. I love you with my open heart."

Keiron smiled. "I think—"

He was interrupted by a shout from the bar. "Hey. Hey, you two, what are you doing down there? What are you doing to my boat?"

"Is this your boat?" Draven asked, bouncing back towards the bar and the clearly drunk and angry young man.

"Yes, it is," he said belligerently, "so stay away from it."

"We were just saying how beautiful it is. Did you do all the paintings on the side and on the buckets and things? I've haven't seen them like that for ever such a long time. And the metal is so shiny. You must have polished and polished it. Do you live on the boat? Are you going a long way in it? Do you live on it all the time? Do you go to different places every day? Oh wow, do you ever go on the sea?"

"Whoa, Draven," Keiron said uneasily. The man's angry expression had been replaced by a puzzled frown. This situation needed careful handling. It could go one of two very different ways.

"Who's this?" a new voice asked, as a young woman appeared behind the man. She linked arms with him. Apparently, he was her boyfriend or husband.

"Someone was looking at the boat."

"It's a really pretty boat," Draven said, his blue eyes innocent. "You're pretty too." He smiled, and Keiron groaned inwardly as the rather well-muscled young man frowned.

"Well, thank you, beautiful. What were you saying about the boat?" She let go of the man and linked arms with Draven. They began to walk back down towards the boat. Draven chattering as he had before, shooting questions at her so fast she had no chance to answer.

"That your kid?" the man growled.

"God, no," Keiron said carefully, wondering which way to go that would be least likely to end in him flat on the floor with two black eyes. "He's my boyfriend."

"You're what? Boyfriend? Are you two...?"

"Yes. Is that a problem?"

The man glanced down towards the boat where the woman had invited Draven onto the deck and was watching him fondly as he touched one thing after another, still talking ten to the dozen.

He visibly relaxed. "Hell no," he said. "Laura loves you gay boys. She's always picking up strays."

While ordinarily Keiron might have been a little put out at being referred to in this way, under the circumstances he was happy to accept and leave things lie.

Simon, as the burly young man was called, and his fiancée, Laura, were taking a trip along the river on their newly renovated barge, of which they were both justifiably proud. They took Draven and Keiron inside, where Draven was almost beside himself with excitement at all the bright shiny things. After the rocky start, both Laura and Simon fell entirely under Draven's spell, and in no time, it was if they had known him all their lives.

An hour later, Keiron found himself sitting outside the bar again, sharing a pint with Simon, while Draven and Laura lay on the grass as he pointed out and named the constellations.

"A long time ago, people used to use the stars to navigate, that's to work out which direction you have to go in," Draven explained seriously. "That star is the North Star. It's the point that everything else is measured from. My father told me if I can see the North Star, I can't ever be lost, and if I can see the Hunter, that's Orion, the one over there, I'll never be alone because he'll guide me wherever I want to go."

"Your father sounds like a wise man."

"Oh he is, very wise. I...don't see him very much. We.... Um.... It's not that we don't get along, just...." He sighed. "Yeah, it is that we don't get along. I frustrate him, and it makes him angry to be around me for too long."

"Oh Draven," Laura cried. "How could anyone be angry being around you? You're so sweet."

"Yes, but my father isn't and he doesn't like sweet. He likes action and confidence and bravery and...doing things."

"He sounds like a prick."

"Oh no, no, no. He's a wonderful man, brave and strong. He has...a lot of responsibility and he needs a son who can support him, and fight at his side. He thinks it may be just that I'm young and need to burn off my wildness. I hope he's right."

"How old are you?" Laura asked, and as Draven opened his mouth, Keiron saw disaster looming and almost choked on his pint.

"Very young compared to him. Not so young compared to you or Keiron," he teased with a laugh. Keiron sighed in relief and took a long drink.

"Where did you and Keiron meet," Laura asked, and again, Keiron tensed.

"I just turned up on his doorstep," Draven said and laughed. Laura laughed with him.

Food arrived, and Draven and Laura joined Keiron and Simon at the table. As always, Draven was deeply interested in what they were eating and managed to secure himself a taste of everything. He was totally honest in what he liked and what he didn't. He found a new favourite in chicken korma but didn't like fries very much and couldn't bear scampi, even the feel of it in his mouth. He spat it on the floor and shuddered.

"I didn't like that," he said.

"You don't say?" Laura laughed.

Even before they had finished eating, Draven ran out of steam and began to nod over the table.

"Are you tired?" Keiron asked, aware that if Draven got too tired he'd just fall asleep, possibly in the middle of the table.

Draven smiled. "Very tired. Can we go home now?"

"But it's still early. Won't you stay just a little while longer?" Laura coaxed.

"I really want to go home now."

"Aren't you enjoying being with us?" Laura was teasing, but Draven completely failed to recognise that and got upset.

"Of course I'm enjoying it. You and Simon are my new friends, but I really am very tired and I don't...." He raised pleading eyes to Keiron. "I don't think I can stay awake for much longer. It's been a very exciting day and I'm not...I'm not better yet."

"Better? Have you been ill?"

"Very ill," Keiron supplied. "We were all very worried about him." He smiled at Draven. "He's definitely getting better, but he's not quite there yet."

"I'm so sorry," Laura cried, throwing her arms around Draven. "No wonder you're so small and pale. We won't keep you. You must go home and rest."

Draven hugged her back and stifled a yawn. "I'm sorry," he said, yawning again. "I know I'm being rude, but I've kind of run down." And that's exactly how he looked, run-down.

Leaving Draven with Laura, Keiron went in search of the captain. He was surprised that they were leaving so early, but as soon as he heard Draven was tired and unwell, he left his pint and was down in the boat before Keiron had extracted Draven from Laura.

Keiron had the sense that Simon was far less sorry to say goodbye than Laura was, although he was friendly enough and was happy to exchange phone numbers. From the glance they exchanged, Keiron was convinced he'd never receive a call.

As soon as they got onto the boat, Draven cuddled into Keiron's side and fell asleep. Keiron held him tight and worried. He felt fragile, as if once the frenetic energy that drove him dissipated, there was nothing left. Brushing the blowing hair out of his face, Keiron stared at him long and hard and realised there was nothing he wouldn't do for this strange creature. He was so much part of his life now that, even if he wanted to, he'd never be able to let him go. It was an uneasy feeling.

When they arrived back at the dock, Keiron woke Draven, who took his leave of the captain in a subdued way that worried Keiron.

"What's wrong?" Keiron asked as they strolled back along the footpath, arm in arm.

"I'm tired," Draven said and sounded it.

"You ran out of steam really fast tonight."

"I know. It was my fault. I forgot I'm not myself. I should conserve energy, but I don't know how. I get excited about things, and I throw my whole self into them, and I don't know how to stop. I keep forgetting there are limits now."

"Never mind," Keiron said, pausing to kiss Draven. "It won't be for long. You'll be better soon."

"Yeah," Draven said with a strange little smile. "Better soon."

It didn't take long for Draven to lag, dragging his feet and leaning more and more heavily on Keiron. "I'm sorry," Keiron said. "I should have thought about the walk home and made sure you had enough energy to take it. I just didn't realise you'd lose your energy so fast and completely."

"Neither did I," Draven replied sadly, then brightened and smiled. "But I'll get used to it. People can get used to anything, you know."

"Really?" Keiron said with a smile and hugged him. "But you don't have to get used to it, do you? Because by the time you get used to it, the limits won't be there anymore. You're getting better every day. Very soon you'll be back to the storehouse of limitless energy you used to be."

"Yes," Draven said with that same little smile. "Very soon."

It was only a few minutes later that he stumbled and passed out, and Keiron had to carry him the rest of the way home.

Chapter Seventeen

KEIRON WAS GETTING used to waking up at the crack of dawn. Today he was late because the sun was already high in the sky, but it still felt early. He was alone, but he thought nothing of it. Draven was often up before him. Feeling warm and comfortable, he rolled over onto his back and stretched, letting his eyes close to enjoy the last moments before he got up. As he was luxuriating, he heard the front door slam.

For an instant, it didn't register, and then he sat up. "What the fuck?"

Grabbing a robe as he ran, Keiron tore out of the room and down the stairs. Someone was moving around in the kitchen.

"What the fuck's going—?" He stopped short. Draven was unpacking a carrier bag onto the kitchen table. There were eggs, bacon, milk, flour, jam, and lemons. Draven glanced up and grinned at him, strangely triumphant.

"I've been reading your kitchen spell-books. I found some things that are good for breakfast. I looked around, but I couldn't find the components, so I went to the shop. I hope you don't mind."

Keiron froze. He couldn't move. Draven's smile slipped a little as he watched. "It-it wasn't bad, was it? I found money in the little bag on the table and I.... Keiron? I...I'm sorry, I...."

"Sorry? No, there's nothing to be sorry about Draven. I'm just...just.... Shit. You did this? You went to the shop and got provisions?"

"I-Is that all right?"

"Yes, of course, but...but how...?"

"Oh." Draven smiled brightly. "Get yourself a coffee and sit down, and I'll tell you everything while I get breakfast on. We're going to have bacon and eggs and pancakes with strawberry jam and lemons."

"Um...well, that sounds nice."

"I thought so. I wanted to do something nice for you so I thought I'd make you breakfast. I remembered about the spell-books so I read them. I looked at the pictures, and I remember you said you liked bacon and eggs, so I thought that would be good, but then I saw the pancakes and I had to try them. Do you know that you throw them up into the air and catch them again?"

"I think you might be slightly confused about the pancakes, Draven."

"No, honestly, I saw the pictures in the book. Shall I show you?"

"No, no it's fine. I know there are pancakes that you do that to, but they're different to breakfast pancakes. Breakfast pancakes are thicker and tend not to have so much sugar."

"Oh. I did it wrong? I'm sorry, I—"

"You didn't do anything wrong. You make the pancakes, no matter how you want to do it, and I'll eat them."

"You will?"

"Of course I will."

"Then I'd better start." Humming softly, Draven took the cookery books over to the counter next to the cooker and smoothed them out. Bending over, he frowned deeply at the page. Tilting his head, first to one side, then the other, he transferred his attention to the cooker and examined it minutely. "What do the runes mean," he asked at last, looking over to Keiron.

"What runes?"

"These ones, the ones on your cooker. Little lines and spirals. Does one of them tell me where the" — he glanced at the book — "grill, is?"

"They're not exactly runes, but never mind. Here, let me show you."

"But I want to do it." Draven pouted.

"I tell you what. I'll show you how everything works and you can use them? Otherwise, we'll be here until dinner time."

Draven considered, then grinned. "Okay."

They worked side by side, Keiron demonstrating and explaining, and Draven doing. It was a lot of fun. Draven was quick and deft, but it was all unfamiliar, and although he tried hard, there were lots of accidents.

"So, how on earth did you do all this?"

"All what?" Draven asked, chewing on his tongue as he beat egg, milk, and pepper in a bowl, splashing it everywhere, and raising smoke where it fell on the hot cooker ring.

"Going out, getting the groceries... For one thing, I thought you were scared of the city."

Draven frowned at him, a thoughtful expression on his face. "I was. I am."

"Then why...?"

"Because I wanted to do something nice for you. You did something nice for me yesterday. And you took me to the...country. I wanted to do the same for you."

"But how...?"

"I know how to do things, Keiron," Draven said firmly. "I know you buy things from shops. I found your bag on the table, and I knew you wouldn't mind, so I took some money out of it. Well, I didn't know how much it would be so I took all the money, but I put back what I didn't use."

"What bag on the table?"

"The little leather one, that was next to your keys."

"Little leather bag?" Keiron was completely mystified.

"Yes. It has lots of bits of plastic in it. Some of them have pictures of you."

"Bit of.... Oh, you mean my wallet?"

"Whatever. So, I took the money and your keys, and went outside. It was quite quiet, not as scary as before. There weren't many people, but the shops were all closed. The hardest thing was remembering how to get back. I went to the park...not the one we went to, but a really little one, and 'hung around' for a while." There was something about the way he said *hung around* that made Keiron both want and not want to ask.

"Then, when the shops opened, I looked in through the windows until I found one that sold food. It was quite hard to find everything, but there was a really nice lady who helped me. She seemed a bit confused, but she was very friendly."

"Confused? Why? What did you tell her?"

Draven paused, about to pour the mixture into a pan of melted butter. "You really have a problem with that, don't you?"

"A problem with what?"

"People knowing what I am."

"Yes, I do. I should have explained it better, but...humans are not very nice to people who are different. If they know what you are, they might hurt you."

"Yes," Draven said dryly, "I know."

"I don't mean just Bren."

"I know. I didn't tell her. I told her I wanted to surprise my boyfriend and haven't done it before. She showed me where everything was, then put them in a bag. She put numbers in a machine, and it told her how much money I had to pay for them. She gave me a list and made me check on it to show she'd taken the right money, then she said she hoped you liked the surprise. I really liked her."

Smiling at the memory, Draven started to hum again as he stirred the scrambled eggs and flipped the bacon. Keiron rested his hands on Draven's shoulders and smiled. His little fairy was full of surprises.

Keiron couldn't honestly say it was the best breakfast he'd ever had, or the least chaotic, but for a meal with—and even more so, made by—Draven, it was incredibly successful. Not only was the food tasty and satisfying, but Draven was so excited and pleased with himself it made Keiron's heart feel warm.

Keiron was surprised Draven managed to eat at all; he didn't stop talking the whole time. Keiron tended to sit back and let him chatter on, nodding occasionally and letting the musical lilt of Draven's voice wash over him.

"Are you even listening?"

"Of course I'm listening."

"Okay, what did I just say?" Draven stood, hands on hips and head tilted to one side. One corner of his mouth was covered with chocolate spread, and he had jam in his hair. Keiron smothered a smile. Draven and jam really did have a chaotic relationship. "Keiron," Draven said again and stamped his foot.

"I'm sorry. You're so adorable. I can't concentrate on what you're *saying* because I'm so lost in how you're *looking*."

"Aww...." Draven smiled and blushed slightly. He danced around the table and put his arms around Keiron's neck. "You say the loveliest things. Even if it is just to get out of having to admit you weren't paying attention."

"Sorry. What were you saying that was so important?"

"I want to go out," he announced.

"What?"

"I want to go out...with you. It was fun this morning, but it would be even more fun with you."

"Oh. Well. Where do you want to go?"

"I don't know, silly. I don't know what's out there. Tell me where it's fun to go."

"With your definition of fun," Keiron said with a smile, "I have no idea. What kind of thing do you want to do?"

Draven pondered. "I want to walk in the street with all the people. And…I want to go in shops and buy things. And I want to… You said we could eat out, right? Before. You said we could eat out…like we did by the river, but here in the city."

"Would you like to go to a restaurant?"

"I don't know what it is, but it sounds fun."

"Hmm…." Keiron thought hard for a moment. "How would you like to see a movie?"

"What's that?"

"It's like television but much, much bigger, and you sit in a room with a lot of other people to watch it. They have much better sound and clearer pictures. We would go see a 3D one where you wear special glasses that make it seem as if the things on the screen are actually coming into the room. We can get snacks to eat while we watch."

"Oooh, that sound fun. Do we have to walk to the get to the…moo-vee?"

"Yes, a little way. It's half ten. Let's go to the park for a couple of hours, and then we can go see the movie and eat on the way home. How does that sound?"

"We won't go up the hill, will we?"

"No. I promise we won't go up the hill."

Draven threw his arms around Keiron's neck. "Yes, yes. I want to go to the park and to the moo-vee."

"Let me take a shower and grab some stuff, and we'll be on our way."

"What shall I do?"

Keiron gazed into the eager little face and shining eyes. It would be downright dangerous to simply leave Draven to wait. "Come here." He led Draven into the living room and sat him down in front of the screen. Loading up the site for the cinema they would be going to, he showed Draven how to find and read the film promotions.

"Choose which film you'd like to see."

"Can I? Can I really? If I find one I like, we can see it?"

"Absolutely. Enjoy yourself. I won't be long."

Draven had already forgotten he was there. He was totally absorbed in the colourful website. Smiling, Keiron turned and headed upstairs.

When he came down again, rubbing his hair dry, Draven was crashing about in the kitchen. With sinking heart, Keiron crept out to find him wiping and neatly stacking dishes he'd washed. The kitchen table was clear and wiped, and all the food had been stored away. Keiron was surprised but very pleased. Draven learned quickly. Keiron was excited about spending the day with him out there in the world.

"Are we ready now? Can we go now? Right now?"

"Yes, we can go right now."

Draven almost skipped beside Keiron as they headed for the park. He winced a couple of times when a big lorry went past or a large crowd of people jostled him but, on the whole, seemed relaxed and comfortable. As usual, Draven was interested in everything and didn't stop asking questions the whole way.

"But why…?"

"Draven," Keiron stopped at the entrance to the park and turned Draven towards him, his hands on Draven's shoulders. "I don't have answers for everything. In fact, I have answers for very few of the things you've asked me. For all of my life, I've lived in the knowledge that these things "just are," and no, that's not the right way to live or the right thing to do, but to use your own phrase, it is at it is. I simply don't have the answers. However, if we take them just one question at a time, I promise I will do my very best to find the answers. Only please, please, can we do one at a time, and can we not do any more today, because I want to enjoy the sunshine and being with you?"

Draven raised himself on tiptoe to kiss Keiron, then slipped his arm through Keiron's. "For you, anything," he said with a smile, resting his head against Keiron's shoulder. And then he was running. "Come on, race you to the place where the wheely people play." It took Keiron a while to work out the "wheely people" were skateboarders.

Keiron was incredibly relieved as he watched Draven play. Draven was bright, sweet, and full of energy again, and it made Keiron warm inside. If he'd regretted for a moment his decision to resign from his job, it disappeared into the distance. After everything that had happened, to watch Draven fly around a skate park with a gang of sixteen-year-olds, his hair streaming like a flag behind him and the sound of his laughter falling like rain in a desert was exhilarating. Keiron was fulfilled as he never had been before, and he realised there was nothing in the world more important to him than Draven's laughter and making sure he heard it at every possible opportunity.

When Draven eventually handed back the borrowed skateboard and said goodbye to his new friends, they were both completely relaxed and very happy.

"I'm hungry now. Will we eat at the moo-vee?"

"No, there's somewhere I'd like to take you first."

"A restaurant? A proper one?"

"Yes, a proper restaurant."

"Cool."

Keiron raised an eyebrow, and Draven shrugged with a smile.

"The wheely people say it, and I thought it was a nice word, although I don't understand why—"

"Just because, okay?"

"Okay," Draven said cheerfully and took Keiron's hand, swinging their joined hands between them as they walked.

The restaurant was a small Italian bistro, and as soon as they walked through the door, Draven's nose twitched.

"Smells good, doesn't it?"

"Yes, like the pizzas you get in boxes."

"It's an Italian restaurant and pizza comes from Italy so there will be plenty of pizza here, much better than the ones that come in boxes, lots of pasta too with all kinds of sauces and cheese."

"What shall I have?" Draven asked, looking around with eyes as big as saucers.

"Anything you like."

"But how will I know what I like?"

"Good afternoon, gentlemen. Table for two?" Draven's attention became riveted on the waiter who showed them to their table. He could have been a hundred years old, with swarthy weather-beaten skin, a kind smile, and a checked cloth tucked into his apron, with which he wiped down the table as they sat.

"Do you come from Italy?" Draven asked, still staring at the man.

"Si, although I have been here a long time now."

"Italy's a long way away, isn't it?"

"It is, but today, with the cheap flights and safe aeroplanes...not so far."

"Does your family live in Italy?"

"Some. My son returned home and is bringing up his family in Campania, among the grapes."

"Grapes?" Draven asked, looking surprised. "Why would they live in grapes?"

The waiter laughed. "It is a saying, piccolo. It means in the region where the grapes grow; grapes for making wine."

"Oh, that's right—grapes make wine and good wine comes from Italy." He grinned, pleased and proud of himself.

The waiter laughed again and ruffled Draven's hair. "You are so precious, piccolo. What can I get you?"

Draven tilted his head to the side. "What does that word mean? The one you keep saying to me."

"Piccolo?"

"Yes."

"Little one."

"Oh." Draven grinned. "That's what Keiron calls me too and I'm not even that little right now."

Keiron almost choked. "Er...what would you like to eat, Draven?"

"I don't know. How will I know what I like?" he asked the waiter seriously.

"Have you tried Italian before?"

"Only pizza in boxes."

The man threw up his arms. "Ai, you have not lived until you have tasted Mama's pizza."

"I haven't?" Draven asked in surprise.

The man laughed. "I will bring you pizza and rich ravioli with garlic bread and good wine, no?"

"Um.... Why—"

"Yes, yes, that would be lovely, thank you," Keiron said quickly, and the man retired, smiling.

"Why did he say he was going to bring all those things and then say he wasn't?"

"He didn't, Draven. His accent is different from ours because he's Italian. The Italian language is very different and Italians use the word no as an enquiry."

"So...he wasn't saying he wasn't going to bring me those things, only asking if I wanted them."

"That's right."

Draven was quiet for a while, during which the waiter brought warm bread, oil, and vinegar. Tearing neat pieces of bread and dunking them delicately, Draven chewed thoughtfully. "Your world is confusing," he said at last. Keiron couldn't help but agree.

When he brought their meals along with wine and more hot bread, the man, Gianni, who turned out to be the owner, and his wife Lucretta sat at the next table to chat. Keiron knew full well they were only interested in Draven, but he didn't mind. That it made Draven happy to chat about all things Italian with two attentive people who treated him like a precious child was good enough for him.

There were tense moments, though, moments when Draven went too far, spoke of things that were far too revealing. Gianni and Lucretta either didn't notice or didn't understand, and their smiles and openness didn't waver for an instant.

"How did you come to be here, piccolo?" Gianni asked, "With your good friend, Keiron?"

"Oh he's not my friend; he's my mate. We are together now. Forever. He won't say he loves me, but he does." Draven beamed and Keiron squirmed.

"You are favoured, my friend," Gianni said to Keiron with all seriousness. "Honoured, indeed."

Keiron watched for sarcasm, but there was none. The whole situation began to seem rather strange.

"Yeah," he said and concentrated on finishing the last of his pizza.

"Would you like more wine, piccolo?"

"No, thank you. It's making me a little giggly, and I think Keiron would be cross with me if I giggled in the moo-vee. There will be other people there, you know. Not everyone understands me," he said thoughtfully, an edge of wistfulness in his voice. "This world is hard."

"All worlds are hard, in their own way, la mio piccolo fata," Lucretta said with a kindly smile.

Draven gazed at her for a while with his head tilted to the side, and then he grinned broadly and threw himself into her arms, hugging her tightly. Taken by surprise, she nevertheless returned the hug, a broad smile on her weathered face, while Gianni looked on smiling and nodding. Keiron was confused.

When the meal ended, Gianni and Lucretta refused to accept payment. "You have paid us with your company and the pleasure it has given to us both."

"But—"

"Hush now. Take the little one and make him happy. That is our payment."

Keiron was confused. Sure, Draven was a sweet angel and easy to love, but this seemed a little excessive.

"Why are you so...? Why has Draven...? Why are you being so nice to him?"

Gianni laughed and patted Keiron on the shoulder. "Their ways are not our ways, my friend. He is precious. He shines a light in this dark world, and you are keeper of that light. It is a hard job but a rewarding one. For this alone, you deserve a pizza and a few glasses of wine."

"But I don't understand."

"I think you do," Gianni said, and Keiron rather thought he did.

"What does 'la mio piccolo fata' mean?"

Gianni smiled. "It means 'my little fairy'." He smiled at Keiron's shocked expression. "Si, my friend. So much is clear when one has eyes to see. Unfortunately, or for you perhaps fortunately, very few do in these dark days. Take care."

Chapter Eighteen

"THEY KNEW," KEIRON said as they walked along the pavement, hand in hand. "They knew what you are."

"Yes," Draven said seriously. "Are you mad at me?"

"Mad at you? Of course I'm not mad at you."

"No, you don't sound mad. I was afraid you would be. You don't like it when people know."

"It's not that I don't like it when people know. I'm just scared of it. There are good people, like the ones we met tonight. But there are those who are not so good. There are people, lots of them, who would hurt you if they knew what you are. People like Bren, and worse."

Draven gazed up at him with his thoughtful eyes and frowned. He didn't say anything, though, and they walked on in silence.

Draven cheered up when they arrived at the cinema. The bright colours, enticing smells, and busy foyer hyped up his excitement level even more, and he was buzzing by the time they'd got their tickets. Spotting something on the other side of the foyer, Draven grabbed Keiron's hand and dragged him across the room.

"Look. Look, what are they? They're so pretty. What are they? Can I have some?"

"They're sweets, Draven. It's called pick-n-mix. You take that cup there and fill it with anything you like out of the little boxes."

"Can I?" Draven asked breathlessly, his eyes glittering in the bright artificial light, very blue even though they were *humanised.* "Can I put sweets in a little cup?"

"Of course you can."

"Thank you, Keiron." Draven threw his arms around Keiron's neck before grabbing a cup and standing in front of the display with shining eyes and a frown on his face.

"Draven," Keiron prompted gently, when he hadn't moved after a couple of minutes. "I think you should choose now? We don't want to miss the start of the movie."

"But there's so many. How will I know what I like? How will I know...?"

"Try a little of everything, and the things you don't like, I'll eat."

"Really?" Draven asked, his enthusiasm rising again. "I can have everything?"

"A little of everything."

"Of course. I can't fit a lot of everything into the cup."

In a frenzy, Draven scooped up sweets and threw them into the cup. While he was doing it, he reached titbits from the top boxes for children, retrieved lost money from the bottom of boxes and under the stand, and gave one little girl an extra pound when the cup he'd helped her fill exceeded her pocket money allowance. Keiron watched, smiled, and was achingly proud. People were attracted to his beautiful boyfriend like bees to a honey pot, and honey was always what they got.

When Draven had paid for his sweets, he started to sniff around the refreshments counter.

"You can't possibly be hungry again, and you've got enough sweets in there to last you a month."

"I know, but what's that smell?"

"I think it's the hot dogs."

"They sell dogs?" Draven's mouth hung open in shock. "To eat?"

"No, no. We don't eat dogs. They're called 'hot dogs,' but they're just sausages in a bread bun."

"What's in the sausages?" he asked suspiciously.

"Mostly beef. That's cows."

"Mostly?"

"Sometimes they have pork too...pigs."

"Pigs?" Draven shook his head, smiling to himself. It was an Oh-God-these-people-are-weird smile.

"I'm not really hungry, and I have sweets. Let's just get a drink."

"What would you like? Coke? Orange juice? Milkshake?"

"Milkshake? Why do they shake the milk?"

"They put flavourings in, like strawberry or banana, and when it gets shaken up the flavour mixes into the milk and it gets frothy."

"Ooh, that sounds nice. Can I have that?"

"What flavour?"

"Umm.... Oooh! What's that? That's not milk."

"It's a drink— sherbet over crushed ice. It's very sharp and sweet."

"Not like milk?"

"No, not like milk at all."

"Will I like it?" Draven peered at the machine, and Keiron knew what attracted him. It was the bright blue colour of the ice in one of the chambers.

"I don't know. Why don't you try a small one? If you don't like it, we can always pour it away and get a milk."

"I don't know. I don't know. I wish I knew if I liked it." He was practically hopping from foot to foot.

"Do you want to try mine?" A very pretty girl with bright green eyes held out her cup, the straw pointed towards Draven. "I don't mind."

Draven practically glowed. "Can I? Oh, thank you, thank you. You can have some of my sweets." He handed over the cup. "Only don't take all of the same kind because I want to try everything."

Keiron smiled as Draven closed his eyes while he sipped the icy blue drink. Draven shivered deeply and gasped.

"Keiron, you have to try this. Oh God, it's so...so.... It's like an explosion, and it makes your head go fizzy. Try it, Keiron. Oh—" He turned to the girl and hugged her. "Thank you so much. I wasn't going to give your drink to Keiron. He can buy me one and try it for himself. Thank you so much for helping me find out how much I like it. Here...." He smiled expansively. "Have more sweets."

The girl laughed and shook her head, returning Draven's hug before running off to join her gossiping friends. Now, Draven was actually bouncing from foot to foot, impatient to have his very own blue sherbet drink. Keiron began to wonder whether it was wise to give him so much sugar, especially as they were about to sit in a dark room and be expected to be quiet for two hours. Oh well, too late now.

Draven was all eyes as they handed their tickets to the doorkeeper and walked down a short corridor, flanked on both sides by screening rooms. Draven counted off the numbers until they got to the one that was running their film. As soon as they got inside, Draven froze and gasped.

"Heck, Keiron, that television is huge."

"I told you that."

"I know but...I mean, Keiron, it's huge."

"Yes, it is. Come on, let's find seats. We're holding everyone up."

When Draven walked out of the end of the short corridor and the theatre opened out, he stopped again, his eyes wide as he stared at the tiers; row after row of seats, about half of which were occupied.

"Where would you like to sit?"

"I...what?" Draven asked, tearing his eyes from the seats to focus on Keiron.

"Where would you like to sit?"

"In one of those seats, please."

"Of course," Keiron said, chuckling. "It's a 3D film so we don't want to sit too far away or the effect's lost. How about halfway? Just there where the walkway goes through so we won't have to keep getting up and down to let people pass?"

Draven followed Keiron to their seats and sat immobile for a while, staring at the screen, which was playing adverts and bright swirling messages of various sorts. At one point, he'd glanced around, searching for where the sound was coming from, but then went right back to staring at the screen again.

When someone sat down next to him, Draven dragged his attention back from the screen to smile at them. It was the girl with the sherbet drink.

"Hello," he said. "I didn't know you were coming to see the same film. Would you like to share my sweets? Keiron was going to share, but I don't think he really wants to. He was just saying it so I wouldn't worry about trying lots of different things."

Keiron smiled and shook his head affectionately, then caught the girl's eye and groaned inwardly. There were four of them altogether, all girls of around fifteen years old, very giggly and hyped. The girl with the sherbet was the quietest. Her friends were nudging and giggling.

"My name's Kathleen," she said. "You can call me Kate."

"Hello, Kate. My name's Draven and this is Keiron. He's my mate." Keiron almost choked, but it was clear the girl had completely misunderstood his meaning.

"These are my mates, Lauren, Christie, and Stacy."

"Your mates? All of them? Ow." The last was for the fact that Keiron had stamped on his foot. "What...?"

"Draven," he said very softly. "People have a different interpretation of words here. She doesn't mean what you think she means. They're just friends."

"So, does she think you're—"

"Probably, yes."

"Should I—"

"No. Absolutely not."

"Oh."

"Be careful, Draven. She likes you."

"I know. I like her too."

"No, Draven, she *likes* you."

"I know. I— Oh. Oh, right. Don't worry. I'll let her down gently."

Keiron groaned when Draven turned to Kate and said brightly. "I hope you're not sitting here just to flirt with me, because I like girls a lot to be friends with and I quite like kissing them, but I don't have sex with girls. That's what I do with Keiron."

Keiron closed his eyes and prayed for the earth to open and swallow him. That was not the sort of thing to say to anyone, let alone a group of fifteen-year-olds. There was a resounding silence, and then Kate began to laugh.

Opening his eyes, Keiron tentatively glanced over. All four of the girls were creased with laughter. "See, I told you," one of them said—Stacy, he believed. "I told you they were *together*."

"I know but...well...I could hope, couldn't I?" Kate said with the kind of smile that indicated she was a little sad but nowhere near devastated. "It doesn't matter. At least I get to sit next to you for the next couple of hours."

Draven beamed and turned to Keiron. "See? I told you it would be okay."

Keiron rolled his eyes and turned his head away, cheeks blazing at the girlish giggles, feeling as if he was the butt of their jokes. A feeling of something close to anger settled into the pit of his stomach, amidst the deep embarrassment, and he fumed silently as Draven chatted to the girls as if he'd known them all his life.

"Keiron, look at this."

Keiron was startled when Draven grabbed his arm and thrust something into it. "What?"

"They're little glasses. Look, they're in the back of the seat. If you put them on and look at the screen, strange things happen. Try it. It's magic, look." Excitedly Draven folded the glasses into his hand and tried to move them towards his eyes.

"I know what they are," Keiron snapped irritably and snatched them out of Draven's hands. Draven stared at him, his lips forming a perfect *O* of surprise.

"I-I'm sorry, Keiron, I—"

"No, no, it's me who should be sorry, Draven. I shouldn't have snapped at you. I'm sorry, truly I am."

"But why...?"

"Here, take these back, because I have my own, see?" Keiron took his own glasses from the pouch on the back of the seat in front. "Now we can both look at the screen with them."

"There's not much to look at," Draven said, his voice and eyes still wary, puzzled.

"There will be when the movie starts."

"It won't be long now," Kate chimed in, and Keiron metaphorically ground his teeth. The voices of all four girls were grating on his nerves, and much as he knew it wasn't fair, he couldn't help it.

Draven seemed hurt and frowned, turning back to Kate who showed him how to wear the glasses and laughed at the faces he made when he sucked down the sharp sherbet of his drink.

Keiron fumed. All four of the girls were laughing and, apparently flirting, with Draven, and he ate up the attention as fast as the sweets, which were disappearing at an alarming rate. Keiron felt bad for begrudging it, but couldn't help but feel cheated that the girls were eating all the sweets he'd bought for Draven and spoiling what Keiron had wanted to be a special experience for them to share together. So he sat and brooded.

When the lights went down, Draven jumped and spun round to grab Keiron's hand and stare at him with eyes that, even in the darkness, shone with fear.

"What's happening?"

"It just means the film is about to start."

"Oh. Oh, I didn't know. It's all right," he said, turning back to Kate and her friends. "There's nothing wrong with the lights. It just means the film is about to start." Their laughter, which might have been mocking with someone else, wasn't with Draven.

As soon as the film began, Draven was drawn straight into it. It was a dark, modern retelling of an old fairy tale with very artistic photography and wild settings. The fantasy element was strong, and there was an ephemeral quality about both the actors and the filming that gave it an almost unreal feel. Draven was entranced.

Keiron had worried a little that Draven might not be able to sit still and watch the film quietly, especially after he'd drunk the whole of the drink and eaten half the sweets. However, instead of making him even more hyperactive, either they, the film, or the general atmosphere seemed to have him spellbound.

Initially, he giggled along with the girls, but as the film progressed, the stunning photography and 3D effects drew them all into silence, other than the occasional gasp.

About halfway through the film, Draven huddled into Keiron and pretty much forced him to put his arm around him.

"Are you enjoying the film?"

"It…it's a bit…scary," Draven said, his voice slightly shaky.

"You don't have to wear the glasses. It's not so scary without them."

"But you're supposed to wear the glasses."

"The glasses enhance the experience, but you don't have to wear them."

"I don't want to. They make my head ache."

"Then don't. Put them back in the pouch." Draven did so and cuddled into Keiron's side again. "Are you cold? You feel like ice."

"The ice I drank, I suppose," he said, then jerked, as a wolf leaped at the screen and turned his face towards Keiron. "It's making me feel weird."

"What is? The film."

"No, the drink. I'm all fluttery inside and tingly all over. It hurts my head."

"That doesn't make sense."

"No," Draven said unhappily.

"Babe, are you all right?"

"No," he said, even more unhappily. "I don't like it, Keiron." He gave a little hiccup. "It's getting worse, and I think I might be sick."

"Do you want to leave?"

"I don't think they would be very happy if I was sick right here."

"No, I don't suppose they would."

When Draven stood up, Kate and the girls complained, but Draven ignored them. Keiron couldn't help the feeling of smugness that came over him about that. He felt dreadful a few moments later, though, when Draven groaned and leaned into his side, hunching over.

"My stomach hurts, Keiron," he moaned. "It feels weird."

"Come on, let's get out of here. Maybe fresh air will make you feel better."

Draven stumbled as Keiron supported him out of the screening room. "Do you still feel sick?" he asked when they were outside the door. He was shocked. Draven looked terrible. "What's wrong? What the hell's going on?"

"It hurts, Keiron," Draven whispered, clinging to Keiron. "It hurts and it's…it's making things weird."

"I don't understand."

"I'm seeing things that can't be there. I want to go home."

"Okay, but you're in no shape to walk like this. Come into the toilet."

Keiron supported Draven into the nearest toilet and splashed water onto his face. He stood with his hands on the basin and his head down, and Keiron could actually see his whole body shaking.

"Fuck, Draven, what's going on?"

"Um…I…I, um…colours…and…wavy things. In my head…music…not there but there inside and…everything…. Have to keep my eyes closed, Keiron. Everything's melting. Bubbles in my head. Bubbles…colours and bubbles."

"Jesus Christ. Draven, are you…?"

Draven giggled and slid to the floor, hugging his knees and moaning. "It hurts, Keiron. It hurts, but it's so…funny." Laughing helplessly and groaning at the same time, Draven gazed up at Keiron with huge eyes, swirling with colour.

"Shit…."

"I don't…I don't think I like the…blue…bl…ue…blue drink anymore."

"No. I don't think I like it very much right now either."

"It's making my head go bubbly, and it hurts my belly. Ow. Ow." He bent over, clutching his stomach, his long hair brushing the floor.

"Are you going to be sick?"

"I don't know. The floor's too scary to be sick on."

"Scary? The floor?"

"You'd better be careful, Keiron. It's melting. The middle's all swirly, and if you step in, you'll get sucked…somewhere."

Keiron raised Draven's head and peered into his eyes, brushing the hair away. "Dear God, you're tripping your head off. You're drugged out on sherbet."

"Am I?" Draven asked, seeming shocked. "Drugged? Is that why I'm so...bub...ub...ub...ubbleubble...bubbly?"

"I'd say so."

"Will I be better in a minute? Wow! Keiron, you'd better get down here. That big black bird is going to...oh...it's not there, is it? No, it's not there. Or the purple holes." Draven licked dry lips and shivered. "Keiron," he whispered. "Please hold my hand."

Keiron took Draven's hand and held it tightly. "How are you doing?"

"I don't know. Keiron, I'm not really sliding into a big hole, am I?"

"Only inside your head, sweetheart."

"Good. Just keep holding my hand...just so I know."

"Do you think you can walk? There are going to be lots of people in here soon, when the film finishes, and they're going to wonder why you're sitting on the floor."

"Keiron, I don't know if I can walk. I'm afraid if I move I'll just...pour away."

"Pour away?"

"Like sand." Draven's eyes were glazing over, and his voice sounded strange and distant. Keiron groaned inwardly. Clearly, something in either the sweets or the drink were sending Draven on a hell of a trip, and he was starting to lose himself in it. What the fuck was he going to do?

"I can't believe I'm going to say this," Keiron said, licking dry lips. "Draven, can you change?"

"Change?"

"Can you get smaller? If you can get smaller, I can carry you home in my pocket. It won't need to be for long, I'll take the shortcuts and run."

"Will you hold my hand?"

"I can't hold your hands when you're that small, but you can hold onto my finger."

"Oh. Okay, I'll try."

Keiron blinked and Draven vanished. "Draven? Shit, Draven. Where are you? Too small, Draven, I can't...." Something fluttered near his foot and rose to rest on the edge of the counter where it swelled until Draven was roughly the size of his hand. Very, very carefully, he reached out and scooped up the tiny figure, which fluttered desperately in the cage of his fingers.

"Ssh, Draven, calm down. It's me, Keiron, I've got you. Ssh now. That right, calm down."

The little creature wrapped itself around Keiron's finger and held on tight. Gently, he eased his hand into his jacket pocket and settled Draven as best he could, then he fled, bundling Draven's clothes in a ball, which he tucked under his arm.

Occasionally on the long journey home, Keiron felt Draven flutter against his hand, but after a time, the fluttering ceased and the little fairy lay quietly, curled in the palm of his hand.

Keiron had never been more relieved in his life to close his front door behind him. Withdrawing his hand from his pocket, he laid it palm up on the kitchen table. Draven seemed to be fast asleep, curled up in the palm, his hands under his cheek and his wings folded over him like a blanket.

"Draven," Keiron called softly. "Draven can you hear me? Wake up."

For what seemed like a long time, Draven didn't stir. He lay quietly, sleeping peacefully. Finally, his wings fluttered and he sat up, yawning.

"Draven, can you hear me?" Keiron asked anxiously. Draven said something, but it sounded like squeaking. "I can't understand you. You need to get bigger again."

It seemed to Keiron as if Draven's change was slower than usual as, instead of going straight from being one size to the other, he actually grew, and he kept his wings.

"How are you feeling?" Keiron asked, helping Draven down from the counter. He staggered and fell into Keiron's arms, giggling. "Just great," Keiron sighed. "Can you lose the wings, Draven?"

"Wiiings?"

"Yes, wings. Those pretty things flapping behind your back."

"P...pretty?" He glanced over his shoulder, seeming to be surprised when he saw a wing fluttering in front of his face. "Ooh yes. It is pretty." He reached behind himself and stroked the opalescent membrane, which fluttered even more under his fingers. "Oh. Oh. Oh, Keiron. Keiron, that feels good. Do it. Do it."

Draven turned round and cast eager, anxious glances over his shoulder until Keiron tentatively stroked the shimmering fabric of Draven's wings. Keiron was surprised by the texture. They appeared to be flimsy and delicate, but he should have realised they couldn't have been too flimsy or they wouldn't support Draven's weight.

"They're beautiful," Keiron breathed, stroking the membrane. It was warm and soft, shivering under his hands, with colours that seemed to shift and change. Draven threw back his head and moaned as Keiron ran his hands over the wing ridges, out to the very edge and back, then down to Draven's back.

"Oh, Keiron, that…that's so…so…so…. Oooh, Keiron, oh, I love that." Draven leaned backwards, his head on Keiron's shoulder. "Touch me, Keiron. Touch me everywhere."

"Draven, babe, you're out of your mind. I can't—"

Draven spun round and threw himself at Keiron, knocking him backwards onto the floor. He landed on top of him in a crouch. "I want you," he growled. His eyes seemed enormous and such an intense shade of blue.

"Draven, you're not—"

"Yes, I am. I am. I am. Iam. IamIamIamIamamamamam," Draven sang.

"Draven, stop it. Get off and I'll—" He was cut off by Draven's lips as they crushed against his, taking his breath away. He couldn't argue with Draven any longer. He couldn't even think.

"Keiron," Draven moaned, breathing hard, his kisses hot and heavy, his hands roving over Keiron's body.

Gasping, Keiron slipped his arms around Draven's waist and drew him close. Draven ground his body against him, and he realised with surprise that Draven's wings were fluttering.

"Do you like me touching your wings, baby? Like this?" Keiron reached up as far as he could and ruffled the downy fur on the edges of Draven's wings. Draven shuddered and moaned.

"Oh…. Oh yes…. Yes, I do. I…. More. More."

Draven's wings trembled violently under Keiron's hands, raising him from Keiron's body to hover free of the ground. Draven closed his eyes, threw back his head, and moaned loudly.

"I didn't realise they were so sensitive."

"Yes, yes, yes. Oh!" Draven gasped and froze.

"What's the matter?"

"Ow," Draven whimpered and dropped to the ground. He rolled away from Keiron and curled on himself. "Keiron, Keiron, it hurts. My belly hurts. Why does it hurt? Why does everything hurt?"

"What's the matter, honey?" Keiron shot to his knees and stroked Draven's shoulder, avoiding the wings, which were now spasming rather than trembling. "Please tell me what's wrong."

"It hurts, Keiron," he cried, rocking. "My stomach hurts."

"You said that before. Is it the sherbet?"

"I don't know. I don't know. It hurts. It hurts."

Carefully, Keiron took Draven into his arms and rocked him helplessly. What could he do? It wasn't as if he could call a doctor when he had an armful of gossamer wings.

Keiron seemed to sit there a long time, cradling and rocking a moaning Draven. He squirmed and writhed, sobbed pleas and curses, deteriorating quickly from a stomach ache to cold sweats and terrifying hallucinations. Keiron was frantic. Should he call Fenn? Could he call Fenn?

When he grew numb from the floor, he lifted Draven in his arms and carried him to the bedroom where more time passed as he held the quivering fairy in his arms. Draven clung to him desperately, burying his face in the crook of his shoulder and moaned, giggled, or screamed, depending on what visions were assailing him or pains gripping him.

Finally, Draven grew quiet. Pacified, Keiron was sure by exhaustion more than relief, Draven lay in Keiron's arms and stared at the ceiling with glassy eyes. Was this really all from drinking sherbet?

"Am I...am I going to die after all?" Draven asked faintly, his breathing fast and shallow.

"No, of course not. The chemicals in the sherbet drink are giving a bad trip, that's all. You're drugged, but you're not dying." He sincerely hoped he was right.

"It's not like before."

"Before what?"

"When you drugged me before."

Keiron frowned, racking his memory. "Oh yes, with the aspirin. No, it's not like that at all. The chemicals put in that kind of drink are much harsher."

"Why?"

"For colour, taste...I don't know."

"Why do you drink it if you don't know what's in it?"

"Because that's the world I live in, little one."

"I don't like your world, Keiron. I don't like feeling like this."

Keiron felt he'd been stabbed through the heart. He stroked the sticky white hair from Draven's pale face and gazed into his eyes, which seemed to be trying hard to focus on him. "We'll be more careful. I won't let you eat or drink things with lots of chemicals anymore. You'll be fine. I promise I'll take better care of you. Now I know this happens, I won't let it happen again."

"I want to go home," Draven whispered plaintively, a tear escaping his eye. "I'm scared, and I want to go home."

Now Keiron felt physically sick. Should he send him home? Fenn said he could go back. He was stubborn and wouldn't listen, but now…. Should he send Draven home? If he did, he'd die inside. Draven hadn't been with him long, hardly a week, but he'd wormed his way into his heart so deeply he was sure it would destroy him if he tore him out. On the other hand, he couldn't sit back and selfishly watch his world destroy Draven bit by bit. Oh God, what to do; what to do.

"When you're feeling better, little one. If you still want to go home when you're feeling better, I'll do everything I can to get you there."

"Thank you, Keiron. I love you so much." Draven sounded totally exhausted and his eyelids were drooping. Keiron held him close and rocked him until he drifted into sleep. Sleep wouldn't come to Keiron, not all that day or through the long night when he watched Draven sleep. It was a restless sleep, punctuated with screaming dreams and pain. Keiron held him, stroked him, petted him, and promised him whatever he asked until sun brought eventual release and Keiron fell into a fitful slumber.

Chapter Nineteen

WHEN KEIRON AWOKE, he knew immediately something was different. Draven was tucked into his side, fast asleep and breathing deeply. His wings had gone. Keiron breathed a huge sigh of relief and stroked Draven's back as he glanced at the clock. Hell, it was 2:30 p.m. He'd never slept in that late. Not that there was anything to get up for. All he needed was right there in his arms.

Then it hit him. Draven didn't want to be in his arms, not really, not anymore. Draven wanted to go home. All the agonising grief he'd suffered when trying to decide if he should send Draven away for his own good had crystallised when Draven said it's what he wanted. Keiron felt sick. He laid his head on Draven's hair. He could cry. But he wouldn't. Draven would cry, no doubt. Emotions were so close to the surface with Draven—he laughed and cried freely, with no reservation. But Keiron would be strong. He wouldn't cry.

"Keiron?" Draven's sleepy voice startled him.

"Hey there," Keiron said softly and tenderly. "How're you feeling?"

"Good." Draven yawned and sat up. "That wasn't very nice. I didn't like feeling like that at all. I'm not going to do it again."

"No," Keiron said sadly, "you're not. I'll help you go home today."

The smile slipped from Draven's face, and he seemed stricken. "You're going to send me away? Is it because I was so bad yesterday? I didn't know the drink was going to make me crazy. Whatever I did. Whatever I said. I didn't mean any of it. I don't remember.... I'm sorry. I'm so sorry. Please don't send me away."

"Ssh, Draven. I'm not going to send you away. I'm just going to help you go home."

"But I don't want to go home. I want to stay here with you."

Despite the fact his heart soared, Keiron shook his head. "Draven, it's not safe here for you. We proved that last night. If something as innocent as a sherbet drink can do that to you—"

"But I know now," Draven begged. "I know not to drink it again. I know if I try something new, it should be just a little. I won't do it again. I promise I won't do it again. Please don't send me away, Keiron. Please."

"I-I won't send you away, but—"

"Keiron, I love you. You're my mate. I keep telling you that, but you don't seem to understand. I love you. I won't leave you; I can't—only if you send me away, and that will break my heart."

"I won't send you away," Keiron repeated softly, holding Draven and pulling him closer. "I won't send you away. It would break my heart too, but you said…last night, you said you wanted to go home."

Draven shook his head. "I was sick and scared, but I'm not anymore. I'm yours now, Keiron, forever and always. I'm yours."

"Don't say that, Draven. You don't belong to anyone, certainly not me."

Draven drew back and stared into his face, gently patting his cheek. "How long are you going to fight it, Keiron?"

"Fight what?" he asked, feeling very uncomfortable. Of course, he knew the answer.

"The bond. We're joined now. Whether you want it or not, you can't break free."

"What bond?" Keiron was alarmed. Was this some kind of fairy magic that—

"Love, Keiron. I love you and you love me and that's an end of it. You can fight it as much as you like, but it is as it is."

And quite suddenly he didn't want to fight anymore. He stared into that beautiful little face, the one he'd been watching so anxiously all night, and he realised he never wanted to spend another day of not seeing it. Somehow, Draven had become so much part of his life he couldn't imagine life without him. Whether he'd known him for five minutes or five days or five years, Draven was part of him now, an integral part, the better part. If that wasn't love, what was?

"I don't want to fight it, Draven. Not anymore. I'm a fool, a complete idiot. What was I thinking? Of course I love you. I love you more than I could ever have imagined loving anyone. You're so much part of my life, I'd cut off my leg before I'd let you go."

"That's good, Keiron," Draven said seriously, "because I'm never going to let you go."

Keiron pulled Draven close and held him tight. Now, more than ever, Keiron fought tears and failed. He sniffed and Draven raised his head.

"What's the matter, Keiron? Why are you crying? Are you sad?"

"I'm not crying, not really. I'm just happy, Draven. I feel.... It feels good to say I love you."

"I know. I love you. I love you. I love you." He punctuated his words with kisses, and Keiron felt weak. Closing his eyes, he surrendered himself completely as Draven carried on kissing all over his body until he was trembling and feverish.

"Oh God, Draven, I love you," he moaned, as Draven squirmed between his legs, still kissing.

"Say it again," Draven gasped between kisses.

"I love you. I love you. I.... Aaaaaah." Keiron moaned deeply when Draven slid up his body to return his kisses to his lips. "Oh God, Draven, you're so fucking sexy, I can't stand it."

"Oh, yes, you can. You can stand a whole lot more. I know you can. Want me to test it out?"

"No, no please, no testing, just lots and lots of sex."

"He-he, you said sex. You can say it now. What do you want me to do?"

"Whatever you want, only do it hard, do it fast, and do it now."

Up to then, their lovemaking had been tender and gentle, but this time Draven seemed to have something to prove. He went crazy, giving Keiron the best afternoon he'd had in years. As soon as they'd finished, Draven curled up, cuddled into Keiron's side, and went to sleep.

The next time Keiron woke, he was alone. For a moment, he panicked. Had Draven had second thoughts? Had he just been buttering Keiron up? Had the sex been goodbye sex? Is that why Draven had tried so hard, been so sweet? Had he gone? Had...?

He leaped out of bed and practically ran down the stairs. When he approached the kitchen, he was surprised to hear voices. For a moment, he was very nervous. Had Draven called his friends to take him home? Was he, even now, arranging to leave him? He cracked open the door.

"I don't know how many times I have to tell you, Fenn. I'm not leaving. Keiron is my mate and he would not be able to live in our world, so I'm going to stay here with him."

"You can't stay here with him. You know that."

"I can," Draven said stubbornly, "and I will."

"For how long?" Fenn asked, crossing her arms. She was leaning casually against the worktop, her long hair seeming to float around her in an invisible breeze.

Keiron hated her for trying to take Draven away from him. She'd never liked him and she'd tried to break them up before. He was about to open the door and enter the kitchen when her next words stopped him in his tracks.

"And how long do you think you're going to be able to hide it from him?" Fenn insisted. "You're dying, Draven, day by day."

"We're all dying day by day, Fenn," Draven said in a sulky voice.

"Not as fast as you are. The poisons in the air are already weakening you. I can tell."

"It's not the poisons in the air. I...had an incident yesterday. Something I drank disagreed with me."

"Whatever, Draven. Sooner or later, you're not going to be able to hide it, and by then, it may be too late."

"I don't care. I'm staying and—"

"No, you're not." Keiron opened the door and stopped short. Fenn wasn't the only fey in the room. In the corner, behind the door, were two cats—one an enormous ginger and the other a sleek black. Both had harnesses and were being ridden by tiny people who looked rather like Draven when he was that size. They both glared at him, as did Fenn.

"Don't you start," Draven said angrily, hands on hips. "Just leave and let me—"

"Why didn't you tell me?" Keiron asked, standing just inside the door where he could see everyone in it. Cat riders? Really?

"I...because it's none of your business."

"It's none of my business that my lover is dying because of me? I beg to differ."

"It's not because of you and I'm not...." He glanced at Fenn and then at the two cat riders who, Keiron noticed, carried tiny spears. "Well...maybe I am, but it won't be for ages and ages and maybe not at all. Maybe I'll get immune to the poison. Sal does that—takes tiny amounts of poison for a long time and gets immune to it. Maybe—"

"Draven, you know that's not going to happen. You've got a couple of months, if that, before you start getting really sick."

"I...I'll deal with it, if and when it happens."

"It's happening already. By then, it will be too late. Why do you have to be so stubborn?"

"I'm not being stubborn. I'm standing by my mate. You understand what that means, Fenn. Our bond is sacred."

"No one is asking you to break your bond, Draven. You can visit—"

"Visit? I don't want to visit. I live here now...with Keiron."

"No, Draven, you don't. I don't want you to live here." It was the hardest thing Keiron had ever done, especially when Draven turned a totally shocked face to him.

"You...you don't want me?" Draven grabbed a strand of hair and started winding it around his finger.

"I don't want you to be sick, Draven, and I certainly don't want you to die. It will hurt me very much to lose you, but I can't be responsible for hurting you."

"Oh, so it's fine for me to hurt you, but not for you to hurt me. That's screwed up logic, Keiron. Besides, it's not your decision; it's mine."

"Actually, Draven, it's not."

"What?" Tearing his eyes away from Keiron, Draven turned to Fenn. He put the end of the strand of hair in his mouth and started to chew. Keiron was fascinated. He couldn't take his eyes off Draven's face, his heart breaking. This might be the last time he'd see him.

"Your father sent us to bring you home."

"My...? My father? But it was agreed. He agreed."

"He agreed before he knew what this would do to you. No one really believed Keiron would be your mate. When it happened, it complicated things but changed nothing. If your father had been home, it would never have got this far."

"My father has nothing to do with this."

"I'm afraid he does. It's his decision whether you will be allowed to stay here, and his decision is that you will not."

"Well, I don't care what my father says," Draven said, tossing his hair. He turned to Keiron, his blue-on-blue eyes flashing in a way Keiron hadn't seen before. "And I don't care what you say either. I'm not leaving."

"That's pretty much what we thought you'd say," Fenn said, "so we came prepared."

"What do you mean you—?"

Fenn nodded to the cat men who immediately rose from the backs of their cats like dragonflies, their incandescent wings fluttering. Draven tried to bat them away as they flew around him, but to no avail. One of them darted past his hands and drove the tiny spear into his neck.

As the men floated back to their cats, Draven turned to Keiron and held out his hands. "Please, Keiron. I love you. Please don't let them take me. Ple...." Before he could finish, his eyes rolled and he collapsed to the floor.

"Draven!" Keiron rushed to his side and knelt. Draven was out cold. "What have you done to him?"

"Saved him, Keiron," Fenn said coldly. "You know it's for the best. I have nothing against you. In fact, for a human, you're a nice person, but I won't let Draven die for you."

"Would he really? Die?"

"Here, yes. The poisons in the air are deadly to our people. That's why we never stay long in or near cities. He's been dying since the moment he came here."

"Then...then he has to go back. I couldn't be responsible for him getting hurt like that. Take him home. Do it quickly."

Fenn nodded and crouched beside Draven. She reached out and touched him gently on the forehead, closing her eyes. Draven moaned and turned his head away from her, but he couldn't fight her, and before Keiron's eyes, he shrank until he was small enough for Fenn to pick up with one hand.

Very carefully, Fenn cradled Draven to her chest like an infant and gave Keiron a wry smile before heading out of the door with the two cats loping at her feet.

Keiron remained kneeling on the floor and stared at the open door long after the unlikely group had left. It was over. It was really over. Draven had gone, and he wasn't coming back. It took a few minutes to truly sink in, and when it did, Keiron wept.

THE DAYS THAT followed were a nightmare to Keiron. From a practical point of view, it should have been one of the best times of his life. Trying to fill his days, he threw himself into setting up his work-from-home business, and the offers poured in, many from old clients. Soon he was earning more than he had working for the company. He worked day and night and tried to fill up the empty space in his life. He failed totally.

Rather than missing him less, he missed Draven more every day and found himself yearning, if not to be close to him, then to be close to somewhere he'd been happy, really happy. On a crazy whim, he bought a house in the middle of nowhere. There was a wood and a stream, a small wooden bridge and a large open field. The house even had a small waterfall and deep pool on its land. Its own private place.

Keiron took to spending his weekends there, sitting beside the pool, thinking and dreaming. He often thought his heart would break, but it kept on beating day by day. When the winter came, he built wood fires in the open grates and in the boiler that heated the house and the water. It had central heating, but there was something about doing it the old-fashioned way that made him feel less hopeless.

It was a week before Christmas when Keiron heard the knock on the back door. His heart soared for a moment, and he scrambled to answer. It was Fenn. She crossed the threshold uninvited, shaking snow from her boots.

"What the hell do you want?" Bitter disappointment made his voice sharp, and Fenn gave him a hard look.

"How much do you love Draven?" she asked.

"That has nothing to do with you. It's over. I'm trying my best to...forget."

"But you can't, can you? You can't forget. You think time will make it easier, but it doesn't. It gets worse every day. You find yourself doing things that would have seemed crazy before, but you can't help yourself. You dream about him every night, and wake crying."

"What the fuck...?"

Fenn met his eyes and she seemed so sad.

"What's wrong? Something's wrong with Draven, isn't it? What is it? Is he all right?"

"No, Keiron. No, he is not all right. The reason I know how you are feeling is because he is feeling it too. But it is different with us, not so easy."

"Easy? Do you think it's easy? You must be—"

"Keiron, Draven is hurt. He has not been able to escape his thoughts of you, and he became sad and melancholy. There was trouble on our borders, and his father called for him. He sent Draven out with the warriors, hoping he would settle and become focussed again. There was a skirmish and he was hurt. Not badly." She hurried on, seeing the expression of horror on Keiron's face.

"The warriors said he was distracted, his attention elsewhere. His heart wasn't in it, and he was careless. After he returned, he withdrew from everyone. The healers treated his wound, but.... They say he has an injury to his psyche that will not be healed. He has become...shut down. No one can reach him, and the healers believe he is suffering because your bond was severed."

"Yes," Keiron said, nodding. He understood completely. He hadn't been able to put his finger on the strange restless melancholy that had been plaguing him, but he realised now that somewhere inside, something had been cut loose and he'd been bleeding from it ever since. It wasn't blood that could be seen, but the more he thought about it, the more he realised it was there. "I feel it too."

Fenn nodded. "With Draven, it is more serious. Serious enough for his father to send me to you. Will you come back with me and save him?"

"Back? To your world? Will I have to stay?" For a moment, he panicked, then he realised what it would mean—he and Draven could be together forever. Isn't that what he wanted more than anything? More than the city. More even than a house in the country. Would he give it all up for the little fairy? Hell yes.

"No, Keiron, you will not be asked to stay. When your work is done, when Draven is healed, you will return."

"Will?"

"You cannot stay in our world."

Keiron shook his head. "If I can't stay, I won't come. It would kill me inside to say goodbye to him again. I think he would be the same. It would be pointless to heal a wound that you're to tear open again."

"I did not say you would have to say goodbye. We know of your house in the wild. It would be safe for Draven. You may take him there."

"What? I.... We can be together? Forever? I-I'd do anything for that."

Fenn smiled. It was the first truly warm smile she had given him. "Your bond is stronger than any I have seen. The gods of our peoples, the energy of the earth and stars have made it so strong it cannot be broken without great pain to both of you. If the gods make a bond that strong, it's not for man or fey to take it upon themselves to sever it. No one will try to separate you again."

"Take me," Keiron demanded.

"You have no hesitation, Keiron? It is a journey into the unknown. Our lands are not as...civilised as yours. There will be danger."

"Take me to him. I don't care about the danger. I don't care about anything but Draven."

"I see it in your eyes. You speak the truth. More than the truth, you speak purity, love, and joy. So follow me, human. Follow me somewhere very few of your kind have ever been."

Chapter Twenty

KEIRON FOLLOWED FENN down the garden path to the shrubbery. "Take my hand," she commanded. Keiron complied. It was soft and warm but still somehow woody. "Close your eyes and, when I tell you, take a step forward. Do not open your eyes until I tell you, or you will lose your mind."

"Nothing serious then," Keiron joked, trying to calm his heart.

"It is very serious, Keiron. Do not doubt that this will be dangerous for you. Humans are not meant to pass through the gates."

Keiron closed his eyes, his heart pounding. He heard Fenn chanting softly in a language like none he'd ever heard. He held tight to her hand and waited.

"Step forward. Now," Fenn commanded, and Keiron complied.

First, a fizzing sensation crawled over his skin, then there was a jerk and he literally felt as if someone had reached in through the top of his head and turned him inside out. It wasn't painful but the strangest sensation he'd ever had. Colours pulsed through his eyelids and deep into his skull, and he began to realise that perhaps Fenn hadn't been teasing when she said opening his eyes would cost him his mind. With a hint of hysteria, Keiron believed Fenn had never teased anyone about anything in her life.

Then, as quickly as it had begun, it ended. A fist punched into the top of his head and continued through his body to his feet. The pulsing colours stopped, and he fell forward onto his knee.

"You may open your eyes now, human," Fenn said, and Keiron did so rather tentatively.

They were standing in a clearing, in a wood. It would have seemed like any clearing in any wood, if it hadn't been for the fact the air was full of tiny glittering beings, like a cloud of dragonflies. They were all chattering and squeaking, and Fenn swatted them away impatiently.

"Very well," she said irritably, "you've seen the human, now buzz off. You all have duties to attend to." The cloud of fairies backed off, out of reach of Fenn's hands, but followed as Fenn led Keiron across the clearing. He noticed other faces peering out from behind branches and leaves, running through the grass and flying above. None of them were as brazen as the little cloud of dragonflies, which still followed, so he never caught more than a glimpse. He knew they were there, though, and it made him nervous.

The ground began to rise steeply, and they soon came to a path that led to a paved road. Keiron was surprised when the road passed through a small village, with human-sized houses.

"Size is relative, Keiron," Fenn said as he gazed in wonder at the quaint thatched cottages with neat gardens and pretty lace curtains at their open windows.

"What do you mean?"

"Nothing here is quite what meets the eye. You see the houses you want to see. Others see them differently. This is not a place to make assumptions. Keep a flexible mind and you'll do fine."

"Do you mean the houses aren't really as I see them?"

"What's real? They are what they are. When you look at them, you see what you see. When I look at them, I see what I see."

"But what are they really? What's actually there?"

"I've just told you, Keiron. Pay attention. These are things you need to know. What you see is real for you."

Keiron thought about it. "So," he said, and Fenn sighed. "When I look at the house and see a thatched cottage, then for me, it is a thatched cottage. I can go inside and sit in the chair and cook on the range. But when someone else looks at it, they see something different. When they go inside and sit in the chair, it's a different chair, but it exists in the same place as mine."

Fenn glanced at him out of the corner of her eye as they passed through the village. "You're not as stupid as you look, are you?"

"I hope not," Keiron responded and got another smile.

The road wound its way out of the village and passed through another wood, where it was overhung by twisted ancient trees that made it impossible to see what was ahead. Keiron began to wonder how much longer they were going to walk before they had something to drink. It was hot and he was parched. They must easily have walked a couple of miles by now.

"How much further?"

"As far as it takes to get there."

"How far is that?"

"How far do you want it to be?"

"Around the next corner," he joked. The road ahead turned sharply to the left, and as they turned the corner, it passed through a gate into a busy walled town.

Crooked streets led off in each direction, and all kinds of people walked them, from blue-haired boys in jeans who leaned against the wall of what might have been a school, to floating women who seemed to be made of cloud, to stiff men and women in medieval costume who passed sedately and nodded in greeting to Fenn.

They hadn't gone far before they were stopped by the strangest little man, dressed all in yellow with green tufted hair peeking from under his pointed yellow hat. Piercing green eyes glared at Keiron, and a gnarled finger with green claws pointed at him. "Is this the human?"

"How many humans are there in Ridgemount, Grundell?" Fenn said, rolling her eyes.

"There's no need for that, Fenn. The Lady is waiting and you know what she's like when she gets impatient."

Fenn rolled her eyes again. "Here then, take him. I should be getting back anyway."

"What? Wait," Keiron said. "Aren't you staying with me?"

"Did you expect me to hold your hand the whole time you're here, Keiron? I have my own work to do. Grundell will show you the way to the Lady."

"The Lady, who's she?"

"The Lord and the Lady are who they are, Keiron. Did Draven not speak to you of them?"

"Oh...right. Why am I going to see them? Can't I just go to Draven? I need to go to Draven."

"You will."

"But—"

"Oh do come along," Grundell said impatiently, grabbing on to Keiron's sleeve and tugging it. "The Lady does not like to be kept waiting."

Keiron threw Fenn a startled look. She smiled her enigmatic smile and turned away, disappearing into the crowd as if by...magic.

"But why do we have to see the Lady first?" Keiron complained. "Why can't I go straight to Draven?"

"Because the Lady has decreed it be so."

"What has it got to do with her?"

"You are in her lands now, human. Everything here concerns her, and nowhere more than her own household."

"Her own household?"

Grundell kept tugging on Keiron's sleeve, walking backwards in his anxiety to hurry Keiron up. With a sigh, Keiron gave in and followed the little man up a steep hill between walls of bright gold-coloured stone that made a graceful arch above.

At the other side of the passage, they passed through a set of ornate gates into a courtyard. If Keiron had ever imagined what a fairy castle might look like, it wasn't anything like this. It was too modern and too square. Where were the soaring turrets and bright flags? Where were the liveried footmen and golden coaches?

Inside, it was no more his idea of a fairy-tale castle, than the outside. In fact, it was quite homely. Again, he had little time to take anything in, as Grundell led him up a flight of stairs, stopping in front of a set of golden doors. *Now this is more like it*, Keiron thought.

"Wait here," Grundell commanded and slipped through the doors.

At last, Keiron had a chance to look around. It was a very strange place, with high ceilings and ornate fixtures but simple wooden chests along the corridors on either side, the kind he could get in a cheap home deco store. Harsh electric lights took the place of the expected chandeliers, and the paintings on the walls either side of the door were abstract and very modern. What a strange place.

Keiron jumped when the doors opened again. He'd been examining a bookcase in a niche at the start of the corridor and hurried back in time to be grabbed by the hand poking out and yanked through the door.

If he'd thought the rest of the castle was nothing like his idea of what a fairy-tale castle should be, this room most certainly was. It was a throne room, with two enormous golden thrones set on a dais at the far end of a space that seemed far too big to fit inside the building he'd seen so far. He walked nervously down a long red carpet past a crowd of interested people of all kinds, some of whom strained his interpretation of "people".

Only one of the thrones was occupied, and as they drew close, Keiron could see the occupant was a woman. She was very beautiful with long white hair bound in a single braid that hung over her shoulder and was decorated with gold ribbon and pearls. She was wearing a dress fit for the most beautiful fairy queen and had a diadem on her head. Keiron noticed all of this in a brief flash of peripheral vision as his eyes were fixed on hers. They were blue. Very blue.

"So you are Keiron," she said when he was standing at the bottom of the dais. For a long moment, she regarded him closely, then rose to her feet and glided down the steps to stand before him. Shockingly, she threw her arms around him and hugged him warmly. "Thank you so much for coming, and so quickly. We've been terribly worried. We should have sent Fenn sooner, but—"

With a sigh, the Lady took Keiron's face between her hands and gazed into his eyes. "If we had only known what a beautiful spirit you are, we would not have fought so hard against it. We were hopeful Draven would come to his senses and leave you behind, but now we see how wrong we were. We have caused him so much unnecessary suffering. We hope that you can both forgive us."

Keiron moved nervously from one foot to another, feeling decidedly nervous. The woman was so intense. And what was with the "we" thing. The royal *we*, he guessed. A dual king/queenship. But wait a minute.... Hadn't Draven said...? His thoughts were cut off as the woman spoke again.

"Before we take one more step, there's something we need to know. We believe we know the answer, but we have to hear it from your lips. Look into our eyes, Keiron the human, and know we will know if you lie, if there is even the smallest deceit inside your heart."

Keiron found himself gazing into the Lady's eyes. He'd had no choice, although he'd not resisted. He could feel the power that emanated from her and was decidedly nervous about what the question would be. He knew for sure he wouldn't be able to lie.

"Do you love our son?"

Oh shit, Keiron thought, but he said with no volition, "Yes, with all my heart."

The Lady smiled and nodded. "Then come with us."

Still tense and nervous, Keiron followed the Lady—Draven's mother—around the side of the dais to a door, where she stopped. "We know you'll find him," the Lady said. "You'll know where to go."

"Where to look, but...isn't he here?"

"In a manner of speaking." She opened the door and ushered him inside, then closed the door again, abandoning him.

The room was dark and silent. It was as if he'd been pushed into a bubble outside time. There was no whisper from the other side of the door, no breath, no sigh. By the light of the shaded lamps, he made out a figure, lying on a mound of bright cushions covered with tapestry rugs. One of the rugs covered the figure.

With a smile, Keiron moved carefully across the room, avoiding more piles of cushions, small stools, and tables. Some of the tables were laden with fruit, and others bore sweet incense that burned Keiron's eyes and the back of his throat.

"Draven?" he called softly as he sat down on the bed. "Draven, it's me." There was no response from the still figure, and Keiron tentatively took his hand. He was shocked by how cold it was. "Draven?" he said again with an edge of fear in his voice. "Draven, it's me, Keiron. Please wake up." His pleas met with nothing but silence and stillness.

"This is what she meant," Keiron said softly. "This is what she meant about finding you. You're not really here, are you? Not really. Your body's here, but you're far away, and now I have to find you. I have no idea how. Help me here, darling, please. Tell me how to find you." He didn't expect a response from Draven, and he didn't get one.

Draven was like a marble statue. Pale and cold and so very beautiful. Keiron was almost afraid to touch him. Dammit. What was he supposed to do? And what would happen if he couldn't find Draven? If he couldn't bring him back?

"Draven, I...." Wait. Something was tugging at his memory, something cliché but maybe.... "Well, nothing ventured, nothing gained, I suppose." Leaning forwards, he pressed his lips against Draven's marble-cold ones. "Do I get to wake you with a kiss, my sleeping beauty?"

He immediately felt a change, but it wasn't in Draven. It was in himself. Keiron's head jerked back as something seemed to open inside him, a core of flame that spread like molten gold through his body and into his head. Like a lotus flower, understanding blossomed in his mind. Draven was in there, everywhere. Layer after layer after layer, he realised how deeply Draven had imbedded himself into every part of him, and it was love that flowed through him, love like no emotion or connection he'd ever experienced before. Was this what Draven had been feeling all along? The connection was so deep and so complete he found himself weeping hot tears, and could almost imagine they were golden.

"Oh God," he whispered, understanding finally dawning. He'd been denying this connection, shutting it off, blocking it. Unwilling to give himself so completely to anyone, not even to Draven, he'd stopped the golden energy that should have been flowing between them. He'd broken the bond and, in so doing, had broken Draven.

"No," he gasped and reached out for Draven's cold hands. Terrified, he couldn't, at first, find the connection at all. The golden energy had all but stopped flowing, and it scared the hell out of him to think it couldn't be started again.

Things like energy channelling and meditating were so far out of Keiron's frame of reference, he had no idea where to start. He tried to calm his mind, as he'd read somewhere, and focussed on Draven's hands. It wasn't hard; they were so cold, like marble in his fingers. Then he tried to picture the golden liquid that flowed through his veins in place of blood, seeping into them, flowing into Draven and running through him, warming his cold flesh, pumping through his slow heart.

Was he imagining it, or were Draven's hands warmer now? Maybe it was just where he'd been holding them. Keiron opened his eyes and sighed. He just didn't know what to do, how to do it. He was failing badly and Draven was slipping away. How could he find him? How could he catch him?

"Draven," he called again. "Please, Draven. I've opened it now, the bond, the…thing. I've done what I was supposed to do. Now what? How can I find you? How can I reach you? Help me."

There was no response, and Keiron began to panic. He had an image in his head of Draven floating further and further away from him, reaching out his hands in supplication, until he was so far away he couldn't be seen anymore and the cold image of him would be nothing more than the marble statue he resembled. Oh God. What if it had already happened? Frantically, he tore away the blanket and laid his head on Draven's chest. The heartbeat was faint and slow, but it was there. He was still alive. Keiron still had a chance.

"You can't speak to me, but maybe you can show me somehow." He closed his eyes and tried to picture that image of Draven again, forcing his mind to see. But the picture was fleeting, flickering and disappearing before he could grasp it.

"This is impossible," Keiron cried and lifted Draven in his arms. The room was beginning to close in on him. The dimness, the smell of incense... It was too much. Wrapping Draven in the tapestry blanket, he kicked open the door and strode into the throne room. Suddenly, it was all so obvious.

The Lady was hovering near the door and everyone else had formed a semicircle around her. Her eyes filled with hope when she saw them, but it didn't last long.

"Take me home," Keiron demanded.

"I cannot. My son.... He...."

"He won't get better here. I can't reach him. I need to do this my way, in my own home, with my things around me. I can't find him if I don't know where I am."

The Lady stared at him for a long moment, then nodded. "Follow me," she said, and the sea of people parted as she strode through. Keiron followed closely, the cold from Draven's body seeping into his own. Draven's head hung over his arm, his long white hair flowing like rippling silk. Keiron couldn't stop gazing at him, drinking in the beauty of his sweet face. No matter what happened, he had to make him whole again, to make him warm and well.

Outside the throne room, the Lady turned left and hurried along the corridor to one of the doors, which she opened. Instead of a room on the other side, there were trees, scrubby trees. "Go," she said. "Do what you have to do. Anything. Anything at all you desire will be yours, only please save our son."

Keiron gazed into her face and saw so much of Draven there. He shook his head. "That's the only thing I desire. I want him back. That's all."

The Lady smiled and nodded. "This is a one-way gate. You won't be able to come back this way once you've left, but if you need it, you will always find your way to us." She quickly unfastened a necklace from among the many she wore around her neck. Unlike the others, it was very plain and simple. A leather thong on which hung a pear-shaped stone. He couldn't quite work out what it was. It seemed to shimmer and flow like a...tear. He glanced up sharply, and she nodded.

Chapter Twenty-One

KEIRON PUSHED THROUGH the branches and found himself in his own garden. Glancing back, he saw no sign of the Lady or the door. He wondered but had no time to linger. He made his way up through the garden as fast as he could and kicked open the back door. Thank goodness he'd forgotten to lock up in his haste to follow Fenn...how long ago?

Carrying Draven carefully, he hurried up the stairs to the bedroom and laid him on the bed. Keiron unwrapped the tapestry and pulled the quilt over Draven, then stripped quickly and slipped under it himself, seeking to warm Draven with his body heat.

"Draven, you're home, home with me. Well...where I live. This isn't going to be my home anymore. It never was our home. I have a new home now, in the countryside. We have our own waterfall and a pool we can swim in. You can have all your friends and...animals around you, and the poison of the city won't touch you. You'll be safe there, Draven, I promise. I'm going to make you safe.

"See, I figured that the reason you couldn't find your way home and I couldn't find you was because that wasn't your home anymore. Now I know what the bond is and what it means, I realise your home is with me. You left that place behind when you came here. You made a new home here, and this is where your heart is, so this is where your body has to be for you to find it. And you have to want to find it, to find me."

Keiron stroked Draven's face, trailing his fingers over his cold cheeks and blue lips. If only they would turn pink again, would part and let him in.

"I hope you want to find me, Draven. I really hope you want to, because if not, I don't know what else to do. I'm so scared you'll go so far away you can't get back and your body will die, and I'll be without you forever. I couldn't live without you, not now. Not when half of what I am would go with you. Please, Draven. Please come home."

Keiron lay for what seemed like hours, stroking Draven's face and body, willing him to come back, to get warm. Then he began to think that maybe the body beneath his fingers was getting warm. He raised his head to find Draven's lips were no longer blue. With his stomach twisting in knots, Keiron laid his head on Draven's chest. Draven's heartbeat thrummed, faster and stronger, throbbing not just in Keiron's ear but all through him, as if it was his own.

"Draven, oh God, Draven, come home. I can feel you. I can actually feel you, and I know you're close now. Come back to me." He gazed frantically around the room, half expecting to see Draven's form floating somewhere in a corner. There was nothing but sparkling motes of dust dancing in the shafts of light shining in through the window.

Moaning aloud, Keiron pulled Draven into his arms and held him close, wrapping him as best he could in the golden glow that permeated his body. It was so strong, he could almost see it. Draven's slender body began to tremble, little tremors running through it, and Keiron held tighter.

"I can feel you, Draven. I can feel you," he gasped, resting his cheek on Draven's fragrant white hair. He breathing deeply of the sweet smell he thought he'd never savour again. The tremors increased in intensity until Draven was quivering in his arms. Then Draven took a deep shuddering breath and gave a strange mewling cry that cut into Keiron's mind and heart.

"Ssh. Ssh beautiful," he crooned. "You're home now. You're home where you belong."

The cry turned to a sob, and Draven stirred, threw his arms around Keiron, and wept on his shoulder. Keiron remained silent, stroking Draven's hair and back until he grew quiet and still.

Carefully and slowly, Keiron released Draven and eased him back onto the pillows. He gasped out loud when he saw Draven's beautiful eyes were open and staring at him with a strange intensity. Keiron smiled and brushed the hair out of the small pointed face. A shaky smile rewarded him.

"Welcome back," Keiron said softly, and Draven blinked.

"Have I...?" His voice cracked, and he licked his lips to try again. "Have I been somewhere?"

"Yes, you've been somewhere. I don't know where, but I don't think it was a very nice place."

"Am I...?" He frowned and looked around, confusion on his face. "I don't think I'm supposed to be here, Keiron. They...they told me I could never come back."

"I know." Keiron stroked Draven's face. "But it's all sorted. I've spoken to your mother and no one's going to keep us apart anymore."

"My mother? You...you have?"

"I have. She's been worried about you."

"Yes," he said with a frown. "They all have, but I didn't know what to do to stop it. I did try. I really did try." He closed his eyes and tears forced themselves out under his lids. "I didn't want to worry anyone, but I just didn't belong there anymore, and no one would listen. I did everything they asked me to, but I couldn't help that I was broken, and everything I did just made it worse."

"Broken? What do you mean, broken?"

"I don't know. It's like...like I was a wineskin with a hole, and little by little, all the wine drained away. I was hollow and empty, and nothing I did could change it. After...after the battle, I-I just felt I was drifting away, and I didn't know what to do to stop it." Draven's voice had grown distant and breathless. Keiron squeezed his hands.

"That's over now. It was my fault. I refused to recognise the bond, to see how it worked. I blocked it out, and when they took you, I think it broke and the...energy leaked out. I know that isn't it, but I still don't really understand and I don't have the words. Our bond is supposed to support and nourish each other, and when it's broken, the opposite happens. Everything that happened to you was my fault, and I'm so, so sorry. I swear to you I'll never let it happen again. I'll never let you go again. I'll hold you close and take care of you and tell you how much I love you a hundred times a day."

Draven blinked. He seemed more...solid, more present, but the more solid he became, the more tired and ill he appeared. It broke Keiron's heart.

"You...you do understand. How...?"

"Fenn came for me. She took me to meet your mother, and your mother took me to you. I thought you were dead. She told me to find you, to bring you back. I didn't know what she meant, but I kissed you and—"

"You kissed me?"

"Of course I did. That's all I ever want to do."

Draven smiled and reached up his hand to touch Keiron's face. The hand was still cold and trembling, but it felt so good. His smile was liquid, and Keiron could see the golden energy flickering behind his eyes. With the same energy flowing through him, setting fire to his blood, Keiron leaned down and kissed his little fairy.

As their lips touched, Draven gasped and cried out, the sound swallowed by the kiss. He arched off the bed and threw his arms around Keiron to steady himself. For the longest time, they held on, their kiss deepening and joining them while the energy flowed through, between, and around them.

When, finally, the kiss broke, they were both trembling, and Keiron lay Draven back on the pillows. He seemed better but exhausted, and he smiled.

"I am home," he whispered before his eyes fluttered closed. At first, Keiron panicked until he realised that Draven was asleep, just sweetly, peacefully asleep, and when Keiron lay down beside him, he murmured something and snuggled close. Rubbing his cheek against Draven's soft hair, Keiron sighed and finally relaxed, falling asleep in moments.

Next morning, Keiron woke with Draven in his arms. He was warm and sweet and responsive, and when Keiron opened his eyes, Draven opened his and smiled brightly at him.

"Good morning, Keiron. I've been awake for ages, but it was so nice to just lie here, I didn't want to wake you. I've missed this so much."

"Oh God, Draven, I've missed you so much too. Wait until you see what I've done. I've bought a new house. It's in the middle of the countryside, just fields and woods all around. We've got our own waterfall and a pool where we can swim. There's a wood and a bluebell grove. You'll love it."

Draven smiled, his eyes sparkling. "Can we stay there sometimes? I-I know you don't like the countryside, but maybe if we spend more time there, the poison won't—"

"Draven, I have no intention of staying there." He smiled at Draven's disappointed expression and gently traced his pouting lips. "When I thought I'd lost you, I started spending more and more time there because it was there I felt closest to you. I was in the process of arranging a permanent move. We're not going to stay there, Draven; we're going to live there."

"Live there? Always?"

"Always. There's no cars or factories or...no poison, Draven. There's no poison there. You'll live free. And I'll be free too."

"I...." Draven was speechless with excitement, his eyes sparkling and his lips quivering.

Keiron laughed. "You're so transparent."

"I am?" Draven sounded alarmed and raised his hand to peer at it anxiously.

"I meant, you can't hide what you're feeling. Every emotion is right there on your face, all the time."

"I'm sorry," Draven said, tears springing to his eyes. Keiron laughed again and kissed him.

"It's not a bad thing, little fairy. It's a good thing, a really good thing."

The sun came out again as Draven smiled brightly. "When can we go? When can we go to the country?"

"Whenever you want."

"Can we go now? Now I know we can leave, I don't want to be here anymore. I don't want to breathe the poison."

"Of course we can go now. Right now. Are you hungry? Do you want breakfast first?"

"I-I'm not really hungry, but I feel...I'm quite weak, so maybe I'd better have something to eat."

"I'm not surprised you're weak after everything that's happened to you lately. Do you want to get up, or shall I bring you something here?"

"I-I should get up, shouldn't I? You can't take the bed with you."

Keiron smiled. "No, I can't. Just wait a sec while I find you something to wear. I didn't think you were coming back, and I got rid of all Bren's stuff."

After a frantic scrabble, Keiron found a very old pair of jeans he'd grown out of since he'd stopped running. They'd have to be rolled up, but that was no problem. A tight-fitted jumper was the only other thing he found that wouldn't swamp Draven completely.

"Right, let's see how you look in these."

Draven observed the clothes. "I can grow to fit."

Keiron laughed. "I forgot about that. Come on then."

Draven grinned and reached out his arms to Keiron. "Help me," he said in a sexy, husky voice. Keiron scooped him up easily and held him in his arms. Draven looped his arms around Keiron's neck and kissed him. "I want to stay here forever."

"Well, you can't, because my arms will hurt too much," Keiron said with a smile and set Draven on his feet. Except that he didn't, because Draven couldn't stand. His legs were too weak to support him. He stumbled and fell with a cry. Keiron was instantly crouching next to him. Draven sighed, looking exhausted again.

"I'm just tired, Keiron. I think...I think what happened was harder than I thought, and my body is weak. I can't...I can't stand up. My head feels weird and my legs won't hold me."

"Then you don't stand up," Keiron said gently. He scooped Draven up and tucked him back into bed. "I should have realised. You've been through a lot. Don't worry. I'll take care of you, and you'll be better in no time. Rest, and I'll bring you something to eat."

"We can still go, can't we?" Draven asked anxiously as he settled back in bed. "We can still go to the country?"

"Of course. Of course, we can go to the country. Eat first, and then you can rest while I pack up a few things, and we can go. We'll sleep in a different bed tonight, with the window open and the sounds of the countryside coming in through it. You'll be happy there, Draven. It's such a beautiful place."

"I can see it through your eyes, your words. I know I'll be happy there. If you are there, I'll be happy."

Keiron hurried to make a simple breakfast of cereal and toast. When he got back, Draven was dozing, but he woke up bright-eyed when Keiron put the tray on the bed. He ate with relish, chatting nonstop about all the things he was looking forward to and excited about, which was just about everything. He seemed to be overflowing with simple joy. Keiron said little but felt very much the same.

Draven dozed again while Keiron packed the car and all the way to the house. Keiron was, of course, worried he was ill, but the worry was a gnat, nipping at a consciousness that was too filled with joy and excitement to really care. He knew Draven would be okay. It wasn't a hope; it was a certainty. He could feel Draven's energy flow through him as he was sure his was flowing through Draven. Draven was weak but getting stronger all the time, as the energy nourished him. If only Keiron had known before what a beautiful, powerful thing it was, he would never have denied it.

Draven loved the house. He insisted Keiron take him down to the pool as soon as they arrived, even before Keiron unloaded the car. Keiron had to carry him, but he was more than happy to hold him close, breathing in his sweetness, touching every part of him he could reach. Draven gazed up into his face with total trust and adoration the whole way.

"Oh Keiron," Draven gasped as Keiron settled him under a tree. There had been heavy rain, although today was a beautiful clear autumn day, and the waterfall was thundering over the cliff and churning the pool, whipping it into frothy waves. Draven stared at it for a long time, then raised a face full of wonder. "It's beautiful," he breathed. "Thank you."

"Thank you," Keiron whispered as he sank down next to him. There were tears in his eyes as he felt the joy that emanated from his little mate. "I'd never have experienced this if not for you. I'd have lived out my life in the city, drifting from day to day in my own little world, with everything in its place—ordered, regimented, sterile.

"I was like an old man, set in my ways, boring, jaded, tired. Then along came this annoying little pixie and turned my world upside down. I feel as if my whole life has been picked up, turned upside down, and shaken. I'm still picking up all the things that fell out."

Draven gazed at him, a strange expression on his face, and then he kissed Keiron on the cheek. "One thing," he said.

"What's that?"

"I'm not a pixie. Pixies are very different, and not really very nice."

Joy flooded Keiron, and he gently scooped Draven into an embrace, setting him on his lap. "Then you certainly can't be a pixie, because you are very nice."

"I am?"

"Oh yes," Keiron said, kissing him on the end of the nose. "Yes, you are."

Something dropped on their heads, causing them to break apart. They both glanced up. "Hey," Draven called. "Quit. Can't a man kiss his mate without interference from you? You'd better not be spying on me for my mother. If you are, she won't be very pleased because this is supposed to happen."

It really shouldn't have surprised Keiron when a red squirrel scampered down the tree and sat on Draven's shoulder, chittering into his ear.

"I don't care," Draven said calmly to the squirrel. "I'm not from around here, but I'm going to be so you'd better pass the word. This human is my mate, and you'd better be nice to him or else. You really don't want to piss me off." The squirrel chattered again and Draven grinned. "Yes, I am, so go spread the word around right now."

The squirrel disappeared back up into the tree, and they could hear the slight rustles and bumps as it leaped to another tree and away to goodness knows where.

"What was that about?"

"Oh, don't worry about it. Some people have a problem with mixed-race relationships. The squirrel was a narrow-minded old fool. No one is going to make things difficult for you. There are benefits to being a prince."

"So...you really are then? A prince, I mean. The Lord and Lady are your parents?"

"Yes."

"Why didn't you tell me?"

"I thought it would scare you off."

"It would have. It kind of does."

"You're not going to be angry with me, are you? Please don't leave because—"

"Draven, I'm not angry with you, and I'm not going to leave you. I've spoken to your mother, and we're all square."

"Square?"

"Everything's fine, Draven. It's all sorted."

Draven smiled and snuggled his head into Keiron's shoulder, toying with a lock of Keiron's hair. It had grown longer in the time they'd been apart. "I like your hair longer," Draven said drowsily.

"I like my hair however it makes you happy."

Draven smiled. "I'd be just as happy if you didn't have any. I hardly see your hair. All I see is how beautiful you are on the inside."

Keiron frowned and was about to ask him what he meant when he realised with something of a shock that, ever since he'd brought Draven back, there'd been a kind of golden shadow overlying his features. They were just as beautiful to him but not as important as that shadow. The more he thought about it, the clearer it became, until he realised he was seeing on the outside what he'd felt on the inside. Their bond was pure gold, and he was seeing that, shining through Draven's outward appearance.

"I've never seen you look so beautiful," he whispered and bent his head to kiss Draven again. This time there was no nut from above breaking them up, and their kisses lingered and stretched and were full of gold.

About the Author

Cheryl was born into a poor mining family in the South Wales Valleys. Until she was 16, the toilet was at the bottom of the garden and the bath hung on the wall. Her refrigerator was a stone slab in the pantry and there was a black lead fireplace in the kitchen. They look lovely in a museum but aren't so much fun to clean.

Cheryl has always been a storyteller. As a child, she'd make up stories for her nieces, nephews and cousin and they'd explore the imaginary worlds she created, in play. Later in life, Cheryl became the storyteller for a reenactment group who travelled widely, giving a taste of life in the Iron Age. As well as having an opportunity to run around hitting people with a sword, she had an opportunity to tell stories of all kinds, sometimes of her own making, to all kinds of people. The criticism was sometimes harsh, especially from the children, but the reward enormous.

It was here she began to appreciate the power of stories and the primal need to hear them. In ancient times, the wandering bard was the only source of news, and the storyteller the heart of the village, keeping the lore and the magic alive. Although much of the magic has been lost, the stories still provide a link to the part of us that still wants to believe that it's still there, somewhere. In present times, Cheryl lives in a terraced house in the valleys with her son, dog, bearded dragon and three cats. Her daughter has deserted her for the big city, but they're still close. She's never been happier since she was made redundant and is able to devote herself entirely to her twin loves of writing and art, with a healthy smattering of magic and mayhem.

Website: www.cherylheadford.com/

Blog: www.cherylheadford.blogspot.co.uk/

Blog: www.nephylim-author.blogspot.co.uk/

Twitter: www.twitter.com/SevenPointStar

Facebook: www.facebook.com/Nephylim.author/

Also Available from NineStar Press

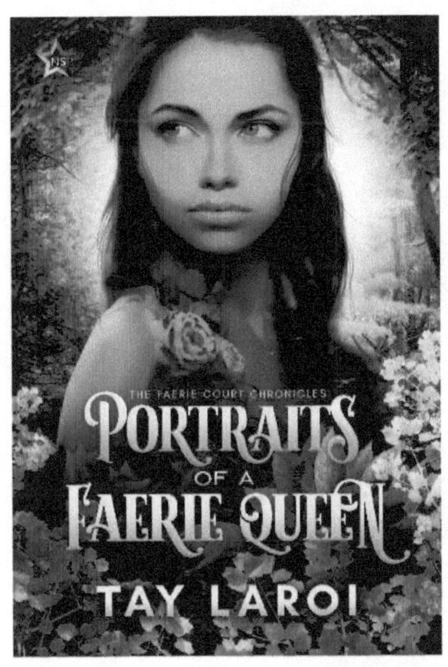

Connect with NineStar Press

www.ninestarpress.com

www.facebook.com/ninestarpress

www.facebook.com/groups/NineStarNiche

www.twitter.com/ninestarpress

www.tumblr.com/blog/ninestarpress